A Dream of Earth and Ash

Madeleine Eliot

Contents

To my readers, for supporting my dream.

Aurelia, Lady of Summer

Aspen, Lord of Spring

Prologue: Aurelia, Six Months Ago

"ARE YOU ALRIGHT?" ASPEN asked, kissing my forehead gently and brushing my hair from my face.

"More than alright," I breathed, sighing happily and admiring the sprites flitting above us under a forest canopy.

"I planned on waiting for this," he said, a little self-consciously, shifting so he was lying on his side next to me, his arm propping up his head to look down at me. "I hope you don't think I'm some kind of rake now."

I laughed, gently lifting my hand to cup his face and running my thumb over his lips.

"I didn't want you to wait," I said quietly, reveling in the feel of his lips beneath my fingers, and the fact that I was here with him like this.

"You are exquisite," he breathed, brushing my hair back over my shoulder and gently kissing it. "Why did you choose me?"

I laughed again, amazed it wasn't obvious to him.

"Because I've been in love with you since I was five," I said, smiling at his raised eyebrows. "You brought me flowers and told me you were going to marry me, remember?"

His eyes widened and he twisted, flopping down on his back heavily next to me.

"Well if I've already proposed, I suppose I don't need to bother with a ring," he joked, putting his arms around me as I lifted myself to rest my chin on his shoulder. I smiled again, but his smile faded a little.

"Aurelia, you know I need my father's permission to..." he began. I stopped him, pressing my fingers to his lips.

"I know," I said quietly. Everything was so wonderful in this moment, I didn't want to ruin it with the difficult parts of our relationship. I felt his arms tighten around me as he sighed a little.

"I would ask you today," he murmured, speaking against my hair, "if I could. I would take you to a priestess right now." I smiled against his shoulder.

"I know," I said again, closing my eyes and focusing on the soft moss beneath me, the chittering of the sprites around us, and the feel of Aspen's arms holding me.

"I'll wait."

Chapter 1: Aurelia

KILLING A MALE WAS never as easy as it sounded.

Getting in was the first challenge, and then having to scale walls or trick guards was the next. It was always easier when I was invited in, but then it was usually much harder to get out again without being noticed.

This particular job was easy in comparison to my usual assignments. Masquerade balls were an assassin's playground. No one expected to know who you were, and it was far easier for me to slip in, do the job, and slip out again unnoticed in a different mask.

I took a glass of faerie wine, sipping it slowly as I scanned the room. I knew my mark was in here, I just had to find him first.

"Aurelia?"

Damn it all. No one who knew me was supposed to be at this ball. I pretended not to hear and continued to sip my wine at the edge of the dance floor, hoping whoever it was would believe they were mistaken and go away.

A golden-haired male moved to stand next to me, a mask of ivy disguising the top half of his face. It didn't work on me. I would know him anywhere. My heart clenched at his nearness as he said my name again.

"Aurelia? What are you doing here?" Lord Aspen hissed furiously.

"My job," I replied coolly. "What are *you* doing here?"

"Also my job," he hissed back. "Leave before you get both of us killed."

"I was here first," I whispered angrily. I had no idea if this was true, but I didn't care. I had a job to do, and Aspen wouldn't stand in my way again.

He grabbed my upper arm and pulled me into an alcove in the ballroom where we were partially hidden from the rest of the guests by a large potted plant of some sort. I had no idea what kind. Plants were more Ember's thing, and now Aspen's too, I supposed.

"Did she really do this again to us?" Aspen growled. "Who are you here for?"

"Lord Abbadon," I replied, staring furiously up at him. His blue eyes blazed like sapphires under the ivy mask, and I had to swallow as a jolt of pain grazed my heart. Looking at him was difficult.

"Who are *you* here for?" I asked, trying to ignore my stupid heart and its ridiculous feelings.

"Also Lord Abbadon," Aspen growled. "Goddess damn it, she *did* do it again. Is he even here, or was this purely another setup?"

"I haven't seen him yet," I said dismissively. "If you'll excuse me, I'll be returning to work now."

I tried to walk out, but Aspen hauled me back, gently but firmly.

"What are you doing?" he hissed again. I gave him as withering a look as I could muster under my golden mask.

In celebration of the newly released seelie magic, the guests at this ball had worn masks representing their re-emerged powers. Aspen wore ivy, representing his gift over the earth. Once Ember's wings had appeared, Aspen had started to move the earth and make plants grow out of control any time he felt a strong emotion, which was almost always around me. My powers had refused to re-emerge, even when I was furious, so gold was the best I could do. I still had the same small magics I could muster before my best friend had been named the Seelie Queen and Queen of All Fae, like simple glamours and shields of air, but nothing else.

Seline, King Hadrian's half-sister gifted with the ability to sense spells, had told me nothing was blocking my magic, and I could feel it burning within me, aching for a route out of me. It just wouldn't come, no matter how hard I pushed it.

"We will surely be identified if we are seen here together," I said, gesturing to the tiny alcove in which we hid. "I'm leaving. If Abaddon isn't here, then there's no point in staying."

"Why would Ember send you to kill Abbadon and me to befriend him?" Aspen asked, still holding my arm. In the wake of Ember's coronation, I had kept up my work as an assassin, and Aspen, Ember's cousin in name, if not in fact, had taken on the role of a spy, using his skills at diplomacy and debauchery to win the confidences of other nobles whose allegiance to his cousin was suspect.

"I wasn't sent to kill him," I said, pulling my arm from his grasp. "I was sent to get information. Killing him is only a last resort."

Below the mask, Aspen's lips twisted into a sardonic smile.

"Yes, well I know how good you are at getting sensitive information from gullible males," he said cruelly. I blinked, feeling my heart crack a little more. Aspen cursed.

"Damn it, Aurelia, I didn't mean..."

"You did," I cut in sharply. "Good night, Aspen."

I turned to leave again, and once more Aspen grabbed my arm to pull me back. This time I was ready. I whirled on him, holding my golden dagger to his throat.

"Let me go, now," I said, trying to fill my words with fury rather than the heartache I felt around him. "Or I will make your cousin extremely angry at me." He released my arm and put up his hands.

"Peace, Aurelia," he said quietly. I could see remorse in his eyes, and I wished I could just not care. I lowered my dagger and he blew out a breath.

Since we had discovered that Ember was the Seelie Queen less than a month ago, Aspen and I had been at odds. I had loved him since I was five years old and he gave me a bouquet of wildflowers he picked on the day of the Midsummer festival. Ember called it infatuation, and maybe it was, but my heart had beat only for him. Then I married another male as part of a mission for the rebellion my best friend now led, and Aspen could not forgive me.

Part of me understood. I had hurt him, unforgivably, even if I had noble reasons for doing it, like saving the whole goddess damned realm. Aspen's persistent refusal to believe the marriage meant nothing and went unconsummated had worn on me. Ember had annulled the marriage, of course, but Aspen grew colder and more cruel with me by the day.

For a moment I flashed back to the fight we had the week before this cursed masquerade ball. We had argued about a mission I had been sent on to extract information from a noble lord who claimed loyalty to Ember but was suspected of selling secrets to the Unseelie King.

Aspen had been there and had seen me let the lord kiss me. He hadn't seen me dispatch him later when I had proof the lord was guilty and he had tried to assault me. Aspen wasn't there when I had furiously scrubbed the blood off my hands, shaking and sick at what I'd had to do, and at the near assault. All he saw was the kiss, and the next day he berated me for not taking my job seriously.

"That *is* my job," I shouted back. "It's my job to make males want to fuck me and tell me their secrets. It's my job to let them kiss me and convince them to take me to their rooms, where it will be easier to dispose of them. It's my job to wipe their blood from my hands and move on when I'm done." My voice had risen to a shrill cry as I finished, "You lost the privilege of judging me when you refused to believe I could do my job and still love you!"

That was when his fury had shattered a window, and he had left me sobbing beneath the broken glass until Ember had found me and held me and cleaned me up. She had insisted he treat me with at least professional courtesy after that. It wasn't going well.

"Stay away from me," I said quietly, "and let me do what I'm good at." I spat this last comment at him, trying to fill my voice with disdain and rage. This time when I tried to leave, he didn't stop me.

Lord Abaddon never showed up. I watched Aspen from the corner of my eye the rest of the night as he spoke and laughed convincingly with some of the nobility and asked several pretty females to dance. I tried to ignore the twist of jealousy. I had been asked to dance too, but had declined. Maybe I should see how he felt watching me dance with other males. I spent several hours contemplating tripping his dance partners while repeatedly stabbing a cherry with a cocktail skewer.

I returned to the palace far later than I hoped I would. The place was asleep, and I navigated through the dark to my room.

Since becoming the Seelie Queen, Ember had moved to the old seelie palace along with most of the rebellion, which included me. Thankfully, I wouldn't run into Aspen as he mostly kept to his father's manor, having assumed the lordship after his father fled from the realm. When he did stay at the palace, he always stayed in the barracks, I assumed to be as far away from me as possible.

My room was dark and cold and my heart was battered and bruised, so once I had undressed and combed out my golden hair, I gave into weakness this one time and cried myself to sleep.

I woke to flames engulfing the palace around me. I screamed, trying to leap out of bed to escape and realizing I was sinking into the earth. A large snake slithered out from the ground and coiled itself around my throat.

I screamed again, and Ember shook me awake. With a sob, I threw myself into her arms.

"It was a dream," she said soothingly, stroking my hair. "Just a dream. You're safe."

"Is she alright?" came a gruff, sleep-worn voice from the door. I peeked over Ember's shoulder to see King Hadrian, her husband and mate, standing there without a shirt. At least he had taken the time to put pants on. I blushed and looked away.

"I'm fine," I said in a small voice. "You should go back to bed."

Ember glanced at Hadrian and he nodded, closing the door as she climbed into bed with me.

"Do you want to talk about it?" she asked. I shook my head. She frowned. "You were screaming."

"It was a bad dream," I said, trying not to let her feel me shaking. I failed, of course. Ember saw everything. Wrapping her arms around me, she held me tightly, stroking my hair soothingly.

"How was the ball?" she asked, trying and failing to both distract me and hide her hopefulness. I sighed. Aspen must be right. She had sent us on the same mission again to try to reconcile us. This was the third time she had done it.

"You know how it went," I said sourly, still trembling at the dream. "Was Abbadon even supposed to be there?"

I felt Ember shift uncomfortably behind me.

"I just hoped that if he saw you..." she trailed off, and I knew that the "he" wasn't Lord Abbadon. I sighed.

"It's time to let it go, Ember. He doesn't want me anymore," I said quietly, my heart breaking a little more. Someday it would crack completely and there would be nothing left of me at all.

"He does," Ember said forcefully. "He's a stubborn fool is all."

"Hmm, who does that remind me of?" I said wryly. "You have to let it go. Aspen has, and both of us need to accept it's not going to happen."

"But he loves you!" she protested, snuggling closer to me. "And you love him. I can't just sit by and watch you both throw it away."

I sighed. Despite the turn of our conversation, I felt a little better in the wake of the dream with Ember, my best friend, and queen, at my back.

"I threw it away when I took that goddess-damned mission," I said sadly, remembering at the time how Ember had sent Hadrian to try to stop me. "And he threw it away when he couldn't forgive me. You've done all you can."

Ember was silent for a while.

"Do you want to talk about the dream?" she asked quietly. I shook my head.

"Later," I whispered.

Eventually, I heard her breathing deepen as sleep claimed her. I lay awake until daybreak, trying to shake the feeling of the flames and earth consuming me.

THE MORNING DAWNED COLD and clear, and I decided to spend it with Mother Vervain in the palace infirmary. This section of the palace was the first that Ember and Hadrian had restored, and the old female, who was also Ember's grandmother and a former Seelie Queen, ran the place like a well-oiled machine. A host of apprentices learned from her and bustled around her each day as she commanded them from a cozy armchair, bundled in scarves and shawls that hid the gruesome scars where her wings used to be.

She was knitting when I arrived.

"Took you long enough," she said, not putting down her knitting. "I expected you a full half hour ago."

I smiled, bemused. Mother Vervain often made proclamations about when and where everyone should and should not be, and I had long ago discovered it was no use arguing with her.

"I'm sorry, Mother V," I said as seriously as possible. "I didn't mean to keep you waiting." I tried to hide a smile as she looked up from her knitting—some pink fluffy thing—and studied me.

"Well, you'd better tell me about the dream," she said looking back down at her work. I blinked in surprise.

"Did Ember tell you?" I asked, frowning.

"Don't be silly, child! It's written plain on your face," she replied exasperatedly. There were many times when I thought Mother Vervain may have the gift of sight, and this was one of them. "Come on then, out with it," she prompted.

With raised eyebrows, I sat on the low stool across from her and recounted the dream. She nodded a few times and added a "Hmm" here and there. When I was done, she put her knitting down and looked at me properly.

She looked older, I noticed. She had already been ancient when she first arrived with all of us back in the seelie court after making a hasty escape from the unseelie palace, but she somehow seemed to be aging more rapidly each day. Maybe it was safety, and the certainty that her granddaughter had been found and recognized as queen that made her determination to outlive the Unseelie King, Hadrian's wicked father, wane a bit.

"Dreams are never nonsense," Mother Vervain said, giving me a hard look. "They always mean something, whether they are a message from the goddess or our minds. What do you think yours means?"

I shrugged, uncomfortable and very much hoping she was wrong about dreams having meanings.

"That I fear fire?" I asked, uncertainly. "Or being buried alive? Or snakes?"

Mother Vervain scowled.

"Try harder, child!" she scolded, picking her knitting back up.

"I truly don't know Mother Vervain," I said with a sigh. "Maybe this one means nothing. Maybe I'm just under stress from work and danger and heartache."

"Hmm," she intoned again, pursing her lips as she continued knitting. "Snakes are a symbol of rebirth. They shed their skins and become new with the changing seasons of their lives. Have you called your magic yet?"

"You know I haven't," I replied, quelling my surprise at the change of subject. "It's come so easily for everyone else, and mine just sits and burns away inside me. Maybe I'm just not gifted with the kind of magic that can be useful."

"I think," said Mother Vervain, with the air of someone who was about to lay some great wisdom on a younger person, "that you're not trying hard enough."

I laughed, and rose, kissing Mother Vervain on the cheek. She was a batty, critical, sometimes pompous old thing, and I loved her like she was my grandmother, not just Ember's.

"I'll take it under advisement, Mother V," I said, "since you're almost always right about these things."

"See that you do," she intoned, waving me off with her knitting needles as I left to do some work, avoiding the bustling apprentices running back and forth.

I spent the morning grinding herbs and pummeling nuts into a cloud of fine dust, which helped to work off some of my frustration. What I didn't tell Mother Vervain is that I was certain something had broken in me the moment Aspen had pushed me away.

Maybe magic couldn't flow from a broken heart.

Chapter 2: Aurelia

I FOUND EMBER LATER in the stables with Nisha, brushing her mane and cooing gently to her. The midnight mare had been a gift from Hadrian for their betrothal, and Ember took prodigious care of her.

"There's my good girl," I heard her saying as she patted the horse's nose. Nisha huffed a breath against her hand, then pricked her ears when she heard me coming.

If I didn't know Ember was the queen, I would have never guessed it from her appearance. Her auburn hair was tied back in a messy braid, and she wore riding breeches and a loose shirt with holes cut in the back for her wings, rather than an elegant dress befitting her status. Even *I* was more dressed up, wearing one of the simple spider silk gowns I favored for day-to-day wear. Then again, I had to keep up the appearance of innocence to maintain my cover as an assassin. Ember was supposed to be fierce and wild.

"Good morning, Nisha," I said, addressing the horse with all the formality appropriate for a royal steed. I patted her soft nose, smiling as she huffed against my hand. Ember smiled at me, stroking the horse's neck. Nisha's mate, a massive black stallion named Erebus who belonged to Hadrian, whinnied in protest at our attentions to his mate and not to him.

"Oh, hush you jealous male," Ember said, scowling at Erebus as I went over to give him a friendly pat too. He nosed my shirt, looking for treats, and neighed in annoyance when I didn't produce any.

"Sorry, boy," I said apologetically. He huffed again as if resigned to go treatless, and I laughed. "Any news today?" I asked Ember as she finished combing and pampering Nisha. Ember shook her head.

"Nothing important," she said, taking my arm and walking with me out of the stables. "The Commander says the training is coming along. Vanth and Seline are whipping the recruits into shape."

"As expected," I said with a smirk, nudging Ember with my hip. "Let's go watch them spar. I know how much you like watching Hadrian fight when he gets all hot and has to take his shirt off."

She blushed faintly and grinned at me.

The training yard was not far from the stables, and the clang of blades and daggers reached us long before we saw any of the fighting. Since it would be impossible to see anything from the ground with the crowd of fae watching the fight, Ember gripped me by the waist and flew us to the roof of the barracks to watch.

I had been flying with her a few times, and it was my greatest joy in the world. Her wings were large, translucent gossamer with the phases of the moon and stars emblazoned around them, and I was more than a little jealous of her ability to fly, even if it was still only for short distances.

We perched on the edge of the roof and looked down at the training yard where Hadrian indeed had his shirt off. I nudged Ember and she blushed even more crimson, which was ridiculous since they were mates and I was certain she had seen him in far less clothing than he wore now.

Mating was the deepest bond a fae couple could form, even more sacred than marriage, although most mated couples also married at some point. Mates tied their lives together, choosing to feel and suffer and love together, bonding their souls and lives and hearts for eternity. Mating bonds were chosen and accepted willingly by both parties, except Hadrian and Ember's had been fated somehow, blazing to life before they even knew they liked each other.

Whatever the reason for it, they were blissfully happy and wholly in love.

Ember had frequently joked in our youth that Aspen and I would one day be mated, and a large part of me had believed her. But that was done now.

Recruits were standing and sitting around the training yard, watching Hadrian spar with another dark-haired, muscular male, who was also shirtless.

"These males," I sighed under my breath. "I hope Seline is watching."

"Oh, she is," said Ember, pointing down to a petite, silver-haired female who stood at the edge of the ring with her arms crossed, looking bored.

Vanth, the unseelie male sparring with Hadrian, shot her a glance and grinned as he attempted to disarm the king. Hadrian dodged and threw darkness out at Vanth, who put up an effective shield of air to block, kicking the king's feet out from under him.

I hadn't seen Vanth use any greater powers when sparring, or ever. I had asked him about it once, and he told me his power was too dark to be used on other fae. Unseelie powers seemed to be the dark twin to our own. Hadrian commanded darkness and death while Ember commanded light and healing. Vanth commanded something so dark it scared even him, while Aspen commanded vines and earth. Seline was a spell breaker, although a weak one, and she commanded some of the same darkness and shadowwalking as Hadrian.

My power had yet to emerge. Maybe I would be Seline's opposite, or Vanth's. I shuddered. The goddess had a wry sense of humor that way.

While I was musing about this, Hadrian landed a wicked blow with his shadows, pushing Vanth clean out of the training ring. The soldiers applauded and Seline gave Vanth a smirk. He replied with a rude gesture. I wondered when those two would finally admit they liked each other.

"Anyone else?" Hadrian boomed, sweat dripping from him. His dark hair gleamed in the weak winter sunlight, and his pale skin shone like snow against the stone backdrop of the training ring.

"Me," came a voice from among the soldiers. I craned my neck to try to see who it was, and my stomach dropped.

Aspen joined Hadrian in the ring, removing his own shirt and taking up his sword.

"You sure you want to be beaten again?" Hadrian joked. He and Aspen had always been on frosty terms at best, but Aspen had turned to him for help in mastering his new magic, and Hadrian had taken on the challenge. There was a grudging respect between them now, although not quite admiration.

"Always," Aspen said, readying his stance. The two of them faced off looking like complete opposites. Hadrian was pale and dark-haired, a winter lord fit for snowy mountains and harsh winter storms. Aspen was golden all over, from his warm tan skin to his blond curls, and he looked more suited for a hot beach than a winter storm.

I noticed he had bulked up some since training to fight with the soldiers, his golden skin marred with new scars and faint bruises from sparring daily. Aspen had always been more of a thinker and a socialite than a warrior, but in the weeks since his cousin was named Queen, he had changed.

No longer was he the slight but strong dancer and noble lord. Now he had muscle and fought like one of the soldiers. He didn't laugh as easily or as infectiously, and his blue eyes, which once sparkled with mirth, were cold and icy now. I knew that was mostly because of me.

"He'll come around," said Ember next to me, clearly seeing where my gaze had gone. "Just give him time."

"He's had time," I said, a little more snappishly than I intended. I softened my words with a gentle squeeze of Ember's hand. "I'm sorry. I know you think he'll come back. But I think the Aspen we knew might be gone."

Ember sighed.

"It's been hard for him to see past his hurt," she confessed, watching her husband and mate begin his match against her cousin. "Especially with his father gone, and his sudden elevation to lord, and discovering the rebellion. I think he aged a decade overnight when Hadrian brought us to him."

I nodded. Hadrian had thrown his darkness at Aspen, who had dodged by throwing up a wall of vines that Hadrian was now attacking with a sword. The vines began to grab at Hadrian's blade and limbs, and he barked a curse. With a clench of his fist, he disintegrated them into black, glittering dust. But Aspen was quick. Hand to the ground, he split the earth beneath Hadrian's feet, causing him to lose his balance and topple over, where Aspen held him at sword point. The watching soldiers gasped.

"Yield?" Aspen panted, sweat dripping down his face and body, making his golden curls cling to his forehead.

"Never," grunted Hadrian with a smirk, throwing up a fist of darkness that hit Aspen in the gut, knocking the wind out of him.

"Males," came a velvety, feminine voice behind us. Seline sat next to me, crossing her legs as she watched her brother pummel her sister-in-law's cousin.

"How did you get up here?" I asked in genuine surprise. I had only ever come via Ember's wings.

"I climbed," said Seline simply, eyes still on the match below.

I hadn't quite figured out what to make of Seline, but Ember liked and trusted her, so I was trying to make space for her in my heart too. It was hard, feeling like I had lost a piece of my friend to this other female who now also claimed her affection, but I kept the jealousy tamped down as best as I could, and I tried to be friendly with Seline. She was not an overly affectionate female, and I found her particular brand of friendship a little difficult to understand sometimes. But I knew she had suffered in her life, losing her mate to the Unseelie King many years ago. It was no wonder she was a little cold, having lost the other half of her soul.

"Is Vanth all right?" asked Ember, concern lacing her voice. "That was a hard hit to the head he took." Seline waved her hand unconcernedly.

"He's fine," she said, glancing down at where he had perched to watch the rest of the fight. "He has an extremely hard head."

Ember snorted and I smiled, as Hadrian, clearly growing tired of the fight, threw Aspen from the ring. He landed with a hard thump as he fell into a group of soldiers. I winced.

"We'd better go down," Ember said, glancing at me, and then at Seline. "Seline, can you climb back down? I can't fly you both."

"Of course," she said, sliding smoothly down the roof and hopping onto the balcony below.

"Show off," grumbled Ember. I smiled as she gripped me by the waist and lowered us, a little faster than necessary, to the ground.

Hadrian had offered Aspen a hand up, grinning at Aspen in smug victory.

"That's the longest you've lasted against me," said Hadrian, a hint of both pride and mockery in his voice. Aspen limped a bit but seemed otherwise unharmed.

"Still, I can do better," said Aspen, somewhat more coldly than Hadrian probably deserved. "Thanks for the fight." Hadrian nodded.

"Any time. Next time you can take on Vanth too," he added, grinning at Aspen. Aspen didn't smile back, and it hurt my heart how much he had changed in the last few weeks. The old Aspen would have joked and bantered and complained. Now he just seemed cold and forever unsatisfied with everything.

"If you're all done attacking each other, then you can come to dinner," Ember said, smiling at Aspen and trying to hide her concern. Aspen glanced at me. I stiffened. The last thing I wanted was to sit through another awkward dinner with Aspen.

"Does my Queen command it?" he asked formally. Ember frowned and went to take his hands.

"No, Aspen, your cousin asks it," she said, looking up at him pleadingly. "Please come? I'll ask the cook to make that meringue dessert you like so much?"

Ember knew exactly how to get people to agree to her plans. Aspen sighed dramatically, as if she had just asked him to run the kingdom for her for a week, instead of coming to dinner and enjoying dessert.

"Very well, if I must," he said, resignedly. Ember clapped her hands with excitement and threw her arms around him. Aspen glanced at me again, then away.

"I'd better go clean up. I'll be there soon," he said, bowing slightly and heading into the barracks.

"Ember," I hissed at my friend. "I don't want to have dinner with him!"

"Please Aurelia?" she said, grabbing my hand. "Aspen never agrees and I want us all to be together just once."

I sighed, rubbing my temple with my fingers.

"He'll come around," she added softly with a sympathetic smile. I was getting tired of her saying this to me. "But you have to let him see that you're still you. No male who looks at you the way he does can be angry forever."

I shook my head and sighed.

"He doesn't look at me like that anymore," I said sadly. "And I don't know if I should either. He's cold now. Cruel sometimes." I also felt like I was changed irrevocably, but I didn't say that. Once

I had been reckless and carefree, rather like Aspen. Now I felt like nothing would ever bring me joy again.

"He's broken," corrected Ember, squeezing my hand once more, "but he's not lost. And I promise you, he still looks." She looked at me with a hopeful smile, and I rolled my eyes.

"There had better be wine at this dinner," I said. Ember smiled.

"So much wine!" she chirped happily, running off to walk with her mate.

I walked back to the castle with Seline, as Hadrian was monopolizing Ember, his arm wrapped around her waist as he dripped sweat onto her shoulder. She didn't seem to mind at all, looking up at him adoringly as he told her some story about his day. My gut twisted, envy rising up again, this time for what they had between them

"I remember what it was like to have that," Seline said, looking wistfully at Ember and Hadrian as well. Her velvet voice soothed something ragged inside me. "You had that with Aspen?" Seline asked.

I nodded.

"There was never a formal arrangement," I said, swallowing rather thickly. Aspen needed his father's approval for marriage, and I had known it would be difficult to get, but he would dance with me at every dance, monopolize my conversation, and stare at me the way Hadrian was now looking at Ember. And we had one perfect night together at Midsummer. The crack in my heart spread a little deeper.

The only reason I had agreed to marry the vile Lord Thorn was because we had intelligence that he had a cache of iron weapons in his manor. Iron is the only thing truly deadly to a fae, and it was illegal to make or sell it in either realm. Yet somehow, Hadrian and I had both been gravely injured with iron blades, saved only by Ember's healing powers.

Thorn had married me to get revenge on Ember, who had refused him, and the arrangement had suited me when I thought I would be able to get some valuable information. Instead, he had locked me up, and I'd been forced into rash action to free myself, setting fire to his house so I could steal letters from his study. The fire had raged out of control, and both Vanth and I had been injured trying to escape. His burn, a dull red gash across his neck and jaw, still pained him from time to time, no matter how much healing salve Ember used on him, and Thorn had escaped in the chaos.

I sighed, remembering the whole mess and how scared, then how angry Aspen had been at me when it was clear I would live. He didn't understand my commitment to the cause or the sacrifices I had made for it.

"If he can't see how much you still love him, then he's a fool," Seline said quietly. I looked down at her, her gray eyes swirling intensely as she regarded me. I sensed that she was a fiercely loyal person, and it warmed me a little that some of that loyalty had spread to include me.

"Or maybe I'm the fool for hoping he will," I said.

Chapter 3: Aurelia

I LOVED EMBER WITH all of my heart, but that evening, I hated her.

We dined in one of the small private dining rooms of the palace since it would only be the six of us. Mother Vervain rarely ate dinner with us, as she preferred to take her tea in her rooms and turn in early, so the dinner party consisted of Ember and Hadrian, Seline and Vanth, and me and Aspen. Nobody bothered to dress up, so we made a motley crew, the males in their partially unbuttoned shirtsleeves. Seline and Ember wore breeches and loose shirts, and I still wore my simple dress.

Matchmaker that she was, Ember couldn't help herself, so I spent an awkward dinner sitting next to the male I had once loved as we tried to make polite conversation over the soup.

Ember and the unseelie fae were all at ease with each other after spending a month in close proximity in the unseelie palace, but I still felt like an outsider, and I got the feeling Aspen did too. He was quiet, offering little to the conversation, which had turned to soldiering and military strategy, as was often the case with Hadrian and his friends.

"You can't send them North without greater numbers," Vanth was arguing. "Better to wait for the king to make his move and defend instead of attack outright."

"We need allies," Seline said thoughtfully, her velvety voice carrying like night over the table. "Our latest reports have the unseelie forces outnumbering us four to one. Perhaps the fae in the Wilds could be rallied to our cause."

"The problem is finding them," replied Hadrian, waving his fork at Seline as he added, "and convincing them, They're scattered and disorganized, and have no reason to pledge us their loyalty."

"Someone could go there," Aspen said, clearing his throat and taking another sip of wine. I watched his throat work as he swallowed. He was not dark or alluring in the way Hadrian and Vanth were, but he was charming and handsome, boyish almost with his golden curls. His figure today had not been that of a boy, and I blushed a little at the memory, which was silly because it wasn't the first time I had seen him shirtless.

Hadrian looked like he was about to argue with Aspen over this point when a steward rushed over to Ember. He whispered in her ear and she nodded, frowning.

"Apparently we have guests waiting for an audience in the throne room," she said, sipping her wine once more before setting the cup in front of her. She stood and we all followed, her loyal army of friends.

"What guests?" asked Hadrian darkly as he took her arm to lead the way to the throne room. Seline and Vanth took up defensive positions in front of them, leaving Aspen and me to trail behind.

"Dwarves," said Ember. Hadrian paused, holding her back.

"What?" he said, bristling. dwarves were historically enemies of the fae, being the creators of the only weapons that could mortally wound us.

"We have dwarves waiting for us in the throne room," she repeated more slowly, giving his arm a squeeze. "They ask for a parley. I have been assured they carry no iron."

Hadrian growled softly as Ember dragged him forward, and Aspen tensed next to me. I know he was thinking of my iron injury, and how close I had been to death. I would have died, if Ember had not broken open her magic to heal me.

The throne room was still in a state of disrepair. Once beautiful marble columns had cracked and crumbled, and the stained glass had been long broken and boarded up. But fires burned merrily in the hearths of the many fireplaces, and guards still at attention along the plush, red carpet that led the way to the dais where the thrones sat.

We entered through the back of the room, and Ember and Hadrian climbed the dais to take their seats in identical marble thrones. Seline and Vanth positioned themselves on either side of the king and queen, leaving Aspen and me to stand at attention at the base of the dais. He put a hand on my lower back to steady me as I stumbled up the dais steps, probably unconsciously. Heat flared at my back where he touched me. I met his gaze for a moment, something molten and possessive flashing in him before he lowered his hand and stepped away.

I pried my eyes from him to study the messengers. One was a dwarf as Ember had said, beard black and long hair bristling all around his face, shorter in stature than the fae of either realm and built like a barrel. He was broad everywhere, leather armor adding to his size, and a mighty war hammer strapped to his back looked like it must weigh hundreds of pounds.

The other member of the party was, to my surprise, an unseelie fae. He was tall and broad, wearing dwarven leathers and carrying a similar war hammer. His skin was the faintest shade of blue, and dark, blue-black hair hung around his shoulders.

Both knelt, bowing their heads before my queen.

"Your majesties," came the cool voice of the unseelie male. He looked up, eyes slightly slanted and the darkest shade of indigo. If he was surprised by our casual attire, he didn't show it. "Lord of Spring, Lady of Summer," he added, addressing Aspen and me each in turn. The formal titles had been given to us by Ember when she took the throne, but I rarely heard them used. I was surprised the dwarven emissary knew them.

"We come on behalf of King Holvard, Protector of the Dwarven Realm. Thank you for receiving us," the unseelie male said, speaking in a slight accent that marked him as living outside the fae realms. "My name is Knox, and my associate is Rourke," he said, gesturing to the male dwarf who knelt next to him. He nodded his head. "We have traveled to you without notice, and we apologize, but the king has sent us to beg the restored Seelie Queen for her aid."

"Why does your king need my help?" Ember asked, voice unreadable as she regarded the emissaries.

The dwarf spoke next, voice gravelly like the rocks he must live beneath, and heavily accented.

"There is a blight, Your Majesty," he said, lifting his head to look at Ember. His eyes were black like onyx, and his bristly beard made it impossible to see his lips moving as he spoke. "It has been slowly destroying our crops for this last year. We have sustained ourselves with hunting, but with winter upon us, the situation grows somewhat desperate."

Ember nodded, and asked, "And what does the king of the Dwarven Realm hope I can do to help with this?"

Rourke spoke again, so deeply I thought I felt the ground rumbling and my shoes vibrating.

"His Majesty has heard of your renewed magic. Your gift of life and healing," he said. "He humbly requests your aid in saving our fields. In exchange, he offers you his friendship and alliance."

Hadrian's brows shot up as he took Ember's hand, stroking the back of it with his thumb. As always, my gut twisted with a pang of jealousy at the intimacy.

"And what of the iron weapons he gifted the Unseelie King?" Hadrian asked, voice harder than Ember's, assessing the risks of trusting this pair.

Knox shook his head, looking confusedly at Rourke. Rourke shook his head slightly in return, face impassive.

"We know of no such gift," said Knox slowly and carefully, "but My King will be anxious to hear if our weapons have been sold to unseelie hands, or stolen from our mountain."

"Why does King Holvard send an unseelie fae with his dwarven Emissary?" Ember asked, gesturing toward the block of a male that was Rourke. "How does an unseelie male find himself swearing fealty to a Dwarven King?"

Rourke answered this time, voice still gravelly.

"The Dwarven Realm has long accepted refugees of your fae war," he said, eyes narrowing in contempt, possibly for all of fae kind. "Some choose to stay and swear loyalty to the Dwarven King."

"I have no love for the Unseelie King," Knox added, voice hard. "He is the reason my people fled my home. I swear loyalty to the king who protects me and mine."

"My King offers his friendship and his armies, and anything else you may wish in exchange for your help," said Rourke, bringing the conversation back to the reason for their arrival. "Soldiers in battle, weapons, armor, whatever you wish is yours if you can help us."

Hadrian and Ember glanced at each other.

"We will need to consider the request," said Ember, standing. "We would be honored to have you stay as our guests while we deliberate. I will give you my answer tomorrow."

Knox bowed. "We are honored to stay and await your response. If you agree, we are prepared to take two representatives of your court to meet with His Majesty to set terms."

Rourke bowed as well, and both were led away to the guest wing of the palace. Ember sighed and stood, stepping off the dais while holding Hadrian's hand.

"Well, I suppose we'd all better go discuss it," she said, giving us all a tired smile. "I'll send for wine."

We met thirty minutes later in Ember and Hadrian's private sitting room. It was connected to their bedroom and was the coziest part of the palace. A roaring fire warmed the room, surrounded by squashy armchairs and plush rugs.

I had changed into my nightdress, a soft silken robe covering me adequately enough for a meeting this casual. Ember was also dressed for bed when I entered, and Hadrian was barefoot, brushing Ember's hair from her shoulder to plant a kiss there, his shadows wrapped around her like a cloak. He rarely showed his shadows in public, not wanting to be associated with his father, but with Ember he let all of himself show freely. She sighed happily, and again I felt the now familiar ache of jealousy at her happiness.

My friend deserved her happiness, which made the jealousy all the worse. I felt like a wretch for being envious of what she had, but it didn't stop the feeling.

The other members of our tiny court showed up one by one, including the Commander, who must have been called in specifically for this meeting. She was a fierce female, one half of her face scarred badly from a fight with the Unseelie King. She had told me the story when I was younger, and it made my stomach turn when she described how it had happened, the king personally carving out her eye on the battlefield.

Aspen showed up last, hair rumpled as if he had been running his hands through it as he sometimes did while thinking. To my surprise, he plopped down next to me, stretching his long arms across the back of the couch. It was such an Aspen way to sit, completely at ease but somehow refined, that my heart leaped a little at the familiar posture, but he didn't look at me.

"So tell me about these emissaries," the Commander said, characteristically impatient to get down to business.

Ember and Hadrian recounted our meeting while I sat listening, trying hard not to glance toward Aspen next to me. I felt a slight tug on my hair and realized Aspen was toying with one of my curls that hung down the back of the couch. I looked at him and he raised an eyebrow, then frowned. He must have done it unconsciously like he had so many times before everything had fallen apart. He lifted the curl over the couch to rest on my shoulder and removed his hand.

"What food do dwarves even grow?" Vanth asked, bringing me back to the conversation which I had been ignoring. "What can grow in the dark?"

"Quite a lot actually," Ember replied, smiling at him. "Various species of mushrooms of course, but also wheatgrass and sprouts and white asparagus and lichen and..."

"My love," Hadrian interrupted, smiling fondly at her.

"Oh, right," she said, blushing at her own enthusiasm for herbology. "Anyway, if their crops are blighted it's no wonder they ask for assistance. I don't know much about the Dwarven Realm, but I have heard their cities are largely carved out from the caves under the mountains. It would be difficult to hunt in there, and the mountains are too inhospitable for farming outside the caves. The winter probably makes hunting on the mountainside equally challenging."

"What do you think about the notion that their king didn't know about the cache of iron?" asked Aspen, brows raised.

"I'm not sure," Ember replied, frowning seriously. "I suppose it's possible they are telling the truth. However," she added, "I don't think it's smart to trust them completely. That's why we need to send a spy as well as an emissary if we do this. And I think we must do it. We don't have the numbers to fight the Unseelie King without additional allies, and he could move on us at any ti me."

"You can't be thinking of going yourself," scolded Seline, looking fierce. "You are needed here to run the whole cursed realm." Vanth grinned at her annoyance for all things bureaucratic.

The Commander, Hadrian, and Aspen chimed in to agree and add various concerns. I was silent. I knew how Ember's mind worked, so I knew where this was going. If she could find a way to further her own agenda while completing this mission, she would. Ember held up both hands to quiet the arguments.

"I do not plan to go myself," she said. "Although I wish I could," she added with chagrin. "I'd love to study the dwarven fields. But I don't have the kind of magic they need anyway. I can heal the sick, but I can't heal the earth, as far as I know. Or grow entire fields of plants anew. That's why Aspen should go."

"What?" said Aspen, brows rising even higher in disbelief.

"As my emissary," Ember continued. "I want you to go as emissary and cousin to the queen. You have studied diplomacy, and your power lends itself to growth and renewal of the earth. Even if we can't cure the blight, you could grow badly needed provisions to tide them over until a cure can be found."

"You want me to knowingly walk into enemy territory, an enemy, by the way, who creates weapons designed specifically to kill me, and help them grow food?" he asked, his voice completely flat as he outlined the mission. "And be your spy?" Ember smiled.

"No, of course not," she said, smiling warmly at him. "You can't play spy if you are also playing emissary. Someone will have to go with you."

"I'll go," Vanth offered, nodding toward Aspen, but the Commander cut in.

"You can't," she said, shaking her head. "You are needed here, both to train soldiers and to protect the queen." Ember bristled as if to argue her need for protection, but the Commander cut her off. "You promised me at least six weeks of training. It's only been four."

"But this is far more important than..." Vanth attempted. The Commander cut him off with a steely glare.

"Nothing is more important than preparing our armies to defend our Queen," she said haughtily. I smirked a little and Vanth rolled his eyes, a grudging acceptance of his orders.

I sat silently, waiting for someone to point out the obvious choice that Ember had clearly already made. However, it seemed that everyone was being obtuse today.

"Then you can go," said Aspen, nodding to Hadrian. "Surely the king will be a better representative than the queen's cousin."

"I'm too dangerous to go," Hadrian said matter of factly. There was no pomposity or false pretense when he spoke, just acceptance of the danger he posed. "They would see my coming as a threat. My reputation precedes me."

"And I?" Asked Seline, raising a brow and glancing at me. Clearly, she had already figured out Ember's plan as well.

"The Unseelie King will gladly kill you on sight," Hadrian said, concern for his sister flashing in his eyes as his shadows flickered agitatedly. Seline was his half-sister, and they shared their monstrous father. He had already tried to have Seline killed once. "If there are any in the dwarven Court working for him, as we suspect there are, you will almost certainly be taken and presented to him."

As usual, it was left to me to state the obvious.

"I'll go," I said, glancing quickly at Aspen before looking at Ember. "That's what you want, yes? Sending your best friend will be a good show of faith. I'm not needed here, and the Unseelie King has no reason to take me if there are spies in the dwarven court. Plus, they don't know that I am an assassin. In that regard, I can serve to defend Aspen should something happen."

"I can defend myself," Aspen said sharply, cutting me a glance before looking back at Ember.

I ignored him, adding, "I am the most logical choice if we wish to find out what really happened with the iron weapons and keep Aspen safe while he works." Ember nodded at me.

"That is what I want to ask, yes," she said, glancing nervously between Aspen and myself. "I won't force you, of course," she added in a rush, "but having you there to…" she hesitated over the word "assassinate," and instead chose, "eliminate the king of the Dwarven Realm or any others should they prove false is an added bonus."

"Will they really be safe in the Dwarven Realm?" Vanth asked skeptically. "My Queen, what will stop the king of the Dwarven Realm from holding them hostage to force your assistance?"

"Vanth, I have told you a hundred times to call me Ember," she replied, looking irritably at Vanth, who smirked under her regard. "And the king has already offered to pay for his assistance. He will have no reason to harm the fae who are trying to help. And we can ask the emissaries to relay terms for us. We can say that all iron must be locked away during their stay and that they may defend themselves with magic if they feel threatened."

I scoffed. My magic would be almost useless if we were attacked. Ember looked up, glancing at me and then at Aspen.

"If you think this is too dangerous, we will decline," she continued, "but we desperately need allies to defeat the Unseelie King. Hadrian's use of his power is weaker here, and we cannot meet the unseelie forces in battle with our current numbers."

"How would we even get there?" I asked, brow furrowing as I thought through the details of the plan. Ember shrugged.

"I assume the emissaries arrived with some mode of transport?" She raised her eyebrow and looked at the Commander.

"I didn't see any," she said gruffly, "but it's possible I missed a wagon or a new horse." Ember nodded, satisfied.

"We will ask tomorrow about the logistics when we give our answer," she said.

"Aspen?" Ember asked, turning to her cousin. "Will you do it?"

Aspen sat, looking thoughtfully at his glass of faerie wine. He swirled it, took a sip, and nodded.

"Yes," he said, "when do we leave?"

Chapter 4: Aurelia

EMBER HAD PRESENTED HER plan to the emissaries the next morning. Rourke, who was very difficult to read, seemed unaffected by the decision, but Knox frowned at the news that Ember would not be coming in person.

"I promise you that Lord Aspen and Lady Aurelia are the best choice," she said in her most regal tone. "Aspen is gifted with earth, and Aurelia is my closest friend. They will represent me perfectly."

Knox was clearly not thrilled, but he accepted this judgment. After discussing the logistics, we had decided that we should leave in two days. Knox told us that they had transportation that would get us to the mountain realm of the dwarves as quickly as possible, but beyond that, he was vague, promising we would have time to inspect his arrangements before we left. Hadrian couldn't shadowwalk us to the mountains, since he could only go where he had previously traveled, so we were forced to rely on the emissaries. I assumed we would be taking horses, and I hoped we could borrow Nisha and Erebus for the journey.

Knox said we should pack only a small trunk each, and I spent the rest of the day trying to decide whether or not I would need formal attire, which knives and blades to bring, and whether I should ask Ember to prepare some poisons for me, just in case.

I decided against the poison and settled on bringing as many daggers as I could fit in my trunk after my other necessities were packed. I'd wear one on my hip and in my boot during travel as well.

Aspen avoided me the whole day. I supposed he was steeling himself for having to spend a lot of time in close proximity with me. I saw him sparring with Vanth at one point, and he spent an hour with Ember in the infirmary discussing seeds and other plants he should carry with him, but other than that he had been scarce.

The next day started much the same; Aspen avoided me like I was plagued while I packed and prepared all morning.

I decided to work off some of my nervous energy by sparring with Seline in the afternoon. I was not strong in combat, relying mostly on stealth and secrecy to do my dirty work, so the exercise was grueling for me as she put me through my paces. A small crowd gathered to watch us as Seline forced me to yield over and over.

"Enough?" Asked Seline, sweat dripping down her forehead as she breathed heavily with exertion. Vanth was watching her with something of a glazed look, and I rolled my eyes at how obviously he wanted her.

"My turn," came a male voice from behind me. I turned to see Aspen striding toward the ring, and nodded to Seline, heading out to take a break.

"No, I'll spar with you, if you'll let me," said Aspen, stopping me with a gentle hand. I raised a brow at him.

"It wouldn't be a fair fight," I said breathlessly. "I've no magic." Aspen shrugged.

"Blades only then," he said, waiting expectantly for me to agree. I glanced at Seline and she shrugged, smirking a little as she went to stand with Vanth.

"Fine," I said. "Daggers or swords?"

"Daggers," said Aspen decidedly, turning to walk to the other side of the sparring ring. From the corner of my eye, I saw that Ember and Hadrian had come to watch too with the dwarven emissaries. Ember had a hopeful gleam in her eye as she cheered for me with the rest of the crowd. Knox raised a brow expectantly, and Rourke looked on impassively.

I sighed, feeling like this was a monumentally bad idea, but also wanting to save face in front of the crowd and the dwarven emissaries.

"Ready?" Aspen asked, taking a defensive stance. I didn't answer, but lunged with my dagger, running for him as fast as I could. The daggers weren't iron, and while it would hurt to be stabbed, we would be fine if we avoided each other's hearts. Maybe it would feel good to stab him a little.

Aspen dodged me and whirled around, sweeping my leg from under me and forcing me into a roll to regain my footing. I wasn't much of a fighter, but I was quick and agile, and I leaned into that strength in fighting a more capable opponent.

Aspen smirked, this time coming straight for me. I jumped, landing a kick to his chest before he got near me with a blade and sending him sprawling back.

"Good hit," Aspen gasped, breath ragged.

"Yield?" I asked, resuming a defensive stance.

"Not on your life," Aspen said, running for me rather gracelessly, clearly hoping to surprise me into yielding to him. I dodged and swiped at him with my blade, grazing his side just enough to draw blood. I hesitated at the sight, meeting his eyes with a question.

"It's nothing," he said dismissively. "Continue." I shrugged and we continued this dance of lunging and defending until the sweat was pouring off us. I rather resented again being unable to remove my own shirt as Aspen's golden tan glowed in the wintry sun.

I was distracted by his chest when Aspen lunged at me next, and without thinking I threw out a wall of air, forcing him back. He snarled, and vines wrapped around my ankles, pulling me down as Aspen knelt over me, pressing his blade gently but firmly to my throat.

"Yield," he commanded. The crowd cheered for him.

"That was cheating," I said as he stood, offering me a hand to help me up. He smirked.

"You cheated first," he said, striding away as if we hadn't just been locked in a furious battle.

"I couldn't tell if he wanted to kill or kiss you at the end there," said Seline as she rejoined me in the ring.

"A little of both, I think," said Vanth, coming over to us with a wide grin.

I looked after Aspen's retreating form and sighed. I was fairly certain he had only wanted to do one of those things, and I rather doubted it was the kissing.

EMBER AND I ATE dinner together just the two of us that evening while Hadrian handled strategy meetings with the Commander. She usually joined them, but said that tonight she wanted to spend time with me instead. My heart warmed at my thoughtful friend, who planned a dinner of only dessert and wine.

"Because I'm the queen, and I can," she said happily when I asked why she didn't plan for any real food. I laughed, agreeing the chocolate mousse and faeberry pie were superior to real food anyway.

I had almost certainly eaten too much, because my stomach just wouldn't settle, and anxiety gnawed at me. Usually, I was more calm before a mission like this. Even my mission to Lord Thorn was met with cool calculation rather than crippling anxiety.

I had been lying in bed wide awake for two hours before I finally gave up on sleep and got out of bed, throwing on my robe and a warm coat and boots and heading down to the palace gardens to clear my head.

The night was very cold. Frost coated the leaves and petals of the winter flowers that bloomed in the queen's garden, and I slipped more than once on the icy garden path as I walked. Luckily for me there would be no one to see me if I fell on my face.

Except of course for Aspen, who had chosen that exact moment to appear directly in front of me walking the opposite direction as I rounded a corner of a high hedge, causing me to slip and lose my balance. I almost hit the ground, but strong arms steadied my waist with an "oof" as I knocked the breath out of him.

"Sorry," I said breathlessly, looking up from where he had caught me. I cursed the goddess for her wicked sense of humor in forcing us together so many times in a single day. Aspen looked down at me in surprise which quickly turned to confusion.

"Why are you out here?" he asked, propping me back up on my feet and taking a step back. "You should be sleeping."

"So should you," I pointed out, reaching out to grab the hedge for support in the absence of his arm. "Can't sleep?" He shook his head.

"You neither, I see," he said. I shook my head, and we stood there for a moment in uncomfortable silence, trying to figure out how to navigate this situation. "Let me walk you back," he added. "It's late."

"I know it's late," I said acerbically. Sighing because I could never just keep a civil tongue in my head around him anymore, I shook my head again. "I need to clear my head. You can go back though. I'll be fine." He sighed.

"I'm not leaving you out here in the dark," he said. I rolled my eyes, torn between frustration at the male and his notions of chivalry, and a fluttering of hope that he cared for my well-being.

"Then I guess you'd better walk with me," I said, stepping around him and continuing down the path. For a moment he stood as I walked on. I tried not to turn and eventually heard a huff of frustration. A moment later he was slipping and sliding on the path next to me. I put my arm out to steady him, and he clasped his hand in mine.

"Your hands are freezing," he said. I winced. I had forgotten gloves, but I rarely felt the cold. I supposed I just ran warm, and I didn't even notice that my fingers were turning faintly blue in the moonlight. He pulled me to a stop, making me slip again, and caught me, taking both of my hands in his gloved ones and blowing hot air into them to warm them.

I looked up at him, startled at this show of tenderness, and not sure what to do with it. He looked down at me, and for that moment it was almost like it had always been between us, tender and hopeful and kind. Warmth filled his blue eyes and turned them the blue of the summer sky, instead of frosty and hard. My heart lurched as he blew a second time, warming my fingers more.

"What are you doing?" I whispered, still looking at him, a riot of emotions twisting in my stomach. Earlier today he had been fighting me like he wanted to do actual damage, and now he was touching me tenderly. I felt I had every right to be confused.

"Warming up your hands," he said quietly, blowing into them a third time. "There," he said, still holding them. "Better?"

I nodded, throat too tight to speak. He turned, still holding one of my hands and made his way down the path. I followed, confusion driving me more than an actual desire to walk now.

We made our way around the tall hedges and toward the rose garden, which was stark and dead in the winter cold, but still eerily beautiful.

"Are you afraid?" Aspen asked, not looking at me as we walked.

"No," I said truthfully. Ember called me recklessly courageous, but it took a lot to scare me. Danger gave me a rush of adrenaline, which was probably a terrible trait for survival, but here we were. "Are you?"

"Yes," Aspen said simply, not elaborating. We walked a little longer in silence as I tried to think of a way to reassure him. I pulled him to a stop and turned to face him.

"I will have your back, the whole time," I said. Aspen took my fingers and warmed them again, and I fought a blush that crept up my cheeks. "I know we are...I know it's..." I struggled to find the right word for what we were and how it was between us.

"Difficult?" he asked, raising an eyebrow at me. I nodded.

"Yes, difficult. It's difficult between us right now," I agreed. He blew on my fingers again to warm them and heat bloomed in my core at his touch. My stupid heart was never going to learn. Whatever this was, I doubted it was more than gentlemanly courtesy. Someone needed to tell my body that. "And I know things can never go back to how they used to be between us. But I'll still have your back. Nothing will happen to you."

Aspen looked at me then, his eyes piercing mine as he frowned.

"That's not what I'm afraid of," he said softly. Before I could ask what he meant, he added, "Please let me walk you back? I'm freezing and I can't leave you out here in good conscience." I rolled my eyes, and he smirked, the old Aspen glinting through again. That smirk made all of me melt and I nodded.

"Fine," I said, trying to sound annoyed. "But if I can't sleep, it will be you who suffers tomorrow. I'm horrible when I'm tired." He laughed.

"Oh, I know," he said.

Chapter 5: Ember

It had been a long day, and all I really wanted was to curl into bed with Hadrian and sleep for a thousand years. The bath water was getting cold, but I couldn't bring myself to leave its remaining warmth, knowing that the cold stone floor of the bathing chamber awaited me.

Aurelia and Aspen would be leaving in the morning, and as confident as I was in their abilities to broker a deal with the Dwarven

King, I was worried about them. I was sending them into enemy territory with only wits and daggers to protect them in the faint hope that the dwarves could turn the tide in the war that was all but guaranteed to break out in the next few months.

I sighed, finally climbing out of the bath and toweling off, careful not to pull my wings too hard with the towel. I had learned, through painful experience, that wings were damned sensitive. Even though my back had fully healed weeks ago from the trauma of their eruption, pulling too hard on them or pressing them hard against a wall hurt. The last lesson I had learned after a painful liaison with Hadrian, and he had been careful to avoid taking me against any walls since.

I smiled, thinking of my mate and hoping he was waiting for me in bed. Hadrian and I had only been married for two weeks, and we had been immediately thrown into ruling and military strategy when we had accepted our positions as Queen and King. We had barely any time with each other except at night, so I hadn't been getting a lot of sleep.

"What's taking so long?" A deep, male voice rumbled from the bedroom. I laughed, opening the door to shout back at him. I laughed harder when I saw him.

He was laid out on his side, completely naked on our bed and lounging with his head propped on his hand. His shadows, which he often kept hidden around the others, swirled around him in a bizarre, undulating dance.

"What is this?" I asked, still laughing and tugging the towel a little tighter around me. I wasn't exactly self-conscious about my body, but I knew I was curvier and more full-figured than the females he had probably been with in the past. Hadrian had the chiseled body of a warrior or a god, and he was on full display, already hard as he gazed at me hungrily.

"You're doing that wrong," he said, standing from the bed and prowling over to me like a sleek jungle cat stalking its prey. I shivered as he stood before me, taking the towel in his large hands and unveiling my body to him. He dropped the towel behind me and ran his large, calloused hands down my side, making me shiver more as his shadows wrapped around my arms and waist.

"You are a goddess," he murmured, leaning forward to kiss the top of my head and running a finger down my spine between my wings. I gasped, feeling heat pool in my center as I pressed my body against his, our chests flush as he stroked down my back.

"What did I ever do to deserve you," he said, pressing his lips to my cheek, just below my ear, the hollow of my throat, and moving lower until he was kneeling before me, his shadows stroking the backs of my knees. I ran my fingers through his dark hair, reveling in the feel of his lips against me as warmth melted me from the inside.

"What did I do to deserve you?" I countered, gasping a little as he grabbed my rear to pull me closer as he licked over one pebbled nipple, then the other.

"Mmmm, so many things," he murmured, kissing down my ribs to my stomach. He ran a pale hand over my stomach and looked up at me, an eyebrow raised in question. I shook my head and he continued kissing down until he reached my center.

He licked, just once, slow and sensual through me as I shuddered, grasping his hair to steady myself against the riot of sensation his tongue created.

"Mmm, you taste like everything I've ever wanted," he growled, licking a second time and making me gasp again. He raised his head, making me whimper in protest, and he smiled, standing to turn me and walk me backward toward our bed. He pushed me to sit on the edge and knelt again, positioning himself between my thighs and pushing them wide. His shadows wrapped around them to hold them apart.

"Let me feast on you," he growled, licking me again until I gasped and fell back on the bed with a moan. My hands tangled in the sheets by my head as he stroked his tongue through me, circling in a deep, steady rhythm as he sucked and tasted. One of his hands reached up to roll my nipple between his fingers and I moaned again, twining one hand in his hair as I began to climb toward release.

Hadrian made a noise of pure male dominance as he felt me building, reaching a second hand up to squeeze the other nipple, his shadows still holding my thighs wide. I ground against his mouth, needing more friction as the pressure built until I was moaning in ecstasy. Release shattered through me as he continued to lick steady circles with his tongue and I shuddered against him.

He turned his head to kiss the inside of my thigh.

"You are perfection," he said, rising to stand above me and pulling me closer to the edge of the bed. He pulled a pillow from the head of the bed and lifted my legs, stuffing it under me to raise me a little higher before he slid into me with a deep thrust, making me cry out in surprise and pleasure.

Hooking my knees over his elbows, he widened my thighs and moved in slow, steady thrusts as I cried out and moaned from the pressure and friction. He leaned down and kissed me, forcing my legs apart almost painfully as his shadows snaked up my arms to hold them above my head.

"My Queen," he said, punctuating the word with a thrust. "My love." Another thrust. "My perfect mate," he groaned, spilling himself into me and taking me over the edge again with his final deep thrusts.

We lay there for a while not moving, kissing and nuzzling and enjoying being close as the shadows cocooned us in semi-darkness. After a few minutes, my thighs began to ache, and I pushed him off me so I could go clean up.

When I returned from the bathing chamber again he was lying in a much less enticing pose, waiting for me with his arm outstretched under the blankets. I went to him, crawling into our bed and resting my head on his wide shoulder as his legs and arms and shadows wrapped comfortingly around me.

"Thank you," I breathed, closing my eyes to take in the smell and feel of him.

"For what?" he asked, kissing my brow and lifting my chin with a finger to meet my eyes. His swirled gray and silver, flashing a little as he took me in, flushed from our lovemaking.

"For helping me relax," I teased, lifting up on my arms to kiss his nose before settling back down into the crook of his arm.

"Anytime," he said smugly, earning a tiny poke in the side from me that made him yelp playfully.

"Do you think I made the wrong call?" I asked. Hadrian didn't need more context. He seemed to always know my exact fears and worries instinctively.

"They haven't left yet," he said, brushing my cheek with his fingertips. "You could still change your mind."

"I know," I sighed, a little annoyed that he was offering me solutions instead of support. "But I want to know if you agree. If it had been your call, would you have done the same thing?"

"Yes," Hadrian said without a moment's hesitation. "Aspen is more magically suited for the task, and I need you here. Who will keep me company if you leave?" He teased. I poked him again.

"And Aurelia?" I asked, still not sure about sending my best friend on a mission with her ex-whatever-it-was she and Aspen used to be. They weren't officially together, but there had been an understanding certainly.

"Aurelia can take care of herself," Hadrian replied tiredly, giving me a little squeeze. "And Aspen too, I expect."

"But they don't exactly get along," I said, worrying my bottom lip with my teeth. Hadrian tilted his head down and kissed me soundly, pulling the worries and misgivings from me with his lips.

"You and I both know," he said, kissing me once more and looking at me with his wicked half-smile, "that nothing combats mutual dislike better than forced proximity on a long and danger- ous mission."

Chapter 6: Aurelia

"GODDESS ABOVE," I SAID, as I stared up into the massive beak of a giant roc. "We're flying?"

The dwarven emissaries had been cagey about our mode of transport, and this explained why. Two great rocs had flapped down on a whistle from Rourke, landing heavily in the castle courtyard with a gust of wind and a mighty squawk.

I beamed at Ember, and she grinned back, knowing how much I loved to fly. As a child, I had once tried to fly by jumping off a tall tree. I was lucky I didn't break my neck, and I remember lamenting my lack of wings to Ember on several occasions.

I had not slept well, but the sight of the giant birds roused me and adrenaline filled me. I laid a hand on one of the giant beaks, feeling the smooth surface vibrate faintly beneath my hand.

"Careful, Lady of Summer," said Knox, hauling one of the trunks past me. "They bite."

"They're beautiful," I said, gazing lovingly into the giant iris of one of the rocs. It had brown feathers and a sharp, golden beak, and black-tipped claws stuck out beneath two huge feathery legs. They were larger than horses, and I wondered where they had been hiding that they hadn't been spotted before this.

"Should we ask the king of the Dwarven Realm to make a gift of one?" Ember asked, laughing when I looked hopeful at the question.

"They take years to tame and train," Rourke said in his gravelly voice, holding a chunk of bloody raw meat up to the bird, who snapped it up in its sharp jaws with a happy squawk. "And they're happiest in the mountains. They like the cold and the thin air."

"Do the dwarves regularly ride rocs?" Aspen asked, coming up behind me, wary of the giant bird.

"Aye, Lord of Spring," Rourke nodded, throwing another hunk of bloody meat to the other bird, who was gray with white tail feathers. He squawked happily as well. "They're the easiest way to traverse the mountains when we have to go abroad."

"My lord, my lady, you two will ride with me on Caelus," Knox said, patting the side of the big brown roc. "Rourke will ride Notus, who will carry your things."

I looked around at the gray bird and saw some kind of netting clutched in his talons. Rourke was heaving trunks into the net for the bird to carry.

"Just 'Aspen' is fine," Aspen said, looking skeptically at the giant birds. "All of us will fit on one of them?" He looked slightly green at the idea of flying, and I smirked. Knox nodded.

"They can carry five if need be, but it's very uncomfortable. The two of you will be no problem," he added, giving me a faint smile.

Ember and Hadrian pulled the unseelie fae aside to discuss the terms for the king, and Aspen gingerly lifted his hand to the roc's beak, laying it flat next to mine on the polished surface. I smiled up at him, more openly and joyfully than I probably had since we fell apart, and he looked down at me, something tender in his expression.

"I'm not sure one would fit in the stables," he joked, patting the bird's beak and shoving his hands in his pockets. "Plus, he might eat the horses." I smiled, looking back up at the roc, who had turned his great head and presented his feathery neck.

"He would never," I cooed, scratching a spot behind his jaw. He closed his eyes and made a purring sound, or as close to one as any bird could make. I laughed. "He's so sweet. He could live on the roof."

I turned back to Aspen and saw he was watching me, his jaw a little slack and his eyes bright. I frowned.

"What?" I asked. After our walk last night, there seemed to be a tentative peace between us that I was terrified of disturbing. The gap between us was bridged now by a thin sheet of ice that could crack with any wrong move.

"Nothing," he said finally, looking away. "You just have ridiculous ideas of what animals make good pets."

"Not a pet," I corrected, turning back to the roc and scratching again. "A valiant steed."

Aspen snorted and I smiled. Knox whistled a long, sharp note, and both birds bent low to the ground, showing that they had saddles similar to a horse's attached to their backs. Rourke swung up into his saddle and patted Notus, who flapped his great wings and took off skyward. I gasped, watching him ascend with our luggage and flap off toward the mountains.

"We'll have to camp tonight to give the birds a rest," Knox said, swinging himself up onto Caelus's saddle. "We will meet Rourke at sunset."

Ember threw her arms around me as Aspen shook Hadrian's hand and bowed his head slightly.

"Be so careful," she said, squeezing me and looking at me for a long moment. "Please, don't be reckless. And take your tea, or my grandmother will never let you hear the end of it." I laughed. Mother Vervain was extremely superstitious about the power of tea in preventing sickness as one traveled the realms.

"I am the epitome of carefulness," I joked, earning another quick hug before she pushed me toward Hadrian. He hugged me as well.

"Stay safe, little sister," he said, calling me by the honorific he had given me the day he and Ember were officially wed.

Seline also embraced me, a little to my surprise.

"Make him regret you," she said, giving me a subtle nod toward Aspen, who quickly turned away from us. I hugged her and laughed.

Vanth, who had guarded me when I had been briefly married to Lord Thorn, clapped me on the shoulder.

"No fires," he said, recalling my semi-disastrous plan to steal Thorn's messages that had resulted in us fleeing his manor, and Vanth being burned and scarred. I winced and nodded, but he smiled warmly at me.

"It's time to go, my lady," shouted Knox. He held his hand out to me, and I grasped his arm as he pulled me up to the bird's back. He was strong, and he swung me around the back of him with ease.

"Just 'Aurelia' is fine for me too," I said, blushing as he gave me a warm smile and settled me behind him.

Aspen climbed up next, taking Knox's offered arm and swinging up behind me. I wasn't sure how I felt about being pressed against Aspen's chest for a large portion of the day, but I felt sure he was similarly conflicted.

Knox passed a leather strap behind him and Aspen pulled it around his back, passing it back to Knox to hook into the front of the saddle.

"Hopefully this will stop you from falling off," he said, grinning sideways at us. "You'd better wrap your arms around me, Lady Aurelia. And Lord Aspen, wrap yours around her. Are you ready?"

I nodded excitedly and we were already rising into the air with a few flaps of the great bird's wings. I felt Aspen tense behind me as his arms folded around my waist, gripping a little too tightly to be comfortable. I grinned, taking in the view of the castle as we rose high above it and took off toward the mountains.

My enthusiasm for the flight waned after a few hours. By the time the sun was setting and we started to descend into the woods at the base of the mountains, my arms and legs were aching from holding their position so long, and my face felt chapped from the blistering winds as we flew.

The mountains loomed above us, gigantic gray monoliths as we spiraled down toward a speck of light on the forest floor. From my place between Knox and Aspen, it was difficult to see much, but I appreciated the warmth they offered on the journey. We hadn't spoken much, as speaking over the rush of air and the flapping of the bird's wings required shouting, and I was soon hoarse. As we landed, I realized the speck of light was a fire pit.

Caelus landed heavily next to Notus and squawked, tongue hanging a bit from his beak.

"Poor baby, you're thirsty," I croaked, patting the bird's back as best as I could as Aspen tried to untangle himself from me.

Knox unhooked us and Aspen slid down the side of the bird rather stiffly, landing a little harder than he meant to, and almost overbalancing. He steadied himself against the bird and looked up at me, lips chapped, cheeks pink with the cold and the wind, and golden curls windblown. I tried to smile, but winced, realizing my lips were equally chapped.

"Aurelia, you next," Knox called hoarsely, holding out an arm to me. I groaned as I pulled my leg around the saddle and slid stiffly down the bird. My legs gave out completely, and Aspen caught me, holding me firmly until I regained my balance. He pulled me away from the bird as Knox slid down, far more graceful and less windblown than either of us. I tried to smooth my braid a bit as he patted the bird and whistled. Both birds rose into the sky and flew off, nearly knocking us over in a gust of wind.

"Where are they going?" I asked, still hoarse from shouting above the wind.

"To hunt," Knox replied, frowning at me. "I forgot you've never flown rocs before," he said apologetically, pulling a small tin of something from his coat. "Here, for your lips."

I took the tin, and opened it, giving it a sniff. I wrinkled my nose. "It smells vile," I said, grimacing. "What is it?"

"Deer fat," Knox said, shrugging and slathering some of the fat on his lips. "It's horrible, but it will save your skin in the wind."

I took a tiny fingerful and passed it to Aspen, who did the same. Now I was tired and sore and I smelled like dead deer. Lovely.

Rourke was already roasting something over the fire pit, and it smelled divine. I had barely eaten all day, except for a few strips of jerky Knox had passed back to us mid-flight. I was also desperate to relieve myself, so I excused myself to try to find a private spot behind a bush or a tree.

When I returned, Rourke was stripping meat off the carcass he was cooking and wrapping it around crude skewers. He handed me the first, and the second to Knox. I sat near the fire, chewing on the meat as the juices dripped down my chin and reveling in how well it filled my hollow stomach. Aspen plopped down next to me and attacked his dinner, and for a while the four of us sat in companionable silence, the sounds of the forest and the crackling fire, and the far-off cries of the rocs the only noise.

"So, Lord Aspen, can we see your magic?" Knox asked. He had finished his dinner and was leaning back on a fallen log, long legs stretched out in front of him. He lifted one of his legs and leaned forward on a knee.

"Just 'Aspen'," Aspen reminded, giving Knox an appraising look. He too had stretched out his long legs. I felt glad that Rourke was at least shorter than me. "What do you want to see?"

Knox shrugged, smirking slightly, his blue-black hair falling over a shoulder. He cupped his palm face up, and a flower of ice blossomed there. It was beautiful and delicate. He looked at me, indigo eyes warm despite his cold, blue face. The fire cast shadows on his angular jaw, and his lips shined slightly with the deer fat.

Aspen smirked and placed a dead leaf in his hand, pouring his magic into it and turning the dry, brown thing green and vibrant once more.

"Impressive," Knox said, smiling and handing the ice flower to me, with a nodded, "My lady." It immediately began to melt in the heat of the fire and my hand. "What about your magic?" he asked, turning to me. I shook my head.

"My magic is...sort of stuck," I confessed, sighing as I watched Aspen grow stocks and blossoms on his leaf. "I'm not sure what it is, and I don't know how to release it." Knox frowned.

"Do dwarves have magic?" Aspen asked, handing me the newly bloomed flower and turning to Rourke.

The dwarf made a noncommittal grunt. "Aye, but not the kind of magic the fae have," he said, voice craggy and rough. "Our magic is in our forging."

We looked at him expectantly, waiting for some elaboration, but none came. Knox turned back to me.

"Can you feel your magic in you?" he asked. I frowned.

"Yes, but it won't move," I said, trying to describe the block of burning something that had taken up residence in my chest. "And believe me, I've tried everything to access it."

"I find that my magic pumps through my veins like my blood," said Knox, creating another ice sculpture in the palm of his hands, this one a tiny version of his roc. "I feel it pumping cold through me, and I pour it into my hands when I need it. How do you experience it, Aspen?"

Aspen started, as if not expecting a question.

"Oh, um," he said, frowning as he thought through how his magic worked. "More like a seed that stretches its roots throughout me," he said, looking at Knox. Knox smiled warmly, and I thought it odd for an unseelie fae to be so friendly toward us, although I supposed we were friends enough with Hadrian and the others.

"Why did you flee the Unseelie King?" Aspen asked. Knox's face darkened.

"My parents fled him," he said, a bit of the friendliness gone as he discussed something that was clearly not a topic he liked to consider. "I was abandoned as a child. The dwarves rescued me."

"Apologies," Aspen said, gently. Knox relaxed a bit and nodded, but said nothing more.

Eventually, Rourke cut in. "We should sleep. Tomorrow is another long flight," he said, tossing each of us a bedroll from the supplies he had taken off Notus.

I grimaced a little, contemplating the hard ground I would be sleeping on tonight, but when no one complained I resigned myself to toughing it out. We spread out a bit around the fire, and I shivered, the night far colder at the base of the mountains than it had been in the Seelie Realm.

I felt the ground behind me shake and move, a rumbling noise coming from all around us. I gasped as a thick wall of vines reached up from the ground around me and curled into a makeshift shelter, a hole in the roof serving to let the smoke from the fire out but keep the warmth in.

"That's a useful trick," said Knox admiringly, putting a finger to the wall of vines and pushing gently to test their strength. Aspen shrugged.

"They probably won't keep out predators, but they'll hopefully keep out the cold," Aspen said, glancing at me before lying back down on his bedroll.

I was exhausted from a night of poor sleep and a day of travel, so I let the sounds of the forest and the crackling fire and the embrace of Aspen's magic lull me to sleep.

I WOKE TO FIND the fire had raged out of control and was swiftly consuming the shelter of vines. I screamed to wake the males, but they were already gone. Smoke filled the tiny hut and I coughed, panic blossoming in my chest as I realized there was no way out. A snake, the same from my dream in the palace, lifted its head to look at me expectantly. Then it lunged.

I screamed and was shaken awake by Aspen, his face pale and eyes wide in the dim firelight, which had burned down to embers.

"Aurelia," he said, giving my shoulders a little shake. "Aurelia, you're fine. Wake up."

I sat up, terrified and confused. The hut was fine, Rourke snored loudly and Knox looked over at us, turning to go back to sleep when he saw Aspen was with me. I let out a sob and he folded me into his arms, holding me against his chest.

"It was a dream," he murmured, stroking soothing lines down my back as he held me and I cried quietly. It was almost like it used to be between us, and I felt myself calming down in the safety of his arms. "Just a dream. You're safe."

"I'm sorry," I choked out, trying to push away and feeling him resist letting me go. "I'm fine, I promise. Go back to sleep."

He tilted my chin up to look at my face, which was probably blotchy and tear-streaked. Sighing, he turned away, and my heart cracked a little with disappointment. But then he was back, laying his bedroll out next to mine. He lay down and opened an arm, an offer of comfort and a truce between us. We hadn't been at war the last couple of days, but again I felt the tentative nature of this renewed connection between us. I hesitated, looking around as if waiting for someone to tell me it was a trick.

"Aurelia," he said quietly, voice gravelly with exhaustion and concern, "come to bed."

I nodded and let him fold me into his embrace, lying with my back against his chest and my head tucked under his. I closed my eyes, imagining that I had never hurt him, that we were just us again, drawing comfort and promises from each other as we had once done.

"I'm sorry," I whispered into the wall of vines in front of me, feeling his arms tighten slightly around me. I didn't say what I was sorry for, and he didn't ask, but I felt a quiet acknowledgment in his arms that he knew I was sorry for more than simply waking him.

I didn't sleep again for the rest of the night, partly because of the dream, and partly because I was afraid if I did I would wake up to find Aspen gone. Instead, I lay in the shelter and warmth of his arms until the gray morning light speared through the top of the shelter he had constructed, and Rourke began to grumble and rustle around as he packed up.

The rocs were back when Aspen pulled down the vine hut, and we wordlessly ate cold meat and drank from water skins without talking about the night. Knox glanced between us warily, as if assessing our relationship.

"Do you want to talk about it?" Aspen asked me quietly as Knox and Rourke packed everything back into storage and we prepared to fly again. I shook my head, not meeting Aspen's eyes as I ran fingers through my tangled hair and attempted to braid it into something civilized.

"Aurelia," he said, putting a hand out to stop my frantic movement and tilting my chin up to look at him. "Is this the first time you've had a dream like that?"

"No," I said, shaking my head and brushing his hands away so I could finish. Knox came over to get us back on the roc, climbing up just as gracefully and fluidly as he had slid down.

"I want to talk about this later," Aspen said, boosting me into the saddle behind Knox and vaulting up behind me. I felt stiff and cold from a day of riding followed by yet another night of miserable sleep, and I was very much hoping that there would be a real bed to sleep in when we finally arrived in the Dwarven Realm.

Chapter 7: Aurelia

THERE *WAS* A REAL bed, and it was made of stone.

After another day of flying, the mountains growing taller and more imposing as we flew to their precipice, I felt more stiff and sore than before and was ready to sleep for a thousand years.

We had arrived at a rookery of sorts, where Caelus and Notus were cleaned and fed and made comfortable with straw as several other rocs squawked in greeting. Rourke had explained that the tame rocs lived in rookeries like this throughout the mountains, and messengers would often fly between them to pass messages more quickly than running through the underground network of tunnels.

From the rookery, we had descended hundreds of stone steps carved into the side of the mountain while wind and ice pummeled us from all sides. It was miserable, and there was a moment I thought for sure I would fall to my death when I missed a step, only to be steadied by Knox, who gripped my waist with firm hands as I regained my balance. I smiled at him gratefully.

"Are you quite well, Lady Aurelia," he asked once we had made it past the steepest part of the stairs. "You seemed very distressed by your dream last night."

"Just 'Aurelia,' please," I said, picking my way carefully as we moved. "And I'm fine now, thank you. Just a nightmare."

After an interminable time, we made it to a stone entrance carved into the mountain itself. Faint blue lights lined the passageways, offering enough light to see by. Knox explained that they were glow worms, kept in glass bulbs and fed a steady diet of luminescent mushrooms to make them glow more brightly.

The passageway went on for what felt like miles, intricately carved columns of stone and great hallways opening up as we moved deeper into the mountain. I'm sure I was limping by the time we finally stopped, my hips and knees aching from the flight. The entrance to the caves was long gone from view when Rourke paused in front of a beautifully carved wooden door.

"These are your guest quarters," Rourke explained, gesturing to the door. "This entrance is the only one that leads back out of the city. You'll find another exit from the main room on the other side that leads down to the city proper. May I?"

I nodded as he opened the door and led us through. I wasn't sure what to expect of an underground city of stone, but it was not glittering walls that gleamed under the light of the glow worms, crystals flaring blue and pink and purple in the dim light with an eerie, beautiful glow.

The room we had entered seemed to be a common room that led to an open balcony with a view of the city before us. It was as if the dwarves had carved their homes into the walls of a huge cave, building cobbled streets and stone gardens and courtyards below. Beyond, a tall structure rose at the back of the cave, glittering like a jewel.

"This is the Crystal City," Knox said reverently, gesturing to the city below us.

"Is that your king's palace?" I asked, pointing toward the spires in the distance.

Knox nodded. "Yes. We are to take you to see the king at first light." He gestured around the room. "I hope this will do. I will have a meal sent to you, and there is a bathing chamber in each of the rooms. Your things will also be brought shortly."

I nodded, not sure how to ask when we would know it was first light. "Will you be staying here?" Aspen asked, sounding like he very much hoped the answer was no. I did too. It would be hard to talk openly if we were constantly under guard.

Knox shook his head. "Rourke lives in the palace," he said, nodding to the broad dwarf. "I have a house in the city."

"You live in the palace?" I asked, turning to the stout dwarf.

He nodded. "Aye," he replied gravely. "The prince is bound to the palace here as he is in your realm."

"Prince?" I squeaked, thinking about how informally we had been treating him. "Why didn't you tell us you were the prince?" I asked, belatedly adding a "Your Highness."

Rourke shrugged. "No one asked," he said. With a nod to Knox, he strode off into the city down a set of narrow stone steps that connected the balcony to the street below.

Knox smiled. "He's a prince of few words, I'm afraid," he said, apologetically. "Will these accommodations do?"

"Yes," Aspen said, always the courtly gentleman. "Thank you." He turned and headed into one of the adjoining rooms, which I assumed must be a bedroom.

Knox gave me a puzzled frown. "Are you two..." he started, pointing between me and the door Aspen had disappeared through.

"Oh, no," I said in a rush. "I mean, we were once, but not anymore." I felt my cheeks turn pink as I tried to explain our situation, but Knox just nodded.

"I see," he said. He cleared his throat, running a hand through his blue-black hair. He wasn't as broad as Aspen was, but he was a fine-looking male. I wondered if he was more interested in my situation, or in Aspen's. "I'll come get you in the morning," he finally added, shooting me a smile and sauntering off toward the city. I watched him walk away, wondering at his reaction. I shook my confusion off. There was no point in worrying about it until a bath and food and a full night of sleep, probably in that order.

Since Aspen seemed to have claimed one of the rooms already, I went through the door to the other. It was a small but elegant sleeping chamber, carved from stone like the rest of the city, walls glittering faintly in the dim light of the glow worms. There was a lamp on a table near the bed filled with fireflies. I tapped it gently to wake them, and the room lit with a warm, golden glow.

The bed was more of a gigantic couch, with furs and pillows piled high. To my chagrin, I noticed the base had been carved from the rock, but there was a soft mattress on top that would make it comfortable. A small dresser and table were the only other furniture in the room, and a bathing chamber adjoined, with running water and a large stone tub.

I ran a bath and dragged my trunk in from the common room. We had no idea how long exactly we would be under the mountain, and I had packed enough for maybe a week if I kept myself clean. When the bath was full, I stripped off my travel-worn clothes, the warm coat stifling in the heat of the bathing chamber, and climbed in. The water was heavenly, and I let it soothe the aches and pains of travel as I sank deeper into the tub.

I found a bar of soap that smelled like lavender and attempted to wash myself and my hair, scrubbing two days of grime from the sky and the forest floor. When I finally felt presentable, I dried off on a length of linen and donned a night dress and robe. I doubted we would have visitors tonight, and I was ready to eat and sleep.

Aspen was already in the common room when I returned, damp hair curling around his nape and temples as he ate some sort of bread with sauce. I remembered we were here to solve a food shortage, and felt a little guilty that we would also need to be fed.

I sat in an armchair next to the table where the food had been placed and examined the options, taking a piece of flatbread and dipping it into a green sauce. It was good—unexpectedly earthy, but not unpleasant. I sighed happily and closed my eyes, letting the bread warm me from the inside.

Aspen was watching me as I swallowed and reached for another piece. "What?" I asked, dipping the bread again and stuffing it into my mouth. He raised a brow, probably shocked at my unladylike manners, but we weren't in a palace right now and I was hungry.

"Tell me about the dream," Aspen said quietly, leaning forward with his forearms on his knees.

I sighed. "It was nothing, just a nightmare," I said dismissively, reaching for another piece of bread.

Aspen caught my hand, and I looked at him. His eyes had lost the icy edge they'd had this last month when he looked at me, and I felt that bridge between us solidifying into something more...sturdy. My stomach gave a little flip at his piercing gaze.

"You screamed like you were dying," he said quietly. "Tell me why."

Whether it was his commanding tone, the concern I saw in him, or the fact that he was maybe softening toward me a little, I didn't know, but I told him. He frowned. "There's always fire? In these dreams?" he asked. I nodded. He was still holding my hand away from the bread, and I was torn between letting him hold it and hunger. He sighed and let go, so I went for the food.

"Maybe it has something to do with the fire you set at Thorn's manor," he said thoughtfully, leaning back and crossing an ankle over a knee.

I shrugged. "Maybe," I conceded. "It was after that that they started."

Aspen nodded. "And the snake?" he asked.

I shook my head. "Mother Vervain said it could be a symbol of rebirth, but I don't feel reborn in any way," I said irritably.

"Will you tell me if you have another?" he asked me seriously.

"Why do you care?" I asked. Until the last week or so, he had made it clear that he was done with me, but now he was acting like the old Aspen. I didn't want to sit around hoping that there might be something between us again if this change in his attitude toward me was all about the mission.

"Mother Vervain says dreams have meaning," Aspen intoned, bringing me back to the present. He quoted her as if quoting a great wisdom from some ancient tome, which was how all of Mother Vervain's wisdom sounded. He leveled a contemplative look at me. "And I care because I never want to hear you scream like that again."

"What is this Aspen?" I asked, throwing caution and timidity to the wind. "What am I to you now? Less than a week ago, you hated me, and we barely spoke. Now you're warming my hands and asking about my dreams and holding me in the night. What do you want from this?" I gestured between us.

"I..." he looked at me, frowning, clearly unable to find the words to express himself. I waited, but he closed his mouth, and my heart gave an almighty crack.

"Do you want us to be friends?" I asked, pushing a little harder. "Lovers? Nothing?" His silence stretched out, and I felt that thin bridge of ice that had grown and solidified between us crack.

"No," I said, standing and walking back toward my room.

"No?" he asked, shaking himself from his confusion and running to get in front of me. "What do you mean, 'no'?"

"I mean, no, I will not tell you about my dreams and I will not spare you from my screaming," I said angrily, rejection and hurt fueling the fury in my chest. If he couldn't voice what he wanted from me, then I presumed he wanted nothing. "You gave up the right to know everything about me when you pushed me away. You can't have it both ways, Aspen. You don't get to have my trust and my confidence and give me none of you in return."

"Damn it, Aurelia," he started as I tried to walk around him. He grabbed my shoulders and shook me gently. "Will you just stop and let me think for a moment?"

"No!" I shouted, pushing his hands from me. "If you need to think, I have my answer. Good night." I left him and slammed the wooden door that separated my room from the common area.

For several minutes I stood against the door, heart pounding and pulse racing. A part of me hoped he was angry. I hoped he was furious. I hoped he would knock down the door and press me hard against the wall and... I shook my head, trying to push the fantasy from my mind. Still, a part of me hoped he might come.

He didn't.

Chapter 8: Aurelia

Knox raised his brows at our snappishness the next morning, but he didn't say anything as he escorted us through the Crystal City toward the palace. He had told us that the palace was indeed made of crystal, carved over generations as a glittering memorial of Dwarvish ingenuity.

I looked on with wonder at the architectural marvel of the city and the palace. Crystals in various colors and cuts gleamed from the walls and streets, lighting our path through the city almost as brightly as if it were day. When we neared the palace, I learned how the dwarves told night from day and lit their city.

A bright beam of sunlight stretched from a tiny carved window in the mountainside and caught the palace, which refracted it across the city, illuminating the crystals and scattering from house to house. The light of day was the glittering of crystal and diamond and quartz spreading around the single beam of sunlight. At night, the crystals glowed from their own magical luminescence, dimming the city and casting it in dark rainbow shades until the sun rose again.

"It's beautiful, isn't it?" said Knox. I turned my attention to him and saw him watching me, smiling slightly at my expression of awe. I wondered again how exactly this male had found himself swearing loyalty to the Dwarven King.

"Very," I agreed, nodding enthusiastically. "Almost better than the rocs," I added. He smiled.

"How long have you lived in this city?" I asked, watching dwarves and unseelie fae mingling about their morning business, all seeming relatively happy. The food shortage must not have hit in full force yet, or the people would have been more pinched and somber.

"I came here as a boy," he replied, looking down at me as he spoke. "It's been several decades now. I know no other home."

"And do you have family here?" I asked, wondering if he had come alone all those years ago, and how in the name of the Goddess he had found this place.

He nodded. "My adoptive family, yes," he said, glancing back to make sure Aspen was still following us. "My father found me on a hunting trip abandoned near the unseelie border. He brought me back on his roc, and I never looked back."

I smiled faintly, torn between sympathy for the loss of his true parents and consolation that he had found a new family to love him. Aspen said nothing, scowling behind us with his hands in his pockets as we walked through the waking streets. It was fairly warm in the caves, so we had both left our coats. I had chosen to wear one of the nicer dresses I had brought for my first meeting with the king, hoping to maintain the illusion that I was harmless and proper. The dagger strapped to each thigh would be a giveaway if not for my flowing silver skirts, a color I had chosen to try to complement the stone and crystal around us. I decided to forgo a glamour, feeling that it might be seen as a deception.

Aspen was also formally dressed in black and navy, his golden curls brushing the collar of his coat and contrasting with the blue. He looked infuriatingly handsome, and I had been doing my best to ignore him completely this morning. When I had first emerged from my room, he had stood, looking as if he wanted to say something. I had given him thirty seconds to decide, and when he said nothing, his jaw grinding as he struggled with words, I threw him a hateful glance and decided to spend the rest of the day being haughty and cold.

The palace sparkled inside as much as it did outside. We met Rourke outside a room and he clasped arms with Knox, saying something in Dwarvish. He laughed and Rourke turned to us with a nod. I began to curtsy. "Only for the king," he said, stopping me with a hand on my arm. "Not for me."

I frowned, but he turned and opened the great crystal doors before us, leading into the room. I was expecting a throne room, but I was wrong. The room was small, a giant stone table taking up the majority of the space. Several dwarves were seated around the table, and a few fae as well, all unseelie. They rose when we entered.

"My guests," boomed the somber, gravelly voice of a great white-bearded dwarf at the head of the table. He carried a war hammer on his back like Knox and Rourke, and he wore the same dwarven armor of leather plates. For being a king of a crystal palace, I was surprised that his crown was a simple ring of stone.

"Lord of Spring and Lady of Summer, you honor my realm. Come, join us," he intoned, indicating two open chairs at the stone table. We sat, Knox and Rourke, standing sentry behind us.

"I hope I can properly thank the Seelie Queen for sending you to help us."

"The Queen of All Fae," I corrected, glancing at the unseelie fae around the table, "for she and King Hadrian rule both realms." There was some whispering and muttering after this pronouncement.

"Excuse the impertinence, my lady, but we hear no such thing," she said, raising a brow at me in challenge. This female was clearly a warrior, like all others in the room. She wore dwarven leathers and carried a war hammer too, and while her figure was slim and graceful, it was strong. Her silver hair was pulled back in a ponytail and her eyes were a pale amber, making her look more ghostly than even Seline as she added, "The Unseelie King still rules and terrorizes in the North."

"He does," said Aspen, cutting in with his most disinterested voice. "For now."

"Bisera, please," said the white-bearded dwarf. Turning to us, he added, "I am Holvard, King of the Dwarven Realm, Protector of the Sacred Mountain." He turned to his council, or whatever they were, and added, "Lord Aspen and Lady Aurelia have been sent as emissaries of Queen Ember. They offer their assistance in relieving our food shortage, and in return, they are our honored guests and friends."

"And what have you promised in exchange for this service, my King?" came a new voice, which sounded like stones being crushed together. A brown-haired dwarven female stood, also in leathers, her hair braided in the typical hanging loops worn by unmarried dwarven females. "What must we give to the fae in exchange for this aid?"

"Friendship, and aid against the Unseelie King," King Holvard replied, nodding to his unseelie council members. "I believe several in our midst will be in favor of such a partnership."

"Pardon my asking," said Aspen, always the diplomat, "but how many unseelie fae reside in your cities? Are all refugees?"

"Refugees or children of refugees," Rourke confirmed from behind me. "And at least two hundred."

"And how will they help us exactly?" another dwarf asked, emphasizing "they" in a way that was meant to be unflattering.

Aspen sighed and held out his hand, placing a single seed in his palm. A sprout grew slowly and steadily in his palm as he poured out his magic into it. The eyes of the fae and dwarves around the table grew wide as he poured more and more power into the plant, which sprouted tiny leaves and white buds that bloomed into honeysuckle. My favorite flower.

"With magic," Aspen said, removing the plant from his hand and placing it on the table, roots twitching in search of darkness and soil and water. "I can't grow from nothing, but if you have seeds, I can help. And I can try to remove the rot from your diseased crops."

There was some murmuring around the room as I gently touched one of the honeysuckle blossoms, their perfume filling the room. I felt Aspen glance at me, but I was determined to keep ignoring him.

"Forgive my council," said King Holvard, looking at me and Aspen. "They hear unfavorable tales of the Seelie fae from our unseelie friends due to your prolonged war. With time, they will unlearn their prejudices." He said this last part as both a reassurance to us and a clear threat to his council that they had better learn to like us. I smiled faintly.

"And you, Lady Aurelia?" said the pale, amber-eyed unseelie female named Bisera across the table. "What power do you bring to aid the king?"

I smiled gently, realizing that now was the time to don my mask of pretty uselessness. "None so impressive, I fear," I said, meeting her amber eyes. "My power did not emerge. I am here only as a representative of my queen, and to aid Lord Aspen with whatever he needs."

"Your Majesty," Aspen cut in, stopping Bisera from saying whatever she had opened her mouth to say next. I didn't think she and I were going to get along. "Please explain the situation here so we can better assist you. Then we will discuss the trade you offer our queen."

King Holvard sighed. He seemed very old, but I wasn't sure how old dwarves grew. I believed they lived shorter lives than the fae, but we had not been taught much about them in childhood.

"We have enough food to feed our people normally for one more week," King Holvard replied, his craggy voice sounding worn and tired. "Then we will have to begin rationing. More than half of our fields are affected by the blight that began a year ago, and the rest do not produce enough to feed all of my people. We have increased our hunting, but with winter on us, game is scarce, and cave rats are barely worth the effort."

Aspen nodded thoughtfully. I grimaced inwardly at the idea of eating rat.

"Can you tell us why the Unseelie King received iron weapons from these mountains?" Aspen asked next. He seemed to have decided that a direct approach was the fastest way to proceed. There was a round of outraged muttering and some shouting at this question.

"Enough," the king shouted, slapping his flat palm on the table loudly. "What is this about iron weapons? I have made no such deal with the Unseelie King." He looked around at his table, and someone coughed nervously.

"Your Majesty, several shipments of iron weapons destined for the human lands have gone missing in the past six months," a dwarven male said nervously, his gravelly voice pitched a little high in his anxiety. "It was such a small portion of our total product that we didn't think..."

"Why is this the first I am hearing of this?" the king bellowed, making his councilors back up slightly in their seats. I raised my brows, trying to look unaffected by the king's fearsome temper.

"We will look into this directly, my King," said Rourke from behind me. "We will find the responsible party."

"My apologies to your queen," the king said, turning his attention back to us. "I will personally see this is taken care of."

Aspen nodded. "If you trade iron with the humans, why have you not been able to trade for food with them?" Aspen asked, clearly weighing the dwarves' allegiances and trying to figure out where their loyalties lay.

"We have some trade with the humans," the dwarven female said, standing again from her chair. "Mostly grain. But it takes many months to transport over land, and our last shipment was partially spoiled by the time it arrived."

Aspen nodded thoughtfully, and I decided to ask a few of my own questions in the momentary pause. "Have you discovered the cause of the blight?" I asked.

The king shook his head. "We know not where it came from or why it struck the fields so suddenly. Our skills lie in forging more than farming. Any expertise you can offer us," he added, nodding to Aspen, "will be appreciated and rewarded."

"And what reward do you offer exactly?" Aspen asked. The counselors looked around at each other a bit nervously, but the king replied with surety.

"We offer dwarven leathers and crafted obsidian blades, as well as my army to fight alongside yours. I have five hundred strong who can assist in your queen's fight against the Unseelie King."

"Many unseelie will join ranks as well," Knox said from behind me. A few of the unseelie present at the table nodded their agreement.

"No iron?" Aspen asked. The king looked uncomfortable. "If you wish it, yes," he replied warily. "I thought your queen would wish to honor the laws of her realm."

"She will. My queen will accept this bargain," Aspen said, standing and holding out his hand to the Dwarven King. The king stood, a full two feet shorter than Aspen at least, and clasped his arm, shaking once. "Well met," said the king, resuming his seat. "What will you need to begin?"

"Seeds you wish planted, for one," Aspen replied. "I brought some that may grow in darkness, but whatever grows naturally in the mountain will be most sustainable. I will also need to inspect the blighted fields to see if they can be salvaged. This will probably take more magic than I can use in a day. It may take several weeks, depending on the extent of the damage. I'll know more when I see it ."

The king nodded. "My emissaries can escort you to the nearest fields beginning tomorrow," he said, nodding behind us to Rourke and Knox. "The blight has spread far through the mountains. You may need to fly to get to the other fields as you begin your work."

My heart did a little skip at the thought of flying above the mountain. I heard Knox breathe out his amusement behind me.

"Tonight, we would welcome you with a celebration," the king continued, standing. The rest of the council also stood. "The feast will be modest under the circumstances, but dwarven music and dancing are always in abundance here."

"And ale," added Rourke, evoking a gravelly laugh from the council.

"I would like a place to spar as well," Aspen said, indicating the king's warhammer. "This is a weapon I have never used. I should like to learn."

The king grinned. "You have the heart of a dwarven warrior then, Lord of Spring," he said approvingly. "You may spar on your balcony whenever you desire it. Knox will provide you with leathers and weapons for practice, as well as a worthy adversary."

Knox bowed his head, accepting the king's request. Aspen and I stood and bowed our heads to the king. "We thank you for your hospitality," I said, smiling as innocently and warmly as I could. The king returned my smile, eyes crinkling a bit at the corners.

"For now, please have Knox show you the city and the crystal gardens," the king added, gesturing to the doors which were being held open by two dwarvish guards. I nodded again and followed Knox from the room, Aspen and Rourke trailing behind us.

Chapter 9: Aurelia

WE SPENT THE MORNING wandering the city and being shown the sights by Knox. Rourke had excused himself to run patrols, so Knox led us through the winding stone streets around the palace, pointing out favorite shops and notable sights.

He guided us through the crystal gardens, which were an odd but beautiful mixture of subterranean plants and natural crystals of all colors and shapes that erupted from the ground. They were strange but captivating, and a tinkling fountain at the center of the gardens made me gasp as tiny diamonds glittered within each tier of water.

Knox had insisted we try pastries from his favorite bakery for lunch and bought the last two tarts from the baker, who was looking worriedly at his stores of grain as he packed up for the afternoon. The sweet, flaky bread disintegrated in my mouth like sugary heaven. Aspen declined, so Knox and I enjoyed the pastries on the balcony of our guest suite while Aspen went off to write a letter to Ember with the terms of the agreement he had struck.

"What are Dwarvish celebrations like?" I asked, looking out over the city as it glowed in the waning afternoon light. Knox chuckled.

"They can be..." he paused, mouth open as he hunted for the right word. He shut his mouth and turned to me with a grin. "Lively," he finished. I raised my eyebrows and smiled.

"What does 'lively' mean?" I pressed, curious about his reaction. He tilted his head to the side, studying me.

"I'm not sure what your celebrations are like," he said slowly, "but dwarvish celebrations are free. Casual. There's no real ceremony or sedate dancing or polite conversation. It's all drinking and dancing and bawdy jokes, and at the moon festivals there are..." he paused again, a faint pink stain rising to his cheeks, "other entertainments to be had as well." I laughed.

"Well, I won't be engaging in those sorts of entertainments I think," I said, smiling faintly and thinking about the last time I *had* engaged in such entertainment.

It had been the Midsummer Festival this past year. I hadn't even told Ember that the male I'd spent the night with had been Aspen. I didn't want her to think I took advantage of his gentlemanly nature, or that he took advantage of me. It was entirely consensual, and I remembered the feeling of his hands on my body, his lips on mine, his warm breath in my ear, and against my neck.

It had been perfect—if not enough—and I remembered the way we had fit together after waiting so long for that moment. I must have let my sadness show on my face, because Knox touched my hand gently, pulling me out of my thoughts and making me look up at him.

His indigo eyes were deep and warm, and he looked at me as if he knew exactly what was upsetting me. He frowned.

"He doesn't deserve you," he said, turning back to look at the city. I sighed, not knowing how I could possibly explain to this male everything that had happened between us.

"You don't know what I did to him," I said, also turning to face the city.

"It doesn't matter," he said, shaking his head. "I see how you look at him. The fact that he can walk away from it means he doesn't deserve your love." I shook my head, a tear sliding unbidden down my cheek. I brushed it away angrily, chastising myself for letting this stranger read me so easily.

"Dance with me tonight," Knox said, turning back to me and brushing a thumb over the trail the tear had left. I was startled to be addressed in such a forward way, but he had said the dwarves lacked the ceremony and pomp of fae society. I smiled faintly, lifting his hand away from my cheek as I looked up at him. He was a handsome male, but he wasn't who I wanted. Still, I nodded. I loved to dance, and there was no way Aspen would be asking me.

"Thank you," I said quietly. "I'd like that." Knox smiled at me and bent to kiss my cheek. Startled, I stepped back from him, putting my hands out in front of me. He lifted his own hands.

"I'm sorry," he said, clearly chagrined at startling me. "I should have realized that would be too forward. Forgive me."

"No, it's alright," I said, trying to ease his embarrassment. "I'm sorry, I just can't..."

"Aurelia," he said, cutting me off and putting a gentle hand on my shoulder. "It's alright. It was my fault. Please don't dwell on it." He squeezed my shoulder, and I nodded. "The dwarves do not share fae notions of lengthy courtship. I have lived here my whole life and have learned to act on every impulse I feel. If it is not too forward for you, I would still like to dance with you tonight."

I nodded, relieved that he hadn't been offended by my rejection.

"Then I'll see you soon," he said, pushing away from the balcony and giving me a friendly wave before heading down the stairs.

"What was that?" Aspen asked behind me. I froze. I had thought we were alone, and Knox must have too. I winced, not turning to meet Aspen's eyes as he came to stand beside me.

"It was nothing," I lied. "Just a friend offering a dance at tonight's party."

"A friend?" Aspen asked, leaning on the balcony and crowding his arms. His eyes were narrowed, brow furrowed. "He looked rather more than friendly."

"Are you jealous?" I asked, incredulous at the gall of this male. To reject me was one thing, but to be jealous of another male's attention was completely unreasonable.

"No," Aspen snapped, turning away from me to face the city. "I don't trust him. I think you should keep your distance." I laughed.

"What about him don't you trust?" I asked, enjoying Aspen's discomfort more than I probably should have. "Is it his dark blue eyes? The cut of his jaw? The fact that he likes me?"

"It's how he looks at you," Aspen said fiercely, whirling to face me. "You don't see how he looks when your back is turned. Like he's trying to figure out how to get you into his bed." I rolled my eyes.

"First, I can take care of myself," I said haughtily, tapping the dagger under my skirts to emphasize this point. "Second, it's none of your business whether males look at me, or how they look at me. Or how I look at them."

"It is my business if it endangers the mission," Aspen replied angrily, taking a step closer to me so only an inch separated us. I momentarily flashed back to that one perfect night, and I met his eyes, something fierce and possessive flashing in them as he looked at me.

"How would my liking another male endanger the mission?" I shouted, aware that our voices were probably carrying from the balcony. Something hot burned in my chest as my emotions overtook my logic. "You don't get an opinion anymore," I added, feeling anger and hurt congeal into a furious fire in my gut. "You

gave up your right to an opinion when you ended things between us
."

"It wasn't me who ended anything," Aspen growled, grabbing my arms gently but firmly. Our chests were touching, pressed perilously close, and I felt Aspen's heartbeat thudding heavily against my own. The stone rumbled beneath me as Aspen lost control of his magic for a moment. He took a deep breath, and the rumbling subsided.

"You walked away!" I shouted, tears pricking at my eyes again.

Aspen was breathing heavily as he tried to master both his anger and his magic. This was the closest we had been since the alcove at the masquerade ball, and I felt warmth flood my core at the smell and feel and nearness of him, at the feel of his hands on my arms and his chest against mine.

His eyes darted to my lips, a fire burning in his eyes as hot as the one burning inside me. An inch separated his lips from mine, and I felt his breath skate over them. I could close the distance if I just stood on my toes, but this wasn't my move to make. Aspen had put the distance between us in the first place. He had to be the one to close it now. He leaned forward a fraction of an inch and I held my breath.

"If you invite him into your bed," Aspen growled, low and deep in his throat, "make sure you keep your dagger on you."

He whirled away so unexpectedly that I nearly fell forward, catching myself on the railing and breathing heavily as he stormed off. It took me several long moments and deep breaths to slow my racing heart and cool the fire that had built in my core.

Goddess damn him, Aspen somehow still had the power to wreck me completely, and I wasn't sure I would be able to survive him much longer.

I TOOK A COLD shower before I dressed for the evening, trying to cool the heated blood that coursed through me after our argument.

Our relationship had always been soft and gentle and tender before we fell apart, and this new hard, fierce edge it had taken on frightened me a little. If I was honest, it also thrilled me, the fire between us burning hot. We had been changed by everything that had happened to us, and I didn't think tender or gentle or soft was something we could easily return to. But maybe I didn't want to return to that either.

Knox and Rourke both arrived to escort us to the castle gardens, where the evening's celebration would be held. Both still wore their dwarven leathers, although they had chosen some that were less scratched and filthy than their usual sets.

Aspen looked like he planned to attend a fine ball. Rourke scowled.

"You should leave the coat," he said in his deep, accented voice. "It's too fancy for a dwarven dance." Aspen raised a brow but did as suggested.

"What about me?" I asked as I emerged from my room, worried I was overdressed. I had chosen a dress of pale blue gossamer that floated around me and pooled at my feet like a waterfall. Without flowers for decoration, I had braided some of my hair into a rough crown atop my head, letting the rest hang loose. I had donned a simple glamour, making my hair shine brighter and my dress glow a bit with an internal light like one of the crystals in the city.

I gave a little twirl and waited for approval. The males all stared a little blankly, no one speaking.

"That bad?" I asked, turning to return to my room and change. Knox darted over to stand in front of me.

"No, my lady," he breathed, clearing his throat and saying a bit more solidly, "No. You are perfect."

"Aurelia," I corrected gently.

"Aurelia," Knox agreed, breaking into a wide smile. I smiled up at him and caught Aspen glowering out of the corner of my eye. Excellent.

"A vision," Rourke agreed, bowing and taking my hand, planting an extremely whiskery kiss on it.

It seemed like the most convenient mode of transport in the city was walking, and dwarves and fae streamed toward the palace as if the whole city had been invited. Maybe they had, I thought with a grimace.

The sun had set, and the city and palace were set in a pale rainbow glow from the crystals' natural luminescence. When we arrived at the palace gardens, I saw that strings of what looked to be tiny blue lights had been hung all over the lawn and paths. On closer inspection, I realized they were tiny glowing mushrooms.

It was both eerie and lovely, and the music was already loud when we arrived. Dwarves and fae laughed raucously and drank heavily, and couples whirled around haphazardly on a dance floor in no clear dance I could recognize. The place was alive, and I felt my skin buzz in the warm glow of the lights and sounds and smells of the city revelry.

"Here," Knox said, bringing over pewter mugs of something a light amber color. "You have never tried dwarven ale, I'm guessing."

Aspen put his hand out over my mug as I lifted it and took a sip of his own first. After a moment he removed his hand and nodded his approval to me. I rolled my eyes.

"It would be reckless to poison you with so many witnesses, my lord," Knox joked, drinking deeply from his mug. Rourke had disappeared, and I caught a glimpse of him spinning around the dance floor with a stout dwarven female, laughing as he spun her to the beat.

"Better safe than dead," Aspen replied coldly, taking another sip. Knox attempted a smile that was more of a wince and looked at me, raising his eyebrows.

"Care to dance?" he asked, holding out a large pale hand. Under the mushroom and crystal lights, he looked even more blue than usual, but it was not alien or unpleasant. If anything, he looked even more vibrant like this.

"I don't know the steps," I said, hesitating as I took in the crowd whirling around. Knox smiled reassuringly.

"There are none," he said, conspiratorially. "I promise, I won't lead you astray."

"Aurelia," Aspen growled. I looked at him, his brows raised in a challenge.

"I'd love to," I said, smiling prettily at Knox. I threw a glare at Aspen over my shoulder as Knox led me onto the floor. He scowled back at me.

Knox led me through the wild dwarven dances until I was sweating and breathing heavily with the exertion. Aspen had planted himself on the edge of the floor several feet away from us and glared the entire time.

"I think I need a break," I said, grinning happily at Knox and fanning myself. I loved to dance and it had been a long time since I had enjoyed myself at one. He nodded, also smiling and breathing hard, and pointed to an area where refreshments had been laid out. Little tables and chairs had been placed haphazardly around the food and drink, and several were taken by laughing dwarves.

"That was fun," I said, moving to a table and taking a long drink from another mug of ale as Knox did the same. He nodded.

"I told you dwarven celebrations are lively," he said, grinning down at me. He had sat next to me, and I was certain he could see my heaving breasts down my dress as I tried to catch my breath, but he was too polite to say anything. I was feeling warm and relaxed, the ale softening the edges of my anxiety and anger at Aspen. I looked around, unable to find him. Knox saw where I was looking and said quietly, "He's there, quite entertained I assure you."

I looked where he pointed and saw Aspen in animated conversation with Bisera, who was dressed in the tiniest dress I had ever seen. I blushed faintly, looking away. Her long, pale legs and an expanse of pale back were fully on display. I raised my brows, and Knox choked on a laugh.

"Are all the females here so brazen?" I asked, feeling bolts of jealousy shoot through my stomach.

"If by 'brazen' you mean 'uninhibited,' then yes," Knox replied, taking another swig of the drink. "You saw my fumbling attempt earlier. We have not been raised with the civilized courtly posturing of the fae."

I smiled. "Courtly posturing is not all it's cracked up to be," I said wryly. "I much prefer the openness and frivolity of this than the stuffy balls of court."

"You do look like you belong here," Knox said softly, gazing at me with something more than friendly approval. I blushed. "Like a moon crystal from the Sacred Lake."

He brushed a wayward strand of my hair back off my shoulder. I was going to have to get used to this more forward culture if I was going to be here for several weeks, but I knew Knox's interest was more than just a manifestation of the culture. Looking at him, I thought he was maybe a male I could have something with if Aspen had never been in the picture. My heart cracked another inch at the thought. I tried to smile, but it must have come out strained. He frowned.

"Are you alright?" he asked, brows furrowing.

"Fine," I said tightly, attempting another smile. "I think I just overdid it a little. Please, you go dance. I'm quite happy sitting here for a while."

"Are you sure?" he asked, looking around as if trying to find something that might revive me. I plastered on a reassuring smile.

"Quite sure," I said. "Go! Enjoy the revelry." Knox nodded and stood.

"I'll come back to check on you soon," he said softly with a squeeze of my hand. He strode off back into the throng of dancing and I breathed a little sigh of relief, happy to have a few moments alone to clear my head.

Aspen staggered over and sat down heavily in a chair across the table, ruining my peace. His hair was tousled and his shirt hung slightly askew, a smear of red on the corner of his mouth.

"You're drunk," I said angrily, taking in his appearance and realizing why he was so disheveled. "Did you get bored of Bisera?"

"I am not drunk," said Aspen, admittedly quite soberly, "and if you must know these females are a pushy lot. I had nothing to do with this," he added, gesturing to his general dishevelment.

"Oh I'm sure you didn't," I said, fury building at the hypocrisy of him warning me off a male only to drape himself all over another female. I stood and began to walk away, trying to move as quickly as I could amid the crush of dwarves and fae.

I heard Aspen swear loudly behind me and move to follow me.

"Damn it, Aurelia, stop," he said, reaching me and whirling me to face him but my upper arm. "Stop running away from me when I say the wrong thing."

"Stop saying the wrong thing and I won't run away," I spat back at him. He sighed and looked around, clearly wanting a private space to speak. Not finding one he leaned closer instead.

"We need information from this court," he hissed quietly, still holding my upper arm firmly so I couldn't easily run from him. "You're not the only one tasked with retrieving it, and it's not my fault if a drunken female misreads the situation. I assure you, I rejected the advance."

"Yes, you look extremely un-advanced upon," I said, giving his messy hair a pointed look. I swiped my finger by his lip and displayed the red coloring to him as further proof. "I'm sure this was entirely her fault."

Aspen smirked, a more wicked look than I was used to seeing from him.

"Now who's jealous?" he purred, rubbing the lipstick off his jaw ineffectually. I glared and stomped on his foot, eliciting a yelp from him, but forcing him to let go of my arm.

"Good night, Aspen," I said angrily, storming off in the direction of the crystal gardens. I wasn't sure where exactly I planned to go, I just knew I couldn't stay there with him.

Aspen cursed again at my back and ran to catch up with me. Before I could go farther he grabbed my shoulders and whirled me against a stone column that secluded us from the view of the rest of the party. His hand was in my hair, cushioning my head as he pushed me against the column. Before I could protest, his mouth crushed mine in a passionate kiss.

My heart leapt and warmth uncurled in my stomach as our teeth and lips and tongue clashed violently. Like no time had passed at all, I felt myself melting into him like I had six months ago. I was suddenly both at home and at war with him, and I twined my fingers in his hair, pulling hard enough to make him hiss and pull back.

"Get off of me," I said, still holding him, not actually wanting him to get off me. He smirked.

"I love how big your pupils become when you look at me like that," he rumbled.

"It's because it's dark, not because I like you," I hissed back angrily. "Now get off me!"

"Ask me again nicely, and I will," he growled quietly, his voice filled with challenge. We stared at each other for a heated moment, both breathing hard and panting as the sounds of revelry continued just out of our view.

And then I was pulling him into me and his lips were on mine again. His hands trailed down my sides, demanding and greedy and not at all gentle or patient. I slid my own hands under his shirt and over the smooth expanse of his chest, his back, trying to memorize the feel of him just in case I woke up from this moment.

"Goddess, I've missed you," he growled in my ear, lifting me as I hooked my legs around his waist. He kissed my jaw, my neck, and my collarbone, and I breathed heavily, hoping this moment would never end. I felt a raw need crash through me as he embraced me,

and I could tell he felt the same from the hard length pressing into m
e.

"Aspen," I breathed, "what is this?" He paused, and I cursed
myself for potentially bringing him back to his senses. He breathed
heavily, heart thrashing in the cage of his ribs.

"Absolution," he growled in my ear, making a shiver run
through me. He tilted his head and stepped away suddenly, leaving
me breathless and disheveled against the column.

"Everything all right here?" asked Knox, raising a brow as he
emerged around the corner.

"Fine," Aspen growled, straightening his shirt. "Good night."

He stormed off and Knox gave me a quizzical look. I stared after
Aspen, feeling like my heart was exploding from my chest.

I had believed we were done with gentle and tender, and I was
right. But whatever that had been, I wanted more of it.

Chapter 10: Ember

HADRIAN AND I WERE in the war room with the Commander, trying to decide where the most advantageous spot for a full-scale battle would be. While we hoped to avoid all-out bloodshed, the Commander had recommended we prepare for the worst-case scenario.

"Here," the Commander said, pointing to the large map of the realms. The Seelie Realm was south of the Unseelie Realm. I cast a glance to the Dwarven Realm in the east where my friend and cousin should be by now, before looking back to where she pointed.

"This spot gives us the high ground with the river behind us," she said, pointing to a place near the border between our realms on the Seelie side. "If we draw the Unseelie King's forces to us here, we can have a dwarven legion flank them from the northeast and trap them in."

"This depends on the dwarves agreeing to our plan," Hadrian said, frowning at the map as if it was purposefully hiding information from him.

"They will," I said, more confidently than I felt. While I trusted Aurelia and Aspen to be up to the task of charming the dwarves into an alliance, I wasn't sure they could work together peacefully enough to make it work. Still, they were our best shot.

Vanth and Seline strode into the war room, both dripping snow and mud and blood on the stone ground.

"You look terrible," said the Commander, glancing up at them before turning back to the map. "Recruits get you?"

"No," growled Vanth, pulling a chair out from the large table and slumping into it. I winced as the disgusting concoction of sludge splattered onto the floor. "This is their blood."

"We let them team up against us," Seline said smoothly, her velvet voice caressing the air as she leaned against the wall behind Vanth's chair. "They still lost."

"I'll start helping you tomorrow," Hadrian said, giving Vanth a dark look. He nodded gratefully. "We need them to be ready, and they obviously need more one-on-one instruction." The way he said 'one-on-one' made me very glad I was not one of the recruits.

"Are you hurt?" I asked, frowning at the amount of blood on them. "Are they hurt?"

"Not enough to need your attention," Vanth said, waving me off. "It will be good for them to feel the bruises in the morning."

I sighed, rolling my eyes. Vanth was an excellent soldier and commander, but he was not a patient male. Seline was hardly better, running the recruits through grueling drills until they were collapsing from exhaustion.

"They're tired," I said, looking to Hadrian for support. He frowned at me, shaking his head slightly. His disagreement was like a punch to my gut, and it threw me off balance for a moment.

"No," he said, "Vanth is right. We need them ready. Babying them won't help."

"We can't drive them so hard they quit," I argued.

"No one is leaving," the Commander said, smiling faintly. "You pay them too well for any grumblings of disloyalty."

"This is barbaric," I tried again, rising from my seat. "I'm going to see them."

Hadrian was before me in a second as he stepped through shadows to stop in front of me. I squeaked out a sound of surprise as he caught me around my upper arms. "Ember," he said, tone serious as he looked down at me darkly. "If they were seriously injured, you would already be on your way there." He looked at me meaningfully. Hadrian could sense death, as well as slowing and speeding it up. I hadn't realized this until one of the recruits had been mortally injured in a training accident and Hadrian had swept me through shadow just in time to save his life. The healing magic pulsed faintly in my veins, itching to do what it was created f or.

I scowled at him, grinding my teeth in frustration. "Fine," I bit out, glaring at both males as I tried to master my temper. "I'll compromise. Tomorrow afternoon."

Hadrian glanced at Vanth, who smirked at him in a way that said he was glad I was Hadrian's problem and not his. "Fine," Hadrian ground out. "Tomorrow. It will probably be good to raise morale anyway, having the queen walk through the ranks."

I nodded, feeling myself deflate a little as the tension in the room diffused.

"Look at you two, compromising like any old married couple," Vanth teased, earning a death glare from Hadrian. Seline rolled her eyes.

"Come on," she said, dragging Vanth from the chair and out of the war room. "You need a bath. Or maybe three baths."

"No more than you do," he replied, bumping her with his shoulder. She smirked as they walked out and I glanced at Hadrian, my brows raised in amusement.

"It's sickening to watch them flirt," he growled, returning to the map and focusing his attention on more serious matters.

"It's adorable," I argued. "I ship them."

"You ship them?" Hadrian asked, raising a skeptical brow at me. "What in the name of the Goddess does that mean?"

"It means I hope they act on their feelings for each other sooner, rather than later," I said, giving him a coy smile that made him smirk at me, his eyes going a bit molten as his mind clearly shifted from war strategy to more pleasurable activities.

"If you're quite done," the Commander said irritably, "then we still have actual work to do today."

Hadrian smirked at me with his wicked half-smile again before turning his attention back to the map and debating the merits of a battle in unseelie territory. I felt myself flush and tried to get my mind out of the bedroom and the gutter, where Hadrian always seemed to manage to push it.

As PROMISED, I VISITED the recruits the next afternoon. Hadrian had rolled his eyes when I had insisted on taking my medical bag and a healthy supply of tea cakes with me, but I ignored him and took them anyway. As my grandmother would say, very little soothes the soul better than a good tea cake.

Most of the recruits had come from common families of both Seelie and unseelie fae fleeing the Unseelie King. I was afraid at first that many would have trouble taking orders from Hadrian. Both groups of fae had good reasons to distrust the son of the king who had tormented them and threatened their families for years.

But to my surprise and relief, Hadrian and Vanth and Seline had managed to create a strong camaraderie among both the Seelie and unseelie recruits, making them live and work and fight together until they were forced to accept that they were more similar than different.

Aspen had helped with this, sparring daily with all three of them until the Seelie fae were also eager to test their magic against their unseelie brethren.

Most of the common fae had magic of some kind, and part of their training included learning to harness and use that magic both defensively and offensively. It was one of the reasons for the occasional almost fatal training accident, and I was relieved that it had been a while since I had been called on to save someone from being accidentally withered or frozen or strangled by vines.

Hadrian had declined the invitation to join me, arguing that it would be a better morale boost to see the queen visiting alone than as an accessory to their general. Vanth and Seline escorted me instead, and I felt a little nervous as we entered the barracks. It was ridiculous, as I'd been there several times before.

Truthfully, my anxiety was due to my guilt. I was risking these soldiers' lives, and while the males and females who had volunteered to fight were paid handsomely for their service, I knew it wouldn't be enough to make up for their deaths if they didn't make it through battle. Many had families and children, and I hated the idea of taking a child's parents from them the way mine had been taken from me.

The soldiers were at mess when we arrived, but all stood at attention with a single word from Vanth, standing stiffly and saluting, wherever they were.

"As you were, please," I said, a little more shyly than I had intended. The soldiers all returned to eating and laughing and drinking, and I moved through the aisles of tables, greeting each fae with a handshake or a nod, and asking about their health.

I doled out a few remedies here and there and healed a rather painful limp and a dislocated shoulder. The recruits stared in wonder at the healing magic that burned gold from my palms. Despite the re-emergence of all the seelie magics, very few healers had emerged. I had recruited two to work in the infirmary with me, and the only other one I knew of was a very young child, too little to be taken from her mother.

As I moved through the crowd, I asked about their families and children. I let each soldier tell me of their sweethearts or spouses or mates, of the children they were missing and couldn't wait to see on their next leave, and of their fears of facing the Unseelie King and his soldiers in battle.

When we left the hall, supplies and tea cakes all gone, I leaned against the wall of the barracks, resting my head on the cold stone and closing my eyes.

"Are you alright?" Seline asked gently, resting a cold hand on my upper arm. I nodded, lips pursed as I tried to put my feelings into words.

"They could all die," I rasped out. "All of them. Because of me."

"No," Vanth said gently, shaking his head. "If they die, it won't be at your hands."

"But I'm the one sending them to their deaths," I said, feeling a tear leak down my cheek. I thought of one of the soldiers who told me about her child, left with her grandmother while she and her husband fought in my army. "Am I any better than the Unseelie King if I'm the reason these fae never make it home?"

"You are," said Vanth sternly.

"They have a choice here," Seline said, giving my arm a gentle squeeze. "You give them the choice to serve. That is different from the Unseelie King. You are nothing like him."

"The unseelie recruits would likely already be dead by his hands if they hadn't fled here," Vanth added, looking briefly at Seline before glancing back at me. "They want to serve to make this place safe for their families."

I nodded tightly, feeling my throat burn at the weight of the responsibility and the lives I carried along with the crown I had accepted.

That night, after I lost myself in my mate and let him love me and treasure me and hold me, I thought of each of those lives and vowed to the Goddess I would do everything in my power to get them out of this war alive.

Chapter 11: Aurelia

WATCHING ASPEN SPAR WITH Knox the next morning was a test of my restraint. Knox had brought a set of dwarven leathers for Aspen, and he looked like a warrior god, swinging a warhammer under Knox and Rourke's encouragement and tutelage.

Both males were sweating beneath the leathers after thirty minutes of sparring with the heavy weapons, and I raised my brows at

Knox as he grinned at me, his blue-black hair falling from the band he had tied it back with as sweat dripped down his face.

"How are we getting out to the fields?" Aspen asked, tan skin gleaming like gold through a sheen of sweat as he gulped down some water. He moved to stand next to me, and I shivered at his nearness. When Knox had escorted me home the previous evening, Aspen had already been in his room, and I hadn't been brave enough to confront him about the kiss.

Knox had been a perfect gentleman. He hadn't tried to kiss my cheek again. I almost wished he had, and that Aspen had seen so he could rage about it.

"That's the best part of this work," Knox said, casting me an excited grin. I raised my brows. "We are riding cave dragons."

I ran to the balcony and looked down. Sure enough, four scaly creatures waited below, bridles tied off on the banister. My heart skipped as I sprinted down to see them. I had heard that dragons lived in the mountains, but I had always assumed my chances of seeing one, never mind four, were as great as seeing a giant roc.

They were smaller than I imagined, and more stout than the lithe, undulating creatures I had seen in books. They were smaller than horses, but strong and sturdy. Their scales were a dark shiny green, so dark they probably blended in with the rocks of the cave for hunting. They had long snouts and a fringe of green spikes down their backs, parted by a leather saddle similar to a horse's.

"Do the dwarves saddle up any and every creature?" I asked, patting a scaly nose as Knox came down to join me. The cave dragon flicked a long forked tongue out at me as I scratched its eye ridges.

"If you can pet it, we can saddle it," Knox replied with a laugh. "These bite too," he said, leaning close in a conspiratorial whisper. I shot a grin at him and caught Aspen scowling from the corner of my eye.

"It's ten miles to the nearest fields," Rourke said in a gravelly voice. "They're not as swift as horses, but the dragons will save us a long, rocky walk." He swung up onto one of the beasts, indicating we should do the same. Aspen swung up into the saddle of the beast next to Rourke, and Knox helped me onto the dragon I had been scratching.

"I think I might need one of these too," I said, cooing over the cave dragon as I patted his scaly snout. Aspen snorted.

"They'd eat the horses," he said, glancing back at me with a small smile. I blinked at him, and he turned away.

All four beasts had saddle bags attached, with what I assumed to be food and drink for the excursion. When they lurched forward I wasn't quite ready for the motion, and I tilted precariously. Knox caught me and pushed me back up, chuckling.

"You have to hold with your knees more than your thighs to keep your balance on these," he said, indicating his grip on the cave dragon. I shifted to sit more comfortably, although the spiked plates of the creature stabbed into my legs uncomfortably where I gripped him.

"Why do you not always ride them?" I asked, patting the dragon's head. He puffed out a small cloud of smoke and I raised my brows. "Do they breathe fire?"

"To answer your first question," Knox replied, "because they don't like crowds. They have sensitive hearing and get easily disoriented by the sounds of the city, so we generally only use them to travel out of the city.

"To answer your second question," he continued, "they can breathe short bursts of flame. We use them for controlled burns and lighting forges mostly." I marveled at the creature beneath me, wondering what other kinds of dragons lived in the mountains.

"Does he have a name?" I asked, gesturing to my mount.

Knox shook his head. "The king keeps many cave dragons. They're a nuisance when they're in the wild. None are given names," he finished. I frowned, feeling a little sad for the dragons that they weren't loved enough to be given names.

"I will think of a good name for you," I assured my dragon, patting his head again. He snorted, another small cloud of smoke bursting from his nostrils. I smiled.

"You certainly have a way with creatures," Knox said, giving me a rueful look. "If you charm all of the dragons, there's no way they'll stay here when it's time for you to go." I smiled.

"Lucky I'm here for a while then," I said, scratching the dragon's eye ridges again. "Isn't that right, Honeysuckle?"

"You can't name a dragon 'Honeysuckle'," Aspen called back irritably. "Stop naming things that might eat you." I grinned.

"It's too late, he's been named. Haven't you, Honey?" The dragon let out another snort and Knox laughed.

We had to stop talking once we reached the edge of the city. The terrain became rockier and rough, even though a road had been cleared for travel to the farms and fields. Without the light from the mountain window, the mountain grew darker as we penetrated its interior. Knox and Rourke brought out several glowworm orbs and attached them to the dragons so that we could see, but Knox explained breathlessly that dragons had excellent vision and didn't need the light to find their way.

We traveled for just over an hour, the city giving way to a harsh landscape of rocks and boulders and sharp crystal edges jutting from the walls and floors and ceilings. The crystals glowed faintly, helping light our way, and by the time we reached the field of luminescent mushrooms, I was aching and my eyes were strained from peering through the darkness.

I knew we had arrived by the light of another small window carved into the side of the mountain, clearly allowing just enough light in for plants to grow. Unlike fields in the fae or human realms, the dwarves allowed their crops to grow wherever they flourished. Mushrooms climbed from the floor up the walls, interspersed by patches of dark green cave moss that stretched to the ceiling to surround the little window. dwarven males and females and a few smaller figures, children I realized, roamed the rows of crops, picking what I assumed to be ripe patches of moss and mushrooms. It all looked healthy enough to me, but Aspen frowned as we dismounted.

He wandered off to the right, pointing out what I hadn't been able to see in the dim light. Several feet of mushroom crops were gray and withered looking, the moss growing with it dry and brittle. A tiny stream trickled by, so water was not the problem, and the patches of rot seemed to be randomly located, so light couldn't be the cause either. Aspen crouched and reached out a hand over the patch of blight.

"How long has this field been blighted?" he asked, recoiling slightly at whatever his magic sensed.

"These patches showed up only recently," Rourke answered, frowning as Aspen inspected a healthy patch of crops. "The other fields started showing signs six months to a year ago."

"And it's the same in every field?" asked Aspen, moving to another patch of rot and stretching out with his magic. I stood, somewhat uselessly, watching his process of testing and feeling.

"Aye, it looks the same at least," Rourke answered, frowning. "Do you know what it is?"

"Maybe," Aspen said, standing and stretching. "I need to examine it more to be sure. Can we take a sample back with us? For today we should harvest the viable crops, burn the rotted sections, and begin growing new plants. It won't stop you from having to begin rationing, but it will take several weeks to rebuild your stores."

Rourke nodded, calling to the workers in Dwarvish and relaying Aspen's recommendations. Knox, Rourke, and I helped, following Aspen through the fields as he ripened sections of crops to be picked. The farmers all carried large baskets, some on the backs of more of the cave dragons, and I ran back and forth with my loads of mushrooms and cave moss, depositing them in any close basket. Rourke instructed us to brush the gills of each mushroom with our thumbs to release the spores back into the field. We did the same with the moss, checking for spores and making sure to release them before gathering the rest.

By midday, the fields were mostly cleared and bare, and all the males had stripped off their shirts to work. I glared at their bare chests, annoyed that convention required me to keep mine on. I rolled up my sleeves as high as possible, sweat dripping down my back.

Aspen collected samples of the blighted crops in an empty saddlebag and nodded at the dwarves to begin the controlled burn of the blighted sections as we broke for lunch. He gulped down water furiously, breath heaving with exertion. He had already used a lot of magic, and I was worried he might overdo it in his eagerness to help.

"We have to irrigate the fields before I can grow more," he said, gesturing to the area around the cave window. While a winter breeze blew through it, the cave stayed relatively warm, especially with the fires of the cave dragons burning away the rot. "Then I can re-grow the field as much as possible to be harvested again." "

Do you have enough magic for this?" I asked, watching sweat drip down his temple. He met my eyes, irises flashing a warm blue. Warmth pooled in my core as I remembered how he had looked at me last night.

He looked away quickly. "I'll manage," he said, taking another long drink of water. He began discussing irrigation plans with Rourke, and Knox leaned over to me, his faint blue skin pale and dusted with faint blue-black hairs and thin scars across his chest from sparring.

"You look beautiful today," he said quietly.

I smiled, raising a brow at him. "I'm currently covered in sweat and mushroom spores, but thank you," I said, laughing.

He smiled and lifted a hand, thinking better of it and dropping it back down. My stomach gave a jolt of relief. "Still," he said. He glanced at Aspen and back to me. "Even *he* has noticed. He's been looking at you all day."

I shook my head, trying to hide my smile. I had noticed him looking at me, but I didn't want Knox to know about the kiss. "Looking is not the same as wanting," I said, feeling a sting. I realized this was true. What if Aspen had given in purely because of lust or attraction? It didn't mean he wanted me.

"Then he's still a fool," Knox said quietly, flicking a wayward strand of hair off my face. Aspen saw the movement, his fist clenched tightly, but he didn't say anything as he drafted an irrigation sketch in the soft soil of the cave.

"Have you heard anything yet about the weapons?" I asked, knowing that frankness might scare him off, but also knowing we didn't have a lot of time to start hunting down answers. Knox shook his head.

"The king has been pouring over trade records since yesterday. The missing shipments were logged, but never reported," he said.

"There's also no indication of who was responsible for logging their loss."

I sighed, frustrated at the lack of progress we were making here.

"We will find the responsible party," Knox said confidently. "It will just take time."

Rourke suggested we stop for the rest of the afternoon so that the fields could be irrigated and return tomorrow so Aspen could grow the new plants and make sure the blight was gone. I thanked the Goddess. I saw Rourke looking concernedly at Aspen, and I had a feeling that worries for his health may have been part of his reasoning.

The ride back on the cave dragons was mostly quiet, all of us lost in thought about different things. My mind wandered to the previous night and Aspen's blazing kiss more times than I cared to count, and I saw him glance at me as if he knew what I was thinking.

"Let's eat out in the city tonight," Knox said when we arrived back at our suite. "There are some amazing restaurants, and you haven't had much of a chance to see the city yet."

"That sounds wonderful," I said, smiling.

"I must investigate these weapons," Rourke said, bowing to us. "I will have to miss dinner tonight." I smiled and nodded as Rourke took the cave dragons and rode toward the palace, cooing softly to them to stop them from becoming agitated in the evening crowds.

"Just us then," Knox said, giving me a wink. "How about you, Aspen?" he asked, turning to where Aspen scowled from across the room. Even though Aspen had told Knox not to call him 'lord,' Knox said Aspen's name with enough irreverence that I could tell it bothered him.

I wasn't sure what I was hoping he would say, but I was a little surprised when he said, "I'll come," in a voice that implied it was the last thing in the world he wanted to do.

Knox told us he would be back in an hour, and Aspen started laying out the samples he had taken from the fields across the table, placing some in water and some to dry. I left him to it and went to bathe, changing into one of my casual but pretty dresses. It was a pale pink gauzy tulle with tiny white flowers embroidered on the bodice, and flowing skirts that hid pockets I found to be very useful in my line of work. I strapped my daggers to my thighs as usual. One of the pockets in this skirt was false, and I could grab a blade in seconds through the hidden slit in the skirts of the dress if I needed to. While I hoped I wouldn't need to gut anyone at dinner, it comforted me to know that I could.

Aspen didn't look up at me when I reentered the common area. I thought I looked particularly pretty, and only maybe eighty percent of my wardrobe choice had been to try to tempt Aspen to kiss me again. Right now, he was examining blackened mushrooms with his shirt sleeves rolled up, hair damp from his own bath.

"Find anything?" I asked, coming to stand around the opposite side of the table.

He shook his head, still not looking up at me. "Not yet," he said, frowning at the table. "I need to try a few things before I can make any guesses for sure." He looked up then and blinked at me, jaw a little slack. I felt a surge of smug satisfaction at having affected him. Smiling, I went to stand on the balcony and wait for Knox.

Aspen followed and my heart did a little leap. "What are you doing Aurelia," he purred, eyebrows raised as he leaned against the balcony rail to face me, arms crossed as if preparing for a fight.

"I have no idea what you mean," I said sweetly, looking out into the city as if anxiously waiting for Knox to arrive.

"If this act doesn't fool me, it won't fool him," he rumbled, inching closer to me. I turned to look at him. His eyes blazed, darting to my lips, which I had glamoured to appear just a little more pink than usual.

"Again, I have no idea what you mean," I repeated, smiling innocently. Aspen pursed his lips and leaned toward me.

"You don't want him," he said—a statement, not a question.

"You have no idea what I want," I said, brows raised in cool regard. Before he could answer, Knox shouted up to me. I smiled and waved at him, then smirked at Aspen before going to meet him.

Knox had changed into more casual attire, and I was a little worried I had overdressed until I saw him smile appreciatively. He nodded a greeting to Aspen and took my arm.

"You look like a summer day," he said to me, smiling warmly. I felt a pang of guilt at the game I was playing with this male. I liked him, certainly, but as long as Aspen was around, I could never let myself love anyone else. Knox had some interest in me, and I knew if I continued I would break his heart too.

"Thank you," I said, trying to tone down my smile a little. I didn't want to hurt him by giving him false hope.

"Where are you taking us?" Aspen asked sourly, noting our linked arms and emanating disdain behind us.

"To enjoy the delights of the Crystal City in the best restaurant our humble realm has to offer," Knox said grandly.

He walked us through the streets, evening crowds of shoppers and diners milling about and smiling. Children darted between their parents' legs, and I smiled at their games. There were far more children here than in the fae realms, where children were a rare blessing.

We arrived at a restaurant where several of the council members met us. To my horror, Bisera was there, wearing a dress with a neckline that plunged to her navel, and she smiled coyly at Aspen as we entered and joined her table. I moved to put space between me and Aspen, but he grabbed my wrist and pulled me down next to him, Bisera on his other side and Knox on mine. Just wonderful.

"This place is known for its exotic dishes and strong ale," Knox said, raising a hand to a server, who brought several mugs of ale to our table. I sipped mine gingerly, remembering how strong it had been last night.

Food was brought on large platters, although I noticed the servings didn't fill their plates. I wondered if shortages were already affecting the city. Tiny cubes of meat were interspersed with greens and mushrooms of all shapes and sizes, and flatbread was served by the basketful. I felt rather guilty, eating so much when I knew that the city would soon be lacking, but maybe Aspen could prevent it from becoming too dire.

Bisera engaged Aspen deep in conversation and one of the dwarves was busy talking to Knox, so I was surprised to feel a gentle stroke on my knee. Knox had both hands on his mug, but Aspen trailed a hand over my skirts beneath the table. Even though he couldn't reach bare skin, I shivered at the touch and pushed his hand away, only to have him grab my fingers and hold them. I kicked him sharply and he choked on a gulp of ale, releasing my fingers.

"Everything okay?" asked Knox, seeing Aspen go a bit red in the face.

"Fine," he coughed. "Just has a bit of a kick." I glared at him, but Knox didn't notice, laughing and slapping Aspen's back.

The night progressed and I felt my inhibitions lower as I slowly sipped the ale. Aspen's hand drifted back to my knee, but this time I didn't push it off as he swept his thumb over my skirts. It was dangerous, sitting next to him like this. Every touch, whether purposeful or accidental, set me aflame, and by the time desserts were brought to the table, I was buzzing with need and frustration and confusion.

"Excuse me," I said, rising from the table and nodding toward the washroom. I went and splashed cool water on my face, seeing that a flush had risen up my cheeks and across my neck. I left the washroom and made my way to the exit, stepping into the cool air and taking several deep breaths.

"You're hiding from me now?" Aspen asked as he sidled up to me from the front doors of the restaurant.

"What are you doing?" I snapped, whirling on him. "Are you torturing me on purpose? Do you want to watch me break?" Tears pricked my eyes, but Aspen's face was hard.

"I thought that's what you were doing to me," he said, voice low and dangerous. He had also had quite a lot of ale, and I wasn't sure how much of our current standoff was due to the drink or to weeks of frustrated desire.

"*You* kissed *me*," I hissed. "And now you're doing whatever this is, and I can't think straight when you're like this."

"Like what?" Aspen growled, closing the distance between us and caging me in with his arms against the wall.

"Like this!" I shouted, waving at his closeness and his presence and his everything. "When you're near me and you're touching me. Why are you doing this? If you don't want me, why are you torturing me?"

Aspen hesitated, face hovering above mine still, as if unsure how to reply. Whether it was the ale or the tension or my own Goddess-damned need, I wasn't sure, but I was so tired of his hesitation that I grabbed his jacket and pulled him to me, crashing my mouth against his. With a groan he responded, tongue sweeping over mine as he deepened the kiss, pressing me harder against the wall.

"I have never stopped wanting you," he rumbled as he broke away, breath skating over my lips. "And I have thought of nothing but claiming you since you appeared tonight in that damn pink dress."

Chapter 12: Aurelia

I DIDN'T EXACTLY REMEMBER the walk back to our suite. I remembered being pushed against several walls for plundering kisses and thinking there was a very good chance we wouldn't make it back at all, but somehow we were there, standing in the common room, the sounds of the city still audible from the open balcony.

We looked at each other, and I was suddenly unsure. What if Aspen was more drunk than he was letting on? What if I was?

What if this was purely physical and nothing more? Could I handle that, if he didn't want anything but my body?

He crashed into me again and I decided that for this one moment, I didn't care. He tore at the buttons at the back of my dress, pulling it down roughly until I was completely exposed. I tore away the buttons on his shirt as we thrashed around the room, not caring that anyone might be watching through the open balcony.

Aspen pushed me roughly against the wall and lifted me, hooking my legs around his waist as he sucked a taut nipple into his mouth. I gasped, throwing my head back and digging my nails into the flesh of his shoulders. He moved to my other breast and continued sucking and licking until I felt fire burn through my limbs. This was a far cry from the tender, slow lovemaking of midsummer, and I was burning with need.

"Aspen, please," I begged, moaning as he continued to lick and suck. He looked up at me, smirking and eyes blazing with desire.

"Do you have any idea how much it killed me to think of that bastard touching you?" he growled, grinding against me with a hardness that betrayed his desires. It created enough delicious friction that I shuddered. His hands twined in my hair as he tortured me so achingly slowly.

"He didn't," I gasped out, eyes fluttering shut at the feel and weight of him. Aspen nipped at my throat and I groaned.

"And no other male ever will," he growled. "Only me. Say it."

"No other male will touch me," I said, desperate to have him in me, trying to rub myself against him as he left me aching and wanting. "I'm yours."

He kissed me then, pressing his tongue against mine in a furious dance for dominance. Belatedly, I realized that this was what he had needed this whole time. To feel in control, to dominate and have me submit. To feel like I was his, unconditionally. To claim me so that no one would take me from him again.

I fumbled at his belt, trying to remove the barrier between us and unbutton his pants. He growled, pushing me harder against the wall until I gasped.

"If I hurt you," he ground out, running his hand up my thigh to the blade strapped there and squeezing, "stab me." He rolled against me again and I moaned, knowing that there would be no way I would stop this from happening, no matter how rough he was with me.

His hands slid further up my thighs to find me bare beneath my skirts already, and he growled, unbuttoning his pants while teasing my wetness with his fingers. I moaned again, digging my nails into his shoulder until he finally thrust up into me in one delicious stroke. I cried out, letting my head fall back against the wall as I felt him fill me with warmth and heat and pressure. He pressed his hand to my throat and squeezed gently as I settled on to him, and I dug my nails harder into his back at the riot of sensation.

He moved, thrusting his tongue in my mouth in tandem with his hips. I felt like he owned me completely in that moment, and I loved it. Our first time together, Aspen had been gentle and hesitant, slow and seductive as he waited to make sure I was ready. Now he was aggressive and passionate and possessive, seeking a release for our fury and a bridging of our injured hearts.

I felt the tension building in me as he moved. I gasped for air, his kisses merciless, and he had me pressed against the wall so hard I knew he was scraping the skin down my back. He lifted his head enough to move his mouth to my ear.

"Come for me," he growled. As if on his command, my body obliged and I shattered around him as he roared through his pleasure.

For a long time, we stayed like that against the wall, breathing hard and staring at each other. I felt somehow as if a weight had been lifted from my chest, letting me breathe freely for the first time in weeks. Aspen rested his forehead against the wall next to me

.

"I'm sorry," he said softly, voice slightly hoarse after our collision together. "I wanted to be gentle."

"No," I said, shaking my head slightly, still feeling rather boneless and unable to move. "Don't apologize. This was right. I don't want gentle."

He slid out of me and lowered me back to the ground gently. I winced, my thighs aching from having been pressed open for so long. I was afraid he would step away, would regret what we had done, so I clutched at him, refusing to let him move as I leaned against the wall for support.

"Don't say it was a mistake," I said hoarsely, looking into his eyes. Pain flashed in them and he shook his head.

"Nothing with you is a mistake," he said, bending down to kiss me gently, the violence and anger of our coupling absent now that we were both spent.

Without another word, he scooped me into his arms and took me to his room, turning on the shower with a free hand and carrying me straight into it with him.

I squawked at the cold water, but he silenced my protest with a heady kiss that warmed me from the inside as the water began to warm me from the outside. We scrubbed in silence, passing each other soap and turning to wash away the hurts from our joining. I had scraped six angry-looking welts down his back with my fingernails, and I could tell my back was in no better shape, having been scraped by the wall. The injuries would be healed by morning, but the longer the silence stretched between us, the more I worried that this thing forged by passion and frustration might crack when we examined what we had just done.

Aspen got out of the shower and handed me a towel, which I used to dry off as best as I could. He scooped me back up, towel and all, and plopped me down on the center of his bed. I sat there, drying my hair as he handed me a blanket to wrap around myself. I was rather sore from our tryst against the wall, but it was the pleasant soreness that I remembered from our first time together, and it made warmth curl inside me again at the memory.

Aspen sat down next to me, fully naked still, his damp hair beginning to curl at his nape and temples. I brushed it aside gently and he closed his eyes, resting his forehead against mine.

"What we just did—" he began, voice low and hoarse.

"We don't have to talk about it," I whispered, desperately afraid he was about to break my heart again. "We can pretend it didn't happen if you want."

He lifted his forehead and looked at me, frowning. "Is that what you want?" he asked.

I swallowed, shaking my head. "No," I said, looking up to meet his eyes. "But if that's what it takes for me to keep you, then I'll pretend." He shook his head, pulling me down next to him on the bed and looking into my eyes.

"You have me already," he said softly, stroking the wet hair back from my face, looking remorseful. "It's me who should worry about keeping you."

"I hurt you," I protested, cupping his face in my hand and tracing his strong jaw with my fingers. He knew I wasn't talking about the scratches down his back.

"And I hurt you in return," he said. "Didn't I?"

I nodded. He had hurt me back, and I had been holding on to my fury and heartache for weeks until this moment.

"Whatever this is now," he said, tracing my collarbone with his fingers, "it won't be the same as it was before. It can't be."

I nodded. "I know," I whispered. "I don't want it to be."

"You don't want soft and tender anymore?" he asked, quirking a brow. "You don't want it to be like our first time? Or when Ember teased you for blushing every time I looked at you?"

"I think we might be beyond blushing now," I said wryly. I thought back again to that first night. To the tentative kisses and touches, the sweet ache of pleasure as I lost myself in him for the first time, the whispered promises of love and faithfulness that both of us ended up breaking.

"I want it to be real," I added. "And raw, and messy, and honest. Even if it hurts."

He nodded and kissed me again, folding me against him and holding me close. "Real it is, then."

THE ROOM WAS ON fire. My skin was burning and my lungs filled with smoke as the blankets and the bed charred away to ash. A snake twisted through the remains, joined by a second that twined with it in a fiery dance as the inferno blazed. A great rumbling shook the room as I screamed through the burning, and the mountain collapsed on top of me.

"Aurelia!" Aspen shouted, shaking me awake. I bolted up, soaked in sweat and trembling from the dream. My throat felt raw like I had been screaming for hours. Aspen felt my face and cursed.

"You're burning up," he said, scooping me up and taking me back into the bathroom. He stepped into the shower and turned the water to cold. I shivered, teeth chattering as the heat inside me was doused by the cold water. Aspen stayed with me, feeling my face and arms until he was satisfied I was cooling down. We were both naked still, I realized. He must have been freezing.

"The same dream?" he asked, turning off the water and fetching a dry towel for me. I shook my head.

"No, and yes," I said, my voice weak and teeth still chattering. "There was fire, but it was here this time. It's always wherever I am." Aspen frowned, feeling my head again, looking worried. "And there were two snakes," I added, shivering.

"Maybe you should go home," he said gently. "Mother Vervain might be able to help with the nightmares, and Ember can help if this is some sickness." I shook my head furiously.

"I'm not leaving until the mission is done," I said, fierceness somewhat undermined by my chattering teeth. "I'm fine." Aspen raised a skeptical brow at me, giving me an appraising once over. "I will be fine," I amended, grudgingly accepting that I probably looked the opposite of fine at this particular moment.

I stood shakily, still wrapped in a towel. Before I had taken more than three steps, Aspen had wrapped his arms around me, holding me tight. We stood like that for a while, accepting that we were not getting back to sleep.

Once I had finally stopped shaking, I looked up into his blue eyes, brushing the damp curls off his brow. "I'm going to get dressed and eat," I said, "and then we have to discuss our plan for how to proceed going forward."

He frowned and nodded, and I went back to my room to dress. Since we would be out inspecting fields today, I chose my riding gear instead of a dress. I wasn't sure how much climbing or walking there would be, and I wanted to be free to move. I strapped my daggers back to my thighs and added one down each boot, then braided my wet hair roughly, lamenting that it may never be dry at this rate.

Aspen was waiting for me when I emerged. The light of early dawn filtered into the city from the mountain window, and I felt like I had barely slept. He handed me a cup of tea wordlessly and we sat, staring into our mugs as we tried to figure out what to say first.

"How do you want to play this," Aspen said, gesturing between us. I sighed, frowning up at him.

"Do you regret it?" I asked, wanting to make sure we were on the same page before I made my suggestion about how we presented ourselves to the dwarves. Aspen shook his head.

"I told you," he said gently, "nothing with you is a mistake." I nodded, a warm glow suffusing my heart as the cracks in it began to slowly knit together.

"You said you agreed to real and messy," I said, my plan solidifying. "This is certainly going to be both of those things."

"What are you thinking?" Aspen asked warily.

"I think we should continue as we have been in front of the dwarves and Knox," I said, keeping my gaze trained on his. "Knox knows we were once lovers. I think he is interested in me now."

Aspen scoffed. "You think?" he said sarcastically.

I scowled at him. "And Bisera has some interest in you," I added accusingly.

"I told you I didn't—" Aspen began defensively.

I shook my head. "It doesn't matter. We need to use it to our advantage," I said. "We need information, and we won't get it without building some trust with the unseelie and dwarves here. I say we act as we have been, at least in front of the others, and let them get close to us. If they know something about the iron weapons that Thorn was storing, we need to find out what it is. Maybe if they truly know nothing, they can help us figure out who does know something."

Aspen growled at my mention of Thorn, and I reveled a little in his possessiveness of me.

"How far do you want me to go to get this information?" he asked, giving me a dark murderous look. "Should I bed her in front of you?" I scowled, my gut twisting at the idea he might do what he did to me last night to another female.

"No," I said, "or I'll cut out your heart with my dagger." He smirked slightly. "But let her think you're interested if she seems to know anything."

"And how far will you go?" he asked, smirk falling away as he frowned. "I can't watch another male with you again. It will break me." My heart ached a bit at his honesty. I stood and walked over to him, sitting on his lap and wrapping my arms around his neck.

"No other male will touch me like that," I reassured him. "Never again."

He nipped at my earlobe and growled, "They'd better fucking not."

Chapter 13: Aurelia

ROURKE AND KNOX APPEARED when the sun was streaking through the mountain window, and we had enough sense to separate ourselves before they arrived. Aspen put on a fairly convincing show of grumpiness at me, aided by the fact that Knox was all smiles and concern about my sudden disappearance last night.

"Are you well?" he asked, stepping close to me, but not reaching out to touch me.

I smiled, trying to make it look pained. "Yes, just a little too much dwarven ale I think," I said, touching my temple as if my head ached. "I felt sick, and Aspen walked me back."

"Aye, it's strong stuff if you're weak of stomach," said Rourke gruffly, saddling the cave dragons for our ride back to the fields. I beamed when I saw that Honeysuckle had returned. He trilled when I patted his scaly head.

Knox seemed convinced by my explanation, brushing a warm hand over my shoulder. I felt, more than heard, Aspen's growl from the other side of the room. I raised my brows at him, trying to communicate wordlessly for him to back off a bit. I stepped away from Knox to keep Aspen from snapping his limited control over his jealousy.

We made the long bumpy ride out again to find that the fields had been watered and were ready for growing. For the rest of the day, I watched in awe as Aspen worked his magic. By lunch he had already managed to regrow a full field, which I helped a small army of dwarves collect in giant baskets, again spreading the spores from the plants as we collected them. The blighted areas had grown back healthy, and he smiled in triumph as we ate a meager lunch.

"I'll study the samples more today," he said, discussing the work with Rourke as we ate cold mushrooms and dry bread. "But if it can be removed like this, then it might be a disease that can be cured, or at least managed through burning."

By the end of the afternoon, Aspen's magic was almost completely spent again, and he was exhausted. He had managed to produce a second immature crop by the time we left, promising to return the next day to finish the job and to check that the blight remained at bay. The sections that had been burned had grown back clean and healthy a second time, and the dwarves cheered as they saw the regrowth that sprang up before them.

As Knox and Rourke packed up the dragons, I went to Aspen with a water skin, insisting he drink more. He took it and downed the water in one gulp. A small dwarven child came and took the water skin from me to refill it. I smiled as he ran off.

"Learn anything today?" Aspen asked, glancing at the child's retreating form. I shook my head. He growled. "If I have to watch Knox flirt with you, I'd at least like it to result in useful information," he rumbled, staring murderously at the male in question.

"Stop that," I said, snapping my fingers in his face. "You need to act more indifferent around him."

Aspen grumbled and I moved away to climb onto Honeysuckle's saddle, patting his scaly head when I had mounted. The ride back seemed twice as long as the ride out, and the sun had fully set outside when we made it back to the city.

"The king has asked if you will dine with him tonight," Rourke said roughly, frowning at Aspen, whose face was ashen as he slumped over his cave dragon. "But it may be best to ask him to wait until tomorrow. He did not know how draining this would be. I will give him your apologies." Aspen nodded, relieved.

"I'll have a meal sent up for you," Knox added, looking between us. To me he added, "Will you be alright?" Aspen growled softly at the insinuation but I pretended not to notice.

"Yes, I'm exhausted. I believe I will eat and go straight to bed," I said, leaning a little against Honeysuckle to prove my point. Knox nodded, and he and Rourke took the two other dragons with them as they headed back toward the palace.

When they were out of sight, Aspen sagged heavily against the railing. I rushed over to catch him under the arm and help him up the stairs. I got him to the couch, where he flopped down heavily. He closed his eyes and ran a hand down his face.

"Rest for a bit," I said, pushing sweaty curls off his forehead. "I'll run you a bath."

I went to Aspen's bathroom and realized there was no tub in there. Sighing, I went to my room and filled the tub with warm water.

Food had been delivered when I got back out to the common room, and Aspen had fallen asleep where he had flopped. I shook him gently and forced him to sit up and eat something.

We sat there eating in an easy silence that hadn't been between us in weeks. The food seemed to revive Aspen a bit because he was able to go to the washroom and start shucking off his sweaty clothes without assistance. I stood leaning against the wall, torn between watching him undress and offering him privacy. He didn't seem in much of a state to do anything that would surely happen if I stayed.

"I'll go to your bathroom to clean up," I said, watching him climb into the bath in all his naked glory, a little disappointed that he didn't argue. He nodded, splashing water over his face and head, and I went to shower quickly in case he fell asleep in the bath.

When I emerged, toweling off my wet hair and wearing my robe, Knox was sitting in the common room. I paused, unsure what to do. I couldn't leave Aspen, but I didn't want Knox to know about us

.

He must have heard me and stood, blushing slightly as he saw me in my thin robe. "I just wanted to check on you," he said, rubbing the back of his neck with a hand nervously. "Do you need anything else?"

"No," I said, smiling warmly, "we are completely fine. Aspen is already asleep I think." Knox glanced curiously back at the door behind me and I cursed inwardly, realizing how strange it looked that I had come out of his room.

"We switched rooms for the night," I said hurriedly by way of explanation. "Mine has the bathtub, and he was too tired to stand." Knox nodded, breathing out a short breath of relief at my answer. My gut twisted at the lie. He would hate me when he found out the depth of my deception.

"Very well," he said, nodding slightly. "Did you eat already? If not, I'm happy to escort you into the city again. There are many more wonderful places I could take you."

I smiled again, genuinely warmed by the invitation. "Another night?" I asked, trying to sound hopeful. "I fear I am too tired to be good company tonight." Knox laughed and stepped closer, running a finger down my silken sleeve.

"I sincerely doubt that, but yes," he said deeply. "Another night." He leaned in a bit, but I smiled and stepped back before he could go further. Confusion flashed across his face momentarily, but he recovered quickly and took my hand, kissing it gently before strolling back down the balcony stairs.

I turned to see Aspen, leaning against the door frame of my bedroom, a towel slung low around his waist, arms crossed, and eyes blazing with jealousy.

"Nothing happened," I said, frowning as I crossed the room to him and putting my hands on his bare chest. "He came to check on me and I sent him away."

"You must think me an unevolved beast," Aspen growled, running his hands down my arms, eyes blazing with fury and desire, "that the sight of another male kissing your hand makes me want to destroy things."

I didn't reply as Aspen crushed his mouth against mine, pushing me back against the wall and claiming me with a searing kiss. His heart was pounding, and I could feel the anger-fueled jealousy roaring through him as he attempted to regain control of the possessive creature inside him.

I moaned as he slid a hand up my thigh, grasping my backside and squeezing hard as he pressed himself against me. A small part of me felt like I should protest at this need for domination Aspen had, but right now it lit a fire in me that could only be doused by him.

"I'm yours," I reminded him as he panted against me, breathing fast as he broke our kiss. He looked at me with a hunger I felt in the core of my being, and warmth flooded me again at the prospect of what he needed tonight.

"I want you to prove it," he growled against my lips, hand reaching back further to dip his fingers into the dampness between my legs. He growled in approval, finding me without undergarments and ready for him. I gasped as he elicited a sweet ache that traveled from my navel to my nipples.

In one quick movement he had turned me, so he was pressed up hard against my backside, my arms bracing us against the wall. His hands trailed down my stomach and my pelvis, brushing the soft hair between my legs and earning another moan from me. He kissed my neck, nipping slightly with his teeth as he moved his other hand to cup my breast beneath my robe. I shuddered as he flicked the sensitive bud there and mirrored the movement between my legs.

"You'll have to do a little better at convincing me," he growled, moving his fingers in torturously slow circles as he teased me.

"Please," I whispered. I felt him smile against my neck as he fumbled to remove the towel between us. I felt him sliding into me, warmth and pressure and delicious sensation between his body at my back and the wall at my front. He continued to move his wicked fingers, circling and kneading until I was shaking with tension, all the while thrusting into me from behind.

I cried out, release shattering through me as he continued moving, building the tension again as he relentlessly pounded into me. His fingers stilled and I let out a little cry of protest, feeling him smile against my neck again.

"Tell me you are only mine," he rumbled, gently flicking the sensitive spot between my legs. His hard length continued to move inside me, and I moaned.

"I'm only yours," I breathed, as he pulled me from the wall and back against him, resuming his attention and making me groan with the ache of him. He stepped back, using the wall behind him as leverage to continue thrusting into me as he teased and stroked, the strong band of his arm coming around me to hold me against him as I shattered for a second time.

This time he came with me, biting down on my neck hard as he came, mixing pleasure and pain and fury and forgiveness all in one intoxicating moment. He slid down the wall with me still against him, breathing heavily as he kissed away the hurt he had inflicted on my neck. I gripped his arm to steady myself, resting my head back against his chest as I worked to catch my own breath. We sat like that until our passions had cooled some.

"I'm sorry," he said, squeezing me with his arm as he removed his fingers from between my legs. "Did I hurt you?"

"You have to stop apologizing," I sighed, tilting my face up to kiss the underside of his jaw. I shivered at the feeling of rough stubble against my chin. "If you hurt me I promise to stab you in return."

"Deal," he said, dropping a scratchy kiss on my shoulder and resting his forehead there. "I keep meaning to be gentle, to take my time with you," he added, still breathing heavily as he spoke into my shoulder. "I don't know what's wrong with me that I can't get a grip on this need I have for you."

I reached a hand up to stroke the back of his head, feeling his soft curls still damp from the bath between my fingers. "It's not just you," I said, closing my eyes as he swept his hand over my stomach, resting his palm there. "Did you prefer me timid and blushing?" I asked, feeling suddenly self-conscious at my brazen response to him. "Our first time was so different..." I trailed off, unsure how to express my uncertainty.

"Things were different. We were different," he said, squeezing me again and running a large hand down my thigh. "I want you exactly as you are right now."

Chapter 14: Aurelia

I SLEPT WELL PAST dawn, and for once, no nightmares of burning plagued me. Aspen was gone from my bed when I awoke, and I hastily dressed, worried I had missed the day's excursion.

I found him sitting in the common room, dressed for sparring in dwarven leathers. The rotted and blighted plants he had collected the previous day were spread out on the small table that we usually ate on, and my appetite for breakfast quickly vanished.

He was gently handling the plants, feeling their roots and pushing his magic through them to try to discover the cause of their decay. He looked up and smiled tiredly when he saw me, then returned to his examination. I came and sat next to him on the couch, cross-legged as I watched him work.

He finally sat back, placing an arm across the back of the couch in a fair imitation of his former self. Looking at me, he frowned. "I know the cause of the blight," he said, tiredly, "but the dwarves and the unseelie are not going to like it. I don't know if we should tell them until we know more."

"What is it?" I asked, frowning at the withered plants on the table. "A disease?"

Aspen shook his head, running a tired hand over his face again. "It's unseelie magic," he said darkly.

I blinked in surprise. "Are you sure?" I asked, looking again at the withered plants.

He nodded. "My magic can't undo the damage, which means it's not natural. No disease could do this. The plants have been killed from the inside." He pointed at the core of the mushrooms which were blackened more than the outer layer of the plants. "Poison would affect the outer layer first, and a natural disease would have more variation in the pattern of destruction."

"What do we do then?" I asked, drawing my hand back from the plants with a grimace.

Aspen shook his head. "If I'm right, the blight will return to the field we just saved," he said. "The magic has probably poisoned the soil itself. My magic will have counteracted it temporarily by not letting it take hold, but unseelie magic would survive the burning without me to speed up the plant growth."

He ran his hands through his hair and looked wearily at me, leaning forward with his arms resting on his knees. "I assume we can trust the king with this, but I don't know if we can trust Knox or Rourke," he went on. "It had to be someone inside the mountain who did this. Maybe several someones."

"Should we write to Ember?" I asked, not sure if we could trust mail leaving this place.

"Not until we know more," Aspen said. He met my eyes, his sharp with resolve. "You're going to have to ask Knox about the situation of the unseelie here," he added, fist clenching at the thought of it.

"You could try charming Bisera at the king's dinner tonight," I suggested, feeling my gut twist in jealousy already at the scandalous dress she would probably be wearing.

Aspen nodded absently. "We need to figure out who is working against the dwarves. And whether the same person killing the crops is also stealing weapons," he said.

"Do you think the king will grant us a private audience?" I asked, remembering the mixed council who advised him, and having no idea who among it we could trust.

"I hope so," said Aspen. "If I'm right, the field I cured will be worse off when we check it today. If someone is working for the Unseelie King, they won't want King Holvard trusting us. They'll want to undermine my success to make the king question his offer of allegiance."

While we waited for Knox and Rourke to arrive with the cave dragons, Aspen practiced with the warhammer Knox had loaned him. I watched him move through exercises and swing at imaginary enemies, and my heart did a happy little leap at the thrill of watching him. He seemed stronger than he had two months ago and more confident in his abilities.

"Do you want to try?" he asked, sweat glistening on his brow. "It's not as heavy as it looks."

"Are you looking to trounce me thoroughly again like you did before we left?" I asked, smiling faintly.

Aspen shrugged and smirked mischievously, but anything he might have said in reply was lost as Knox and Rourke arrived for training and our daily outing. The males spent an interminable time discussing the finer points of warhammers with Aspen. I entertained myself by naming all of the cave dragons they had brought with them.

Honeysuckle wasn't with them this time. Knox laughed when I chose 'Primrose' for my new mount, especially as she had a particularly fearsome personality.

"I'm not sure flower names suit cave dragons," he said, as I pointed out all of the dragons I had already christened. His was Dewberry, and Aspen was riding on Bluebell while Rourke rode on Hyacinth.

Aspen was too tense about what we might find at the fields to join in our conversation or tease me about doting on fire-breathing monsters. He rode in silence the entire trek, looking as if he expected the worst.

When we arrived, his fears were confirmed. He hopped off his dragon before it had even stopped and put his hands on his head.

Where the day before there had been no blight present in the nearly-regrown fields, now more than half the field had been destroyed. The dwarves who had been present yesterday muttered darkly, casting accusing looks at Aspen as if blaming him for the failure of the field.

"How?" I asked, staring in horror at the destruction. Aspen shook his head.

"Someone is trying to undermine our efforts here," he said darkly, running his fingers through the blighted soil and studying his hands. They were red. He began directing the dwarves to harvest what was salvageable, pouring his magic into the unspoiled plants to help them mature.

"Aspen," I said, catching up to him as we finished pulling the healthy crops. I cast a shield of air around us to ensure we weren't overheard. "You can't waste your magic on this again today. If you're right, it will be the same or worse tomorrow and you'll be fit for nothing if you keep draining yourself."

"I know," said Aspen, sweat running down his face as he surveyed the ruined plants. Rourke and Knox were approaching, so I quickly dropped my shield.

"What should we do, Lord Aspen?" asked Rourke, crossing his large arms across his chest in a posture ready for battle. "Do you know why the sickness spread?"

"I have a theory," Aspen said, hedging the truth, "but I want to share it with your king first to see if he agrees."

Rourke nodded, his eyes taking in the devastation of the field with remorse. Knox had been mostly silent when we arrived. I knew Aspen would view it as a sign of his guilt, but I rather thought he was just as shocked as everyone else.

"Can you fix it?" he asked Aspen, gesturing to the blighted land.

Aspen shook his head. "If I'm right, it will come back unless we replace the blighted soil," he said, wiping a forearm over his brow. "I need to speak with your king as soon as possible about bringing in new soil from the Seelie lands. It's the only way I can think to solve the problem long term, other than finding the responsible party."

Knox nodded. "You are requested at dinner tonight," he reminded us, glancing between us as we looked at each other. "You can hopefully speak to him then and share your recommendations."

We rode back to the city in silence, Aspen brooding over what to tell the king, and my mind working to puzzle out who was responsible. Someone had been shipping weapons to the Unseelie King, and it had to be someone powerful and influential enough to do it behind King Holvard's back and without his knowledge. Someone else, or possibly the same someone, was killing off the fields, forcing the dwarves to face starvation. But to what end?

Rourke seemed an obvious suspect. He could want to take his father's position and be using the blight to undermine him. But he seemed to genuinely care about his people, and he acted just as surprised as the others about the weapons shipments to the Unseelie King.

"Has anyone suggested trading with the Unseelie King for food since this all began?" I asked Knox as we neared the city limits.

"Yes," he replied. "We discussed every option possible. That suggestion was quickly squashed by several unseelie council members, but I believe it was suggested."

"Do you remember who suggested it?" I asked, hoping that Knox might unwittingly have all of the answers I needed.

He shook his head, and I felt my hope deflate in my chest. "Several suggestions were made," he repeated. "I know that was one of them, but I don't know who suggested it." He looked at me, eyes narrowing. "What do you suspect is causing this?"

"I'm not completely sure yet," I said, which wasn't a total lie. "But I suspect there's a link between whoever is selling iron weapons and whatever is poisoning your fields."

Knox raised his brows. "You don't think the blight is natural?" he asked.

I cursed internally, realizing that I may have revealed too much. "It's just a theory," I said, shrugging as if I wasn't already sure.

When we arrived at our dwelling, Knox stopped me with a hand on my shoulder before I could go in to change for dinner. "I hope you know you can trust me, Aurelia," he said, giving my shoulder a gentle squeeze. "I won't ask you to reveal your secrets to me, but I vow to you, I want what is best for my people. These people."

I nodded, patting his hand as I gently removed it from my shoulder. "Thank you," I said.

"I'll be back for you in an hour," he replied. Rourke bowed and left with the cave dragons as Aspen and I went to dress for dinner.

"YOU THINK IT COULD be Knox?" I asked Aspen as he glared at me across my bedroom while I combed my hair. "Are you sure this is not your jealousy getting the better of you?"

Aspen growled slightly, bending one of the few hairpins I had brought with me out of shape.

"Hey," I said, taking it from him and lamenting the lost hairpin. "Take out your aggression on your accessories."

Aspen sighed. "We need to play this close to the chest, Aurelia," he said, running his hands through his hair and making it look wilder than usual. "If someone on the council is responsible, they may already know all of our moves. They will be ahead of us every step."

"Do you think we shouldn't tell the king?" I asked, dusting some powder on my cheeks and admiring my reflection.

My goal was to appear young and pretty and useless tonight. Aspen would take the lead in diplomacy, while I would attempt to flatter and flirt information out of the guests. People were more likely to talk if they thought you were too young or naive to understand what they were saying, and my goal was to get someone to talk to me if Knox and Aspen would let anyone else get near me.

To assist my ruse, I had poured a little extra magic into my glamour, hoping it made it look like I was trying to impress the dwarven court. My dress was one of pure white, as I wanted to exude innocent naïveté. The skirts flared out ridiculously and the sleeves puffed over my bare upper arms, leaving my shoulders exposed. Aside from my pointed ears, I looked like a porcelain doll, all pink cheeks and shining golden hair, but I supposed it had the effect I desired.

"I don't think we have a choice," Aspen said, pulling me back to the conversation. "We just have to hope the responsible party is stupid enough to reveal their hand."

I stood and turned to Aspen, giving a small twirl for his approval. He looked at me gravely, frowning. "What is it?" I asked, going to him and putting my hands on his cheeks.

He sighed and ran his hands over my bare shoulders, making me shiver. "You're just so Goddess-damned beautiful," he said, running his fingers through my hair and dislodging the comb. I sighed and fixed it, and he gave me a sheepish smile. "I don't know how I'm going to keep it together tonight if every male is lusting after you."

"Luckily, I don't think the dwarves are all that interested in fae females," I teased, kissing him gently.

"Lucky indeed," he replied, running a thumb gently over my lips.

I felt warmth curl in my belly. This was the first truly tender moment between us since whatever we were doing now had started, other than when he had held me after my nightmare. All of our other moments had been fierce or aggressive or born of need or heightened emotion. I looked into his face, still sad but now also hungry.

"I don't want anyone else," I reminded him. "I'm utterly yours."

He nodded, pressing his forehead to mine. "And I'm yours."

Something glowed in my chest as he said that, sealing yet another crack in my heart. I felt a warmth between us that had been absent for so long that I hadn't realized how cold I had been.

Aspen pulled back a little, looking surprised. "Do you feel that?" he asked.

"Feel what?" I asked, not sure if he was referring to the warm buzzing glow between us, and not sure I wanted to be the first to admit its presence.

He looked at me a moment longer and shook his head. "Never mind," he said, kissing me lightly and smiling faintly. "We should go."

Chapter 15: Aurelia

KNOX WAS WAITING AT the bottom of the balcony stairs to escort us to dinner. He did a bit of a double take when he saw me, mouth splitting into a wide grin as he took me in.

"Goddess above, Aurelia," he said, kissing my hand. "No one will be able to focus on dinner if you come looking like that."

I blushed prettily and heard Aspen grinding his teeth behind me. I let Knox take my arm and escort us through the city, the crystals on the walls and roads beginning to glow as daylight faded. We moved more slowly than normal because my shoes were not designed for walking, but I enjoyed seeing the city at dusk.

The Crystal Palace loomed like a great, glittering heart beating at the center of the city. I had always pictured dwarven architecture as being largely carved from stone, but that this crystal art had been hidden from us was truly a tragedy. I felt lucky to be able to see it.

Knox spoke all about his childhood running around the streets of the city, and he led us through the massive crystal doors of the palace to a new room.

The dining room of the Crystal Palace had walls that gleamed pink and gold in the dying light of day. A long stone table was set with stone plates and goblets, and long stone benches were placed along its length for guests to sit. The king greeted us warmly, the council a little less so, and we sat to dine.

dwarven fare seemed to be all the same—bread and cave plants, with small cuts of meat as the hunting in winter was poor. I hoped that none of the meat was cave rat, but I wasn't brave enough to ask. There were sautéed mushrooms in an excellent wine sauce, but I noticed the portions were small in size for such a large party. Clearly, the rationing had begun.

"Lord Aspen," said Bisera, who was seated across from us at the table wearing a red dress that should not be classified as a dress at all, it was so scant. "Tell us, how fares the farming?" Her tone was condescending, but it was impossible to tell if she meant anything by it.

"Yes, my lord and lady, tell us how you fare," boomed King Holvard from the head of the table. The table quieted, waiting for Aspen's answer. He looked at Knox and Rourke and cleared his throat.

"Not well, I fear," said Aspen. Assorted murmuring followed his statement and he cleared his throat again before continuing. "I was able to mature the fields and burn away the blight our first day with some success," he continued, "and we reseeded before leaving for the night yesterday, but this morning it appeared the blight had spread over half the field."

The table was quiet, the guests realizing the implications of this.

King Holvard frowned. "I appreciate your efforts, despite this setback," he said, gravely, "but what could have spread the blight overnight? It has never moved so fast before."

"Do you believe it was your magic?" Bisera asked, looking at Aspen appraisingly. I tried to read her tone, wanting her very much to be guilty, but she sounded genuinely concerned.

Aspen frowned. "No, I do not," he replied curtly. "Your Majesty, if I could have a private word..."

"Nonsense," said a dwarf near the head of the table. "We are the king's trusted council. You can have nothing to tell His Majesty that we should not all hear."

Aspen looked at me, and I shrugged. "I really feel—" Aspen tried again.

The king waved his hand dismissively. "Speak freely, Lord Aspen," he said. "I trust my council. I permit them to hear everything of importance about our realm."

There was some political conflict going on here that I couldn't quite parse. Several dwarves and unseelie fae exchanged wary glances, while others appeared almost smug at this pronouncement. It was impossible to know which I should be paying attention to.

"Very well, Your Majesty," Aspen said, bowing his head. "The cause of the blight is most likely unseelie magic poisoning the soil."

Outraged cries and muttering broke out from all sides of the table.

The king stared hard at Aspen. "How can you be sure?" he asked, craggy voice dropping even deeper in fury at this news. Aspen explained it the same way he explained it to me, mentioning the blackened cores of the plants and the staining red dirt.

"This is Seelie trickery," shouted one unseelie fae, rising angrily from his seat. "They seek to paint us as the villains to win your favor, Your Highness. All unseelie in the city are loyal to you."

"And what of the unseelie outside the city?" Aspen asked, pinning the unseelie male with a glare.

"That's enough," said King Holvard, bringing an end to the outbursts. "This is news I should have taken in private. Lord Aspen, do you believe this is the case for all our fields?"

"I can't be sure without inspecting them," Aspen said. "But it seems likely. I think the best course is to send out scouts to map the damage and try to find a common pattern or element, while I focus my magic on growing as much as I can with your limited resources. In the meantime, you should write to my cousin requesting emergency supplies of grain and dried meat to get you through the winter, and larger shipments of fresh soil to replace the poisoned land."

"You cannot trust these fae," the same unseelie male shouted again. "They seek to undermine us and exterminate our kind with their war and their magic."

"That is not true," I said angrily, fury rising in me at the implication. "Our king is unseelie. Some of our closest friends are unseelie. Lord Aspen speaks the truth to you. We came here to help."

"If you do not wish for our help in light of this discovery," Aspen said coldly to the unseelie male, "we can leave at dawn."

"My king," broke in Rourke, always formal even with his father. "I believe the lord and lady wish to help and speak true. I saw Lord Aspen grow new crops for us with my own eyes, as did many others in the nearest fields, and I believe his course is the best one for us."

"So you agree that this is somehow our fault?" Bisera asked, bristling with anger at the assumed insult.

"It may be that no one here is responsible," I threw out angrily, glaring at Bisera. "But someone has been withering your fields, and someone has been stealing iron and selling it to the Unseelie King. It is not a coincidence that this is happening at the same time."

"Your Highness, something must be done," an older dwarf said seriously. "We have no way to tell where everyone's loyalties lie."

The king ran his hands over his face, looking haggard. "Place all unseelie in the city and the nearby outskirts under house arrest," he said tiredly, waving his guards out.

"What?" shouted Knox and Bisera, both standing in shock and protest. "Your Majesty," Aspen started, "this isn't—"

"I am King under this mountain, Lord Aspen," King Holvard interrupted fiercely, "and this blight threatens my people. Until the culprit is caught, I have no choice but to detain any possible suspects."

The unseelie at the table stood in protest, and the king rose, motioning more guards forward. "My trusted council," he said, "we have important work to do and I look to you to set an example. I will ask you to remain in the palace until the culprit can be found. Rooms will be provided and you will be my guests."

"Prisoners, you mean," snapped Bisera, looking daggers at me. I sighed, knowing she would blame me somehow even though Aspen had delivered the truth.

"Guests," corrected King Holvard. "And to be safe and ensure no foul play is at work, Lord Aspen and Lady Aurelia will be relocated here too." I started to rise to protest, but Aspen gripped my hand under the table in warning.

"You will be supervised by Prince Rourke and my guards when you visit the fields until the guilty party is caught or you have provided all the aid you can to meet our bargain," the king said. "Your things will be brought here, and I will write to your queen explaining this decision and begging for her cooperation."

Aspen nodded in acquiescence, still gripping my hand tightly to stop me from reacting.

The dwarves at the table grumbled their approval of this plan. I looked to Knox, who was furious, but he nodded slightly. He would follow orders, I realized, and we should too.

The unseelie council members were led away to guest rooms by guards, and Rourke personally escorted Aspen and me to the guest wing.

"This shall be Lady Aurelia's room," he said, gesturing to an ornate stone door. I was about to say thank you when Aspen cut in.

"No," he said, gripping my hand and pulling me back next to him. Rourke frowned.

"It is not acceptable?" he asked, his accent more thick than usual after the stress of the dinner.

"If we are to be your father's guests here, surrounded by potential enemies, then we will share a room," Aspen said, still holding my hand tightly. "Lady Aurelia was sent as my guard, and I expect to keep her close."

Rourke raised a brow, giving me an appraising look, but nodded. "There are no suites free," he said apologetically, "but I can find a room with a couch for you." Aspen nodded his assent and we continued down the hall, Rourke poking his head into any doors that were not guarded. I realized that we would have a guard outside our door too. It should have made me relieved, but I didn't like having no means of escape on hand.

Finally, Rourke picked a room he deemed satisfactory, and left us, saying our things would arrive shortly. He introduced the guard that was stationed outside our door, whose name was Brokk, then left us, reminding us to lock the door and open it only for meals or for him or the king.

"What about Knox?" I asked, worried about what would happen to my friend.

Rourke shook his head sadly. "I do not know," he grated out, "but I will ask my father. Knox is a trustworthy friend." He nodded once and left. Aspen shut the door and turned to me. "Goddess damn it all," he said.

I nodded in agreement. "It certainly could have gone better," I said, moving to sit on the bed. Like the beds in our guest suite, it had a solid stone platform piled with feathery mattresses and furs. The room looked a bit like a cave that had been carved into the mountainside. A small washroom adjoined it, and there was a tiny window carved into one wall, but no balcony. The window looked out over the city. We weren't high up, but the window was very small. Aspen wouldn't even be able to get his shoulders through if we needed to escape through it.

"I feel like we are trapped underground here," I said, looking around at our new accommodations.

Aspen was pacing the room and nodded. "We are," he agreed. "I'll write to Ember. I'm not sure how she can help, but maybe Vanth and Seline can be spared and sent as backup. I'd rather they guarded our backs than Brokk," he added, nodding toward the d oor.

"Agreed," I said, shivering slightly. This part of the palace was colder than the dining room and our guest quarters in the city.

"The best way forward for us now is to figure out who is responsible for all of this," Aspen said, coming to sit next to me on the bed. He took my hands in his, flooding me with his warmth as he had done that night in the garden. "Any theories?"

I shook my head. "I don't know any unseelie with the power we saw in the field except for Hadrian," I said, remembering the withered black cores of the mushrooms Aspen had been studying. "And his father. Could the Unseelie King have come here himself?"

"Unlikely," said Aspen. "But it would be something to look into. Can that power be transferred in some way other than touch? Maybe through blood? I'll ask Ember when I write. Maybe she and Hadrian can figure it out."

I leaned my head on Aspen's shoulder, suddenly exhausted. He kissed the top of it. "Let's go to sleep, Aurelia," he said.

"But there's this beautiful bed here," I whined teasingly. "You've never actually ravished me on a bed." Both times in our guest suite had been against a wall, and our first time had been in a grassy patch of moss in the forest under the moonlight. I sighed, remembering how beautiful that night was.

Aspen chuckled, realizing I was right. He lifted my chin and placed a gentle kiss on my lips. "There will be time for ravishing another night," he promised.

Chapter 16: Aurelia

ASH FLOATED AROUND ME as I woke to a room filled with smoke. I tried to move, to call out for Aspen, but vines of ivy had wrapped tightly around me, pinning me to the bed and gagging me. I felt tears sting my eyes as the ash around me intensified. I finally managed to move my head to the side enough to see where Aspen had been sleeping. A black, charred husk was all that remained of him, a snake slithering from his open, screaming mouth.

I bolted up in bed and ran to the bathing room, bringing up my dinner as I heaved from the sight and smell of his charred corpse. Aspen was there instantly, holding my hair back and mumbling soothingly. I couldn't make out the words over the sounds of my sickness. Eventually, I stopped and sat back, sweaty and tear-stained as he wiped my face with a cool cloth.

"You're burning up again," he said anxiously, feeling my brow. "Was it the same dream?"

I shook my head but I couldn't elaborate. I tried to croak out something, but my throat felt raw as if I had breathed in the ash of my dream. Aspen filled a glass with water and crouched before me, a hand on my shoulder as I drank.

"You were dead," I choked out. "Burned." Aspen frowned.

"You are safe from the fire," Aspen said tenderly. "You got out in time." I nodded, resting the back of my head on the wall. I wasn't as convinced as Aspen that the dreams had to do with the fire I'd set at Thorn's estate, but I had no idea what else could be causing them. That fire hadn't scared me, and it didn't explain the cave-ins or the vines or snakes or anything else from my nightmares.

Knowing I wouldn't get back to sleep, I stood shakily. He helped me up, holding me gently by the waist.

"Go back to sleep," I croaked. "You need it if you're going to be expending magic all day."

Aspen scooped me up wordlessly and took me with him, despite my croaked protest. "I won't sleep," I said, as he curled up next to me and wrapped his arms and legs around me.

"Then I won't either," he said, kissing me behind the ear.

"You need to sleep," I argued, trying to turn to face him. He held me fast and nuzzled my ear again.

We lay there for a while until my breathing had calmed, Aspen running his fingers down my arm in soothing strokes. He kissed the back of my neck again and I shivered.

"I can help you sleep if you want," he purred, trailing his fingers down my body. Something must have been wrong with me because despite the nightmare and the terror and the shakiness I felt, warmth pooled between my legs at the suggestion.

"Aspen," I said, thinking of something we hadn't discussed yet. I wasn't sure how to bring it up, but if this was going to continue, we needed to discuss it. I cleared my throat awkwardly, starting again. "Aspen, I'm not taking anything," I said somewhat self-consciously, "to prevent pregnancy."

Fae pregnancies were rare. We were long-lived, and as a result, the Goddess had seen fit to make pregnancies difficult and infrequent. Still, most children who were conceived were done so within marriages or committed partnerships, even though our morals and sensibilities were less prudish than those of the humans to the south. I wasn't exactly sure where Aspen and I stood, and while I knew a pregnancy would be considered a blessing, as all were, I wanted to make sure we had a plan for that possibility.

"If this is going to continue, we should probably discuss that," I added, waiting for him to jump in and say something. He nodded behind me.

"We should," he said, running his fingers gently down my thigh. "Do you want to stop?"

"No," I blurted out, making him chuckle. I blushed. "No, I just mean, do you want children?"

"With you?" Aspen asked, still stroking gentle lines down my leg.

I frowned. "With anyone," I said, realizing I hated the idea of him siring a child with another female.

"Yes," he breathed, kissing me behind the ear, "although maybe not right this second, as I'm very much enjoying having you all to myself."

"Then what should we—" I began.

He stopped me with a hand stroking higher and I gasped. "I'll start taking something tomorrow," he rumbled against my neck. "Ember was already prepared for this. She sent me here with all the plants I'd need for it."

I blushed again, cursing and thanking my very nosy, very thoughtful friend. "You don't have—" I gasped as he hitched my nightgown up my thigh and stroked me over my undergarments.

"I want to," he growled, slipping a finger beneath the fabric and feeling the wetness there. I let out a shuddering breath as he stroked me, more gently and tenderly than he had since we had come crashing together several nights ago. "Now let me help you sleep."

"Aspen," I breathed as he moved his other hand to cup my breast, still stroking me with the hand between my legs.

"Mmm?" he breathed, running his teeth gently over my neck in a way that sent shivers through me.

"Have you forgiven me?" I asked breathily.

He paused momentarily, then resumed what he was doing. "Oh, I'm still very, very angry," he teased, sliding his finger to my entrance and circling there. I moaned again as he whispered, "This is my revenge."

I gasped and thrust my hips forward, seeking the feeling he was withholding from me. Aspen nipped my neck, squeezing my breast over my nightgown.

"If I were truly angry," Aspen continued, circling and stroking and squeezing until I was writhing against him. I could feel that he was hard and ready against me, and I tried to reach between us. He pressed against my rear with a groan. "If I were truly angry, I would stop right now and leave you wanting all night."

"Don't stop," I breathed, feeling him slide a finger into me as he continued to squeeze and knead my breast. He removed the finger and I whined in protest. He chuckled as he repositioned his hand so that his thumb pressed against my sensitive flesh as he plunged his finger into me again.

"You should say please," he growled, kissing down the column of my neck and shoulder as he continued moving in me.

"Please," I gasped, as he swiped his thumb over the aching spot where my thighs met, caressing and stroking until I was gasping. Release shuddered out of me, and Aspen clapped his hand over my mouth to muffle my moans.

"Brokk is outside," he breathed, holding me through my pleasure. In seconds he had rolled me and pinned me beneath him, his mouth replacing his hand as he swallowed my cries with his tongue and his lips. He shifted his breeches down and entered me, groaning as he felt me still pulsing from my first release.

He lifted his head and looked into my eyes, the blue light of the glowworms casting him in eerie, beautiful shadows. He moved gently and I urged him to go faster, hooking my legs around his hips and pressing him to me.

He nipped my lip in gentle admonishment. "Tonight will be gentle," he said, kissing me again. "And tender." Another kiss paired with a gentle thrust. I scrabbled at his back to try to make him go faster, but he held firm. "And slow," he added, with another kiss and a slow roll of his hips. I gasped again as his weight hit me in all the right places and he kissed me, deep and slow and sensual, until I was humming with need.

He didn't speed up as he maintained the steady rhythm he had established, making me beg for him to go faster and harder instead of this slow, aching torture. He kissed my neck, my shoulders, my ears, my mouth, and pressed his forehead to mine as he came. He groaned deeply, spilling warmth inside me as I met him over the edge.

His brow and chest were sweaty, but I didn't care as I clasped his face in my hands and kissed him, reveling in the feel of him in me and on me. To my embarrassment, tears welled in my eyes as I felt the cracks in my heart heal with warmth and love for this male.

"Don't cry, my love," he said, brushing away the tears that fell down my cheeks. He kissed them away and wrapped me in his arms, stroking my hair and holding me close.

My heart felt like it might burst at the endearment, and I whispered my own sliver of truth into the darkness as, miraculously, sleep claimed me again. "I love you too."

I AWOKE STILL IN Aspen's arms, the pale sunlight of early morning filtering through our tiny window. He was already awake, kissing my face and neck in possibly my new favorite way to be woken.

"Good morning," he said, kissing my nose and brushing his own against it. I sighed, feeling like I had slept well for the first time in days, despite the nightmare, and feeling oddly light. My heart, which had been bruised and battered when we had arrived in the Dwarven Realm, finally felt whole again, and while I knew not everything could be entirely resolved between us, I felt like we had finally come back to near where we had begun.

Another cursed tear slid down my cheek, and Aspen frowned. "What is it?" he asked, brushing it away with his thumb. "Did I hurt you?"

I shook my head. "No," I whispered. "No, I just feel..." I paused trying to find words to explain it to him. "I feel whole again," I finished.

Aspen kissed me again, sweeping his tongue over mine in a way that promised a lifetime of pleasure and romance and joy. "I'm sorry it took me so long to forgive you," he said quietly, speaking against my forehead as he held me. "I was an ass."

I laughed. "You were," I agreed. I felt him smile against my brow. "I did try to tell you that."

"You did," he agreed, moving his head back a little so he could look at me. "Will you forgive me for being unbearable and cold and cruel for so long? I know I don't deserve it, but—"

I cut him off with a kiss. "It's forgiven," I whispered, feeling the thrum of something hum between us.

He looked at me again, frowning slightly. "You said you were mine," he said, still frowning.

"I did, and I am," I agreed, now frowning at him too. "What's wrong?"

His face cleared and he shook his head, kissing me again. "Nothing," he said softly. "Nothing is wrong."

A knock at the door startled us from our reverie. "My lord, my lady," came Rourke's voice from beyond the door. "The king asks for your attendance at breakfast."

"Coming," Aspen called, turning over with a groan and standing to stretch his arms above his head. I smiled, admiring him for a moment before getting up and dressed as well. I assumed we'd be heading out to more farmland today, so I wore my riding gear and braided my hair loosely down my back.

"I know we have to pretend out there," Aspen murmured as we headed for the door, turning me to face him and placing a gentle kiss on my lips. "But don't forget that you're mine."

I smiled. "Fae males are so over-possessive," I teased. He pinched my bottom as we opened the door, and I had to hide my squeak of surprise as Rourke met us.

Despite the situation with the unseelie fae and the dwarves' lack of trust, I felt hopeful that we would make some headway today in solving both mysteries that plagued us. But as we entered the breakfast room, the hopefulness drained out of me and cold dread encased my heart. Aspen grasped my hand, heedless of any onlookers.

"Lady Aurelia, Lord Aspen," came the oily voice of a male I had hoped to never see again. "What a pleasant surprise to see you both alive and well."

Across the room, Lord Thorn stood from his seat at the side of the Dwarven King.

Chapter 17: Aurelia

"WHAT IS *HE* DOING here?" roared Aspen, striding toward the king and pushing me behind him. I squeezed his hand in warning and he stopped short, breathing hard.

The king stood, looking confused. "Lord Aspen, is Lord Thorn not your ally and friend?" the king asked, lifting a paper from the table. "I have a letter of introduction here from your queen saying as much," he added.

Aspen laughed derisively, but I took the letter from the king and scanned it. It was a fair imitation of Ember's handwriting, but I knew it to be false.

"This is a forgery," I said, handing the letter back to King Holvard. "Lord Thorn is an enemy of the seelie court, and of our queen. She would never write in his support."

"But he tells me he is your husband?" the king said, still not sure if he should believe us.

I bristled. "The queen annulled the marriage after Lord Thorn tried to murder me," I said coldly, feeling a phantom lick of pain in the iron stab wound at my side. The injury would have killed me if not for Ember's healing. "This is the male who has been caching stolen iron weapons for the Unseelie King. I saw them with my own eyes in his estate."

Thorn held his hands up in surrender, feigning shock. "My dearest wife, you are confused," he said, moving around the table.

"How dare you address her as your wife," growled Aspen, pushing me behind him again.

I rolled my eyes and pushed my way back next to him, perfectly capable of dealing with Thorn myself. "Come near me and I will make you wish it had been you who was stabbed with iron," I said, touching the dagger at my thigh.

Thorn stopped and turned beseechingly to the king. "Your Majesty, my poor wife doesn't know what she is saying.' I glared at Thorn, but he continued in his oily, wheedling voice, "Lady Aurelia suffered a terrible injury when my manor was attacked. She doesn't remember what happened, and I have been searching for her for months. Queen Ember assured me that this would all be easily cleared up by the letter you have before you."

The king frowned at the letter, at Thorn's placating hands, at Aspen's growing fury, and at my obvious dislike. I leaned in a little toward Aspen and the king furrowed his brow and sighed tiredly, clearly not having the energy to deal with yet another complication in his growing list of concerns.

"Lord Thorn, we do not force females to stay married to males, and I will not force Lady Aurelia to go anywhere with you," he said, sounding tired and frustrated. "You may stay as my guest in the palace, as Lady Aurelia and Lord Aspen are until I have written to and received a response from the Seelie Queen asking her to verify this letter."

Aspen began to protest, but the king raised a hand, turning to me. "Lady Aurelia and Lord Aspen, I hope you will continue your work today despite this added distraction," the king said, sitting back down and taking a swig from the drink in the mug placed before him at the table. "Lord Thorn will keep his distance from your work until I hear from your queen."

"I want to write to Ember as well," Aspen said firmly.

The king nodded his acceptance. "Yes, yes, of course," he said, waving a hand at the table. "Please eat something. You will be using a great deal of magic today."

I nodded tightly, squeezing Aspen's hand. Thorn returned to his seat next to the king, and Aspen and I sat across from them. I could feel Aspen vibrating with fury all through the mostly silent, very awkward meal. Rourke, who had skillfully disappeared into the background during our confrontation with Thorn, sat beside his father, discussing where we should focus our efforts for the day. Aspen stared murderously at Thorn and I dearly regretted my decision not to ask Ember to send me with a stash of poisons.

King Holvard had paper and pen brought to Aspen so he could write a quick message to Ember before we left for the day.

"We should fly out to the neighboring peak to check their cave nettles," Rourke said in his deep growl. "Our people cook them to extract their sting before eating. The last time I checked, there were only a few patches of blight, but now I fear it may have spread if what you say is true and someone is poisoning the land."

Aspen nodded his agreement and we stood to follow him out. Lord Thorn stood and bowed to me, before returning to his seat to chat animatedly to the king.

"Someone is working with Thorn," I murmured to Aspen as Rourke led us through the city back to the rookery that housed the rocs. We had retrieved coats and supplies to make the trip out to the next peak, and we were sweating in the warmth of the cave as we made our way to the outdoor staircase that led up the mountain. I cast an air shield around us so we wouldn't be overheard.

"We can't prove it yet," Aspen agreed. "But yes. It's too convenient that he happened to come here right now."

"Any theories?" I asked, walking close to him, but resisting holding his hand lest it draw Rourke's attention.

"A few," Aspen replied darkly. "But none with evidence."

I was winded by the trek up the steep staircase, and the winter wind had grown more biting, snow whipping around us and making visibility difficult as we climbed. "How can the rocs fly in this?" I shouted to Rourke as we neared the top.

"They are skilled navigators," he shouted back. I waited for more explanation, but nothing came.

When we reached the rookery, I shook the snow from my hair and shoulders as best as I could. Rourke saddled up Notus as Caelus gazed mournfully at us, looking like he would quite like to go flying too. I went over and patted his beak. "Don't worry, boy," I murmured soothingly, stroking the smooth surface. "Knox will be back soon."

Riding behind Rourke was more challenging than riding behind Knox had been. Because he was a good foot shorter than me, I struggled to keep hold of Rourke's waist in the battering wind, and by the time we landed half an hour later, my back was aching from my hunched posture.

This mountain opened up much the same way as the first. Another dwarven city sprawled before us, this one less glamorous than the Crystal City. There were no crystals to reflect the light of day. Instead, paths of blue glowing mushrooms lined the streets to light them. This city marked the hours by way of a giant clock tower, and the stone buildings were squat and old and more ramshackle than in the Crystal City.

Flying through the winter winds was also much more terrifying than the flight to the mountains had been, and my momentary joy in our upward swoop was quickly quelled by my lurching stomach as Notus fought the winds. I was not sad when it was time to dismount, and I spent the entire trek down the mountain dreading the return trip.

"This is Dunmarra," Rourke said as we traversed the streets. "It is one of the oldest cities in our realm. The fields are just outside the city limits."

"Do any unseelie live here?" I asked, looking around for the diversity that was present in the Crystal City, and not seeing it.

"Aye, a few," Rourke said, "but most prefer the capitol. The Crystal City has more to attract foreigners than the other cities in the realm."

We traversed the city in half an hour, leaving stone buildings and glowing pathways for darkness. Rourke lit a globe and led us forward. Aspen and I both kept a hand on our daggers, less trusting of the almost complete darkness in this part of the realm.

After another fifteen minutes, the space brightened. A skylight was cut in the ceiling about fifty feet above us, snow swirling slowly down in a shaft of weak sunlight. The skylight must cut deep through the mountainside—the light was dim compared to that which streamed through the little window in the wall of the Crystal City.

Fields of cave nettles grew around us in the dim light. Rourke stopped me with an arm before I could move any further. "They sting," he reminded me, looking down at my uncovered hands.

He pulled out a pair of thick leather gloves and put them on, calling out to the dark shapes moving in the field, which I eventually recognized as other dwarves. They came toward us dressed head to toe in thick leathers to protect their skin from the sting of the plants.

"My lord," Rourke said, turning to Aspen. "How do you wish to proceed?"

Aspen directed the dwarves to begin mapping the blight, starting from the outer ring of the fields and spiraling inward. While they began their survey, Aspen crouched and started pouring his power into the leaves, closing his eyes as he concentrated on the plants without getting close enough to be stung.

I watched in wonder as the leaves fanned and grew, section by section until a square mile of the field looked almost overgrown. It took two hours, and I stood guard over Aspen as he worked, ready to be his knife in the dark if someone came too close.

Aspen gasped and opened his eyes, and I crouched down to offer him water. "I hit the blighted section," he croaked, guzzling down water as if he had poured out everything in him into the fields. "I couldn't pass it with my magic. It cuts off this half of the field from the rest right down the center."

I nodded, calling out to Rourke to tell him Aspen's findings as Aspen pulled on an extra set of gloves and gathered some of the blighted soil and plants to study. Again, the soil left red stains on the fingers of the gloves.

Rourke nodded, heading back out and shouting orders in Dwarvish. The dwarves soon returned, looking grim.

"It is as you say," said Rourke, voice rough with tension. "Half the fields are gone, lost to the blight."

Aspen took another drink and nodded. "I think you'll have to harvest the section I just grew for now to make sure the blight doesn't spread to it," he said. "How many unseelie have access to these fields?"

"None, as far as I know," Rourke grunted. He shouted something in Dwarvish to the others. I made out the word 'unseelie' and realized he was repeating Aspen's question. He turned back to us. "The others say none as well," Rourke said, running a thick hand through his beard. "But there are no guards on watch at night. Could a dwarf be responsible for this instead?"

"It's possible," Aspen said thoughtfully, "but only if they somehow had access to unseelie magic. I have asked my Queen and King to look into that."

Rourke nodded, shouting some more orders in Dwarvish and turning back to us. "We have a library with much information on fae magic," Rourke said. "I will ask some of the scholars to look into this."

Aspen nodded his agreement and Rourke continued. "I'll have this field harvested today. The cities send a tithe to the king, but I am not sure there will be enough of a harvest to merit it here," Rourke said, scowling at the blighted fields.

"Best to have your crew burn the blighted sections just in case," Aspen said, following his gaze. "Tell them not to replant the field for several days and to dig out the blighted soil. You'll need to find new soil to replenish these fields properly. And maybe set guards on rotation through the night at all the fields until we figure this out."

Rourke nodded, relaying some more instructions in Dwarvish to the male who was some kind of foreman. When his back was turned, Aspen leaned heavily on me for a moment.

"Can you make it back?" I asked quietly.

He nodded, face pale in the dim light. "Yes, it's not that bad," he said, straightening as Rourke turned toward us. "But If we had to travel any farther I don't think I could. Using all of this magic is more draining than I anticipated."

I nodded, taking his arm as we followed Rourke back toward the little city. I hoped it looked like I was leaning on him for support, rather than the other way around.

Chapter 18: Ember

"WHAT IN THE NAME of the Goddess is the matter with you today, child?" my grandmother scolded as I accidentally burned the third bushel of sage I was supposed to be gently smoking.

I sighed, batting out the small flame in frustration as my grandmother waved away the smoke and called for more sage from the herb garden. "I'm sorry," I said irritably as I threw the ruined sage into the bucket the gardeners used for compost. "I'm just distracted today."

My grandmother regarded me thoughtfully, understanding lighting her face as he looked at me sympathetically. "Let's take a break," she said, putting down the sage and taking my arm, leaning on me a bit as I helped her to a chair in the corner of the little workshop.

The infirmary in the palace was located next to the kitchens, and we had turned a little pantry into something of a workshop for drying and mixing herbs and tinctures so that there was more room in the infirmary for patients. When I wasn't needed for strategy meetings or political meetings, I spent most of my time here, preparing bandages and potions and teas and training the recruits in battlefield healing for the inevitable injuries we would see if and when war came.

I had a small army of apprentices now, most without healing magic, but eager to learn what they could. Aurelia usually helped me here when she didn't have other assignments, and I missed her. I loved my grandmother, but no one could replace a best friend.

"Tea?" my grandmother asked.

"Of course," I said, smiling as she poured tea into two floral, pink teacups. She wrapped her shawls around her a bit more tightly as she passed me a cup and I frowned. I had told her she could remove the shawls here, that her scars were a testament to her strength in surviving the Unseelie King. She had smiled and patted my hand, telling me she liked to be cozy.

"Are they still hurting?" I asked, gesturing to her with the teacup. She had let me infuse the scars with my healing magic, and it seemed to help the pain for a few weeks before it wore off and she needed another dose. I had treated her just a week ago, and I feared that the healing magic might not be working anymore.

She shook her head, sipping her tea placidly. "Don't worry yourself, my dear," she said, smiling at me as she lowered the cup. She picked up the pink fluffy thing she had been knitting for several days and for a little while, I let myself be soothed by the clacking of knitting needles as she worked.

"So it's your time then," my grandmother said. I frowned at her. She had an eerie ability to sense things that no ordinary fae should be able to, and I wondered for the hundredth time if she was a seer.

"Yes," I said, sighing and lowering my cup.

"It's early days, my dear," she said, clicking away as she worked. "These things take time. Especially for you two."

"What do you mean?" I asked. "Why should it be harder for us than anyone else?"

She sighed and looked up at me a little sadly, putting down the knitting so she could clasp my hand. "My darling girl, you are a Seelie Queen mated by fate to an unseelie Prince," she said, stating the fact like I had somehow forgotten it. "Your situation is unprecedented. There has never been a child of both courts, as far as I know."

My gut twisted painfully as sympathy filled her eyes. I knew what was coming next, but I didn't want to hear it.

"There may be a reason for that," she said gently. "Perhaps your magic isn't compatible in that way."

"I can't believe the Goddess would have brought us together only to deny us a child," I whispered, throat constricting as I said the words. As much as I wanted to believe this with every part of my being, a small rebelliously sensible part knew my grandmother might be right.

"I know," my grandmother said, sitting back in her chair and regarding me warmly. "I too have faith in the Goddess. But it can take couples decades, even centuries to conceive. You shouldn't fret over a matter of months."

"What will I do if I can't?" I said, looking at her mistily, my eyes swimming with unwelcome tears. I brushed them away, irritated with myself for crying over something that was merely a possibility. My grandmother was right, it had only been a short while. Fae cycles came only once or twice a year, which was not a lot of chances to conceive. We were long-lived and hard to kill, and I supposed this was the Goddess's way of making sure our numbers remained under control.

"Then you will name an heir and all will be well," my grandmother said, smiling reassuringly as she handed me her handkerchief. I wiped my eyes again as she added, "And there is more than one way to become a mother."

"PASS THE SALT," VANTH said through a mouthful of bread. Seline grimaced and passed him the salt. I smiled and Hadrian laughed at Seline's displeasure.

The four of us were having a casual dinner in our private sitting room. There was no point having a big fancy meal when there were so few of us in the palace, and I was much more comfortable anyway with just my friends and my mate and a warm fire and a glass of faerie wine.

Hadrian was sitting at his desk, going through the day's mail. There were usually several communications from various scouts and outposts, as well as a daily report from the Commander and messages or complaints from the noble houses all over the realm that had to be dealt with. To my relief, Hadrian had taken on this onerous task and only bothered me with the mail that required some decision to be made.

He choked on his wine, and the three of us looked over to him. His shadows were escaping the control he usually maintained over them to leak out and bleed blackness up the wall.

I frowned. "What is it?" I asked, standing and moving to his side. I looked down to see a familiar rolling script. "Aspen?"

Hadrian nodded, flipping the page before I could read it to scan the rest. Vanth and Seline came to join us by the desk, and we all looked expectantly over Hadrian's shoulder as he finished reading. "They need reinforcements," Hadrian said, turning the page over and handing it to me. I scanned the letter, eyes going wide as I read.

"Thorn is there?" I asked incredulously. "And he says I sent him?"

"What?" growled Vanth, fists clenching in anger as he read over my shoulder. Vanth had saved Aurelia from Thorn once before, and he held a hatred for the male with which I completely sympathized.

"I'll write to the king at once," I said, hunting for clean paper and a pen to write my reply.

"It will take a few weeks to arrive," Seline reminded me. "Thorn could have done a great deal of damage by then."

"Aspen asked if we can send Seline and Vanth to assist them," Hadrian said, standing and touching my hand to still the frantic writing. "He's asking the king to send a roc for them and for us to also send supplies of grain."

"We don't have a lot to spare," I said, worrying my lip between my teeth. "We have to feed all of the recruits through the rest of the winter."

"We'll manage," Hadrian assured me, squeezing my shoulder. "Write your reply. Vanth, Seline," he said, turning to his sister and his best friend. "Are you willing to go?"

Vanth nodded. "Yes," he growled darkly. "But I can't promise not to kill that snake when I get there."

"Just don't start a war and we should be fine," I said, finishing my reply and assuring King Holvard that Thorn was most certainly not a trusted friend and should be arrested and returned to me immediately.

"Do you think Aspen and Aurelia are all right?" Seline asked, her normally cool voice sounding worried. Seline cared for very few people, but I knew that Aspen and Aurelia had been added to the list, whether they knew it or not.

"They'd better be," I growled. "And if they're not, I give you permission to unleash your magic on that whole Goddess-damned mountain," I added, giving Vanth a pointed look.

"It would be my pleasure," he replied.

Vanth and Seline left to pack and Hadrian came to me, holding me gently by the waist as he placed a kiss on my collarbone. His shadows snaked around me in comfort and I smiled a little at the trust he had always put in me by not hiding them.

"They'll be fine," he said soothingly, misinterpreting my mood as concern for my friends.

I smiled faintly. "I know," I said, placing my hands on his broad chest. "It's not that."

"Then what is it?" he asked, placing another kiss just below my ear, making me shiver. A shadow curled up around my neck in comfort.

"It's…" I faltered, not sure what to say. I didn't want to make him worry too, and I knew in my head that things like this took time. My stupid heart was the organ that needed a reality check. I looked up at him, trying to express my sadness and worry without words. I sighed heavily.

"Oh," he said, frowning sympathetically as he cupped my face in his hand. "It's still early days, my love."

"I know," I laughed, resting my forehead against his chest as he wrapped his arms around me. "You sound just like my grandmother."

"She's a smart female," he said, speaking against my hair as he stroked soothing lines down my back, careful not to get too close to the sensitive wings. "I am not my father. Producing an heir is not my only goal, my love."

"I know that," I said, trying to reassure him. Hadrian's father had attempted to sire him for almost seven centuries and had discarded or executed many females when they didn't produce an heir. I stepped back a little and gently stroked the hair from his eyes. "I wasn't thinking that, I promise."

"There are many, many reasons I love and want you," Hadrian replied, leaning forward and skating his lips down my neck slowly, eliciting more shivers from me. "I would be happy to show you three or four reasons right now if you're not in any pain."

I laughed. "Three or four?" I asked, feigning shock. "My king, you are utterly insatiable."

"I am," he said, closing his lips over mine and sweeping his tongue into my mouth in a plundering kiss. "For you only, my mate."

I sighed, wishing that the Goddess could have made our cycles a bit less messy. "Hadrian," I protested as he kissed down the column of my throat and ran a finger up my sensitive spine. "It won't be pretty. If you keep doing what you're doing..." I gasped a little as he dug his fingers into my ribs. "We'll have to get new sheets."

"Damn the sheets," he said, kissing my shoulder as he swept my shirt down and undid the laces at the front. He paused, looking up to search my eyes. "If you don't want to, I'll stop," he said seriously, looking at me with that molten, needy gaze. "But I don't mind a little mess."

He kissed me again, and I came to realize that I didn't mind a little mess either.

Chapter 19: Aurelia

I TRIED TO GET Aspen to beg fatigue that night when we returned to the palace, but when he realized that I was determined to go to dinner, he insisted on joining me. I wanted to go to keep an eye and an ear on Lord Thorn, and Aspen wasn't happy about it.

"You shouldn't go anywhere near him," he growled at me as I got ready. I chose a black dress with silver plates on the bodice that looked a bit like armor. I felt I would need it in Thorn's presence. "I can't believe the king bought his rocshit about you not remembering anything."

"The king doesn't know any better," I argued, styling my hair into a braided crown atop my head. "The letter looked real enough. I only know it's not because I know Ember's writing as well as my own. And because we know Thorn is a snake."

Aspen huffed, looking exhausted as he lounged on the couch waiting for me to finish. I frowned at him, the bags under his eyes worrying me.

"You should stay here," I said, moving to sit next to him and cupping his face with my hand. "You look half dead."

Aspen raised a brow. "You always did know how to compliment me, my love," he said, taking my hand from his face and kissing the palm. "I'm not letting you go alone."

"You do remember I'm an assassin, don't you?" I said sardonically, tapping the daggers strapped to my thighs. The black dress had slits up each side, making access to the daggers easier than in another gown. It was one of the reasons I chose it.

"You do remember that he nearly killed you, don't you?" Aspen replied, no humor in his expression as his eyes flicked to the place where I knew there would always be a scar. He tapped it gently with his finger.

"If he gives me a reason, I'll happily repay the favor tonight," I said darkly, bending down to kiss him.

"King Holvard would have to punish you," Aspen said, shaking his head as I lifted back up. "Until Ember's reply comes, we cannot act against Thorn, at least not overtly."

"Hateful male," I mumbled.

Aspen sat up and kissed my temple. "Promise me you will keep your distance," he said, leveling me with a hard look. "If you even think of pretending to seduce him for information, I'll be forced to rip out his tongue, and then we'll both be in trouble."

"You'd stain your jacket," I said, trying to keep my face serious as I teased him. He didn't smile, and I sighed. "I promise. I will stay with you or Rourke or Knox the whole night."

"With me," Aspen corrected, planting a small kiss on my nose.

I sighed again at the possessiveness of fae males. "I wonder if Hadrian was like this around Vanth when he first took Ember to his bed," I mused, giving him a beleaguered look.

Aspen raised his brows, waiting for my promise.

"I promise, I will stay with you the whole night," I said.

Aspen nodded, finally satisfied. "And promise me," he added, "that you will not enact violence against Lord Thorn until after the king agrees he is a treacherous snake."

I sighed resignedly. "What if he provokes me?" I asked, pouting my lip at him. "Just a little violence?"

He pulled me to my feet with a laugh and a playful pinch on my thigh above a dagger. "Maybe just a little."

DINNER WAS A TENSE affair. The unseelie members of the council had been locked in the palace all day, and the dwarves were even more distrustful of them after Rourke reported our findings from the fields outside Dunmarra.

The tension was heightened by the meal itself, which was significantly smaller than the previous night's, Thorn's presence adding a mouth to be fed at the table. The only bright spot was how he scowled at the mushroom courses, which the king took notice of.

"You do not care for our food, Lord Thorn?" he asked harshly, eliciting some disapproving murmurs from the table. I made it a point to pop an entire mushroom in my mouth and smile sweetly at him as he tried to come up with an answer.

"Forgive me, Your Majesty, I find my stomach is rather sour tonight," he said. "I mean no offense to your excellent cooks." I vaguely wondered how satisfying it might be to watch Thorn slowly starve in the Dwarven Realm when the discussion turned to his magic.

"We have seen Lord Aspen's gift of earth," Rourke said craggily to Lord Thorn. "I am curious what gift the Goddess has blessed other Seelie fae with, now that the curse upon you is lifted and your queen returned."

Thorn smiled obsequiously and held out his palms. Clear water pooled in them, and he took a sip to the applause of the table.

"This is a mighty gift indeed," said the king. "Water is life. Lord Aspen, will you consent to Lord Thorn joining you to assist in watering the fields you visit next?" Aspen stiffened.

"I would be happy to assist as a humble servant of my Queen," Thorn said, turning his snakelike smile upon me and earning a scowl from Aspen.

"I will consent on the condition that our own guards be allowed to travel with us," Aspen said, turning to the king. "I asked the queen in my letter this morning that they be sent to assist us, with Your Majesty's blessing. If you send riders to retrieve them, they will also surely come with supplies of grain and dried meats from the Seelie palace."

Some muttering broke out from the assembled dwarves at the table at the prospect of additional supplies and fae in their realm.

"More Seelie fae to undermine us, Lord Aspen?" Bisera asked acerbically.

"No indeed," I said before Aspen had the chance to reply. "Seline and Vanth," I emphasized his name and was satisfied to see Thorn pale slightly, "are both unseelie and loyal friends of our Queen. And us."

The unseelie at the table seemed somewhat mollified by this, and Bisera pursed her lips.

The king frowned. "You would have me invite more unseelie into my realm, despite the origin of the blight?" he asked, thundering a little at the perceived threat.

"Our friends can be in no way responsible for the blight," I reasoned, growing irritated that the king did not just agree to our very reasonable request.

"The alternative is our departure," Aspen announced, to more muttering around the table. "Without your trust, we cannot continue our alliance, and we do not trust the male you have invited to this table." Aspen nodded at Thorn, who pretended to be offended fairly convincingly.

"This is a plot to steal my wife from me," Thorn said in outrage, standing and pointing accusingly at Aspen.

"Your wife?" cut in Knox, who was seated several seats away from me flanked by dwarves. We hadn't been able to speak since he had been confined to the palace, and I winced at what he was about to learn. He looked at me, hurt flashing in his eyes.

"Lady Aurelia is my wife by law," Thorn bit out.

"The marriage was annulled by law," Aspen reminded him, grinding his teeth so hard I feared they may crack. I subtly put my hand on his leg under the table and squeezed.

"Enough," said King Holvard, rolling his eyes at the petty squabbling. "It matters not. As I already told you, Lord Thorn, dwarven law permits any female to leave a marriage for any reason. And Lord Aspen," he said, turning toward us, "I grant your request. Rourke, choose two of your most trusted dwarves to fetch these guards. I trust they will return quickly and with the promised supplies."

Aspen nodded his thanks and Thorn scowled across the table. I patted my blade at my thighs again for comfort and strength. I had nothing to fear from this male. He should fear me.

Dinner ended with more awkward and stilted conversation, and it was a relief when the king called for an end to it.

Knox caught me before we could escape back to our room. "You didn't tell me you were married," he whispered, frowning as he lightly grabbed my arm.

Aspen stiffened and I shot him a warning look. "I am not," I said quietly. "As Aspen told you, the marriage was annulled."

Knox looked between me and Aspen and released my arm. "He hurt you," he said, a statement, not a question.

"He nearly killed her," Aspen growled, his temper quickly coming loose from the tight leash he had held it on all night. Knox's face darkened. Of course, it would be this they found common ground on.

"I see," Knox said, looking at me for confirmation. His eyes flicked to the slit in my dress where a dagger peeked out. He looked at Aspen again and nodded as if deciding something. "The male stays in a room that has a balcony exit two floors below yours," he whispered, raising his brows meaningfully. I nodded, and Knox walked away casually as Rourke approached to escort us to our room.

"What was that about," Aspen said when we were behind the privacy of a locked door.

"I think Knox just told me how to kill Lord Thorn," I said, pulling off my dress and making Aspen's eyebrows shoot up.

"What are you doing?" he hissed, torn between delight and frustration when I began to put on my riding leathers.

"Going to investigate," I said, smirking coyly over my shoulder at him.

"This is a terrible plan," Aspen growled when I explained what I intended to do with the information Knox had given me. "He will almost certainly be there, and I may not be able to pull you back fast enough."

Knox had meant, I thought, for me to eliminate Thorn by telling me how to get to him. But his death before Ember publicly condemned him might backfire on us. Instead, I planned to sneak into his room and search for any clue as to who he was working with among the dwarves.

While Aspen was too broad to fit through the window in our bedroom, I could just make it if I didn't mind squeezing. With a sturdy rope, I could rappel down the wall of the palace to Thorn's balcony two floors below and search his rooms. That was where Aspen would come in.

"Just make sure whatever you use is strong enough to hold my weight, and I'll do the rest," I said. He scowled at me. "Or I can just knot the bedsheets together," I added. "Either way, this is happening."

Aspen rolled his eyes and pulled three seeds from one of the pouches he had brought with him. Vines of ivy began to grow from his palm, twisting and braiding into a length and thickness I would be able to climb. I took the ends and tossed them from the small window, watching their progression so I could tell Aspen when to stop.

Since everything was made of stone in our room, there was nothing particularly convenient to tie the ivy to. Aspen knotted the ends and placed them under his trunk, sitting on it to make sure they didn't shift. He held the ivy rope as an added precaution, wrapping it around his fists.

"Two tugs mean pull me back up," I said, lifting myself through the window and dangling my legs down to wrap around the ivy.

"Be careful," he growled. I shot him a smile and slid down the vine.

Getting down was the easy part. Getting back up was going to be the challenge, but I was trusting Aspen to help haul me back up the wall and through the window.

I carefully skirted another window on the floor below, which was thankfully shuttered, and lowered myself until I was hanging just over Thorn's balcony. His room was dark, and I listened for a minute before deciding the coast was clear enough for me to drop onto the balcony itself. It bothered me a bit that his room had a clear escape route where ours didn't, but I didn't have time to dwell on petty jealousy.

I made sure the ivy was hanging low enough for me to clamber back up when it was time and eased toward the open entrance to Thorn's room. There was no light or movement, and I waited in the darkness for my eyes to adjust, cursing myself that I hadn't brought a light. I felt a flicker of something pulse in me at the thought, but the feeling passed so quickly that I decided I must have imagined it.

Once I could see a little in the dimness, I realized the error of my plan. There was no way I could see anything useful in the dark, and I couldn't just grab papers wildly and hope they'd be both useful and not missed. I was about to tug on the ivy to get pulled back up when I heard voices outside the door.

Flattening myself against the wall next to the open entryway, I strained my ears to hear who was with Thorn. I could hear his oily, nasal whine, and a deep rumbling voice speaking to him. A dwarf then, almost certainly. But it was impossible to tell who. The stone door opened with a thump, and a bolt of panic jolted through me.

"It won't matter what your council believes now," I heard Thorn saying as he opened his door and stepped into the room, a faint blue light filling the darkness. "That whore's letter will arrive and out me in a matter of days, and that's if the unseelie guards don't arrive and gut me first. We have to act now, and I need to get out." I clenched my jaw at his disrespect of Ember but held myself fast against the wall.

"It takes years to carve the mountain with the wind," the deep, gravelly voice replied in heavily accented tones. "We will proceed as planned. Nothing can be gained by rushing."

"But everything may be lost by delaying," Thorn snapped. I scrambled up the vine as I heard his steps grow closer and tugged sharply twice. The vine started to slowly pull upwards, and I began walking up the wall as quietly as possible.

The dwarf's reply was lost to me as I climbed and I cursed myself for not staying a moment longer to try to make out the suspect. When I reached our window, Aspen was there, grabbing me by the waist and hauling me through into his arms.

"Well?" he asked, checking me over for injuries. I shook my head, panting after the exertion of climbing up two stories of sheer stone.

"Nothing," I breathed. "It was too dark to see." Aspen cursed and I added, "But he's working with a dwarf. I heard them speaking as I left."

"Did they see you?" he snapped, looking at me sharply.

I rolled my eyes. "Yes, they saw me and are currently holding me prisoner to interrogate me," I said sarcastically. "No, they didn't see me, you idiot."

"I'm the idiot?" Aspen growled, whirling on me and backing me up against the wall. "I told you this was a foolhardy plan."

"But we learned something," I argued, pushing my hands against his chest as he closed in on me.

"Not anything we didn't already expect," he growled, caging me in between his arms and glaring down at me. We stood there both breathing heavily for a moment.

"Now would be an excellent time to ravish me," I breathed out.

He barked a laugh and crashed his lips against mine, relief mingling with desire as he swept me up into his arms and crushed me to him. "Promise me you are done with scaling the walls, and I'll consider it," he said, quieting me with another kiss.

Despite this bravado, Aspen did not have the energy for ravishing. A day of using his magic on the nettle fields, then growing vines and hauling me up and down walls had exhausted him, and he fell asleep almost as soon as he climbed into the bed.

I lay awake for a while, watching his sleeping face and admiring the strong lines of his jaw and nose in the dim light. Some of his boyishness had returned to him over the last few days, and the hollow seriousness that had plagued him was retreating as we climbed back into each other's hearts. I ran a hand down his shoulder, his strong arm, admiring the muscle beneath and sighing a bit at my blessings. My last thought as I curled up next to him was that I would die happy if I could just sleep like this every night for the rest of my life.

Chapter 20: Aurelia

I WOKE AGAIN TO flames. This time, my mind seemed to recognize it as a dream, because the same panic that usually filled me was absent. Instead, I sat in the bed as fire engulfed the small room and ash floated around me like rotten leaves in an autumn wind.

Aspen was not present in this dream, and there was no burning heat from the fire. Instead, I lifted my arm curiously as flames licked my skin, gently tingling as they traveled up my arm to my shoulder. A snake twined around my other arm, lifting its head to look at me expectantly. It undulated, shedding its skin as it slithered away.

With a thought, I doused the flames, blinking them out of existence one by one until I was sitting in the dark. Then I relit them.

I woke with a start, sitting upright in bed, causing Aspen to groan as the movement shook him awake. I was drenched in a cold sweat, not from fear I realized, but from the effort of subconsciously controlling the magic burning within me.

"What is it?" Aspen asked groggily, sitting up and rubbing his face. "Another dream?"

I nodded, holding out my hand in front of me, and not quite believing what I saw there.

Aspen squinted at the brightness, then cursed, trying to leap out of the bed to find water to smother the fire. I stopped him, grabbing his arm to keep him next to me. "No, look," I whispered. In the palm of my hand, a tiny flame flickered and pulsed. I snuffed it out and relit it.

Aspen stared. "Aurelia," he said, looking at me with wide eyes as I continued snuffing and relighting the flame. "You have fire magic."

I nodded, remembering the moment on Thorn's balcony when I had wished for a light and felt something spark in me.

"It doesn't burn?" Aspen asked warily, inching his hand over my tiny flame, then drawing it back with a hiss. I shook my head, dousing the flame and lifting his palm. A faint line of red was already healing over where my fire had burned him.

"Aspen," I said, as panic began to claw its way up my chest. "What if I can't control this? What if I hurt you?" I scooted away from him, as if distance would save him from my fire.

He hauled me back and knelt, placing his hands on my shoulders and looking into my eyes. "You have been controlling it, my love," he said, feeling my brows and arms and frowning. "You're burning up again. I think your dreams must have been a manifestation of your magic. You couldn't release it in reality, so your subconscious came up with a way to do it for you."

I shook my head as he scooped me up and took me to the bathroom, turning the shower on cold. "Dreams aren't real," I said angrily, "and magic doesn't work that way."

Aspen laughed. "We have no idea how magic really works," he said, laying a cool palm on my cheek. I did feel hot, and I wondered faintly if this fire had always been simmering under the surface of my skin. "But you haven't hurt me, and I don't believe you will."

I swallowed, fear encasing my heart as I remembered the mental image of his burned corpse next to me in bed. I fought down bile.

He plopped me in the cold shower and I hissed, feeling steam rising from my fevered skin. "Why is it coming out now?" I said, starting to feel the cold as I sat under the water.

"Maybe you just finally called it. Or maybe it had welled up for so long, that it needed a way to escape," Aspen said, watching me as I stood there soaking wet. "Try releasing some of the magic now, under the cold water."

I called flame into my palm again and it came instantly, hissing and spitting as the water drenched me and doused it. It still didn't hurt, so I called more until I was wreathed in flame while cold water splashed all around me.

"Remarkable," Aspen breathed, watching me burn. When I felt the pressure of the magic under my skin finally lessen, I turned off the water. Aspen wrapped me in a towel and held me tightly. "Seline will be here in a few days," he said, resting his forehead on mine. "She's good with magic. Maybe she can reassure you that you have control."

"You don't always have control," I said, remembering Aspen's magical tantrum before the masquerade ball, and the near earthquake caused by our argument on the balcony.

"When angry, no," he agreed. "I am still working on that." He kissed me gently. "Which makes it extremely important that you don't get angry at me," he added, smiling against my lips.

"Don't even joke about such a thing," I whispered, the image of the blackened corpse still floating before my vision.

"I'm sorry," he said, sighing as he pulled me tighter into his arms. "I trust you, even if you don't trust yourself. You won't hurt me."

A tear trickled down my cheek and he brushed it away gently, cupping my chin so I met his gaze. "Aurelia," he breathed, voice full of wonder. He smiled, his mouth forming a devious grin. "You have fire magic. Just think of all the havoc we can wreak on the Unseelie King."

We returned to the bed and Aspen held me through the rest of the night, sleeping soundly against my shoulder. I lay awake, terrified I would ignite if I let myself fall asleep for even a minute.

The next day tested my patience more than any other day of my life. Now that my magic had emerged, it seemed I couldn't turn off the gushing faucet of fire that longed to drip out of me all day, eager to escape into the world.

Tiny accidental fires trailed me, from igniting my napkin at breakfast to incinerating one of the saddlebags on my cave dragon— I named this one Dewdrop, which Aspen later said was very ironic since I set him on fire—and even lighting the cuff of Aspen's shirt as I fought the wave of magic for control.

"We need to get you somewhere you can practice without setting anything vital ablaze," Aspen grumbled, patting out his singed cuff as I apologized profusely for lighting him on fire. "Your magic has been suppressed for so long, I think it's like a festering wound. You need to drain it so it can begin to heal over."

I grimaced. "Why in all the stars is that the analogy you chose," I asked, pulling our meager lunch out of a saddlebag and handing it to him, deciding I maybe wasn't hungry after all. Rourke was supervising the other dwarves who were working in this field. The blight was not as bad here, and we had been able to salvage a lot more of the crop for harvest than we had in the nettle field.

Aspen shrugged, chewing on some dried meat. "It seemed fitting," he said, grimacing a bit as he contemplated his lunch. He put down the food and looked at me seriously. "Help me think. How can we get you out of the mountain to purge some of the magic without letting our gracious hosts know about it?"

We had decided it would be best not to share my newly emerged gifts with the king or the other dwarves or unseelie present. Better to let them think me weak and unthreatening than give them even more reason to distrust us.

"We could say you need a day off to recover your magic?" I suggested. "But it would be hard to explain why you have to go out in the snow to do it." I cursed as the piece of flatbread I was holding started to smoke at the edges, and I tightened my leash on the magic.

At least in the snow, there'd be no chance you could destroy anything," Aspen said, considering my suggestion. "But if we leave, Rourke will be sent with us. I don't want him finding out about this yet."

"You don't trust him?" I asked, glancing at his distant form as he barked orders in Dwarvish.

"I don't trust anyone here," Aspen said darkly, "except for you."

SINCE WE COULDN'T FIND a way to help me practice my magic properly, I used the cold shower to drain the excess magic from me. It didn't completely stop the spate of mysterious fires that broke out all over the palace, but it seemed to help a bit.

I calculated that Vanth and Seline should arrive with supplies and a condemning Thorn in approximately two more nights, so we had only that much time to find out what he was up to and who he was working with. Best case scenario, King Holvard would imprison him on receiving Ember's letter. Worst case, he would already have fled when it was received.

The days of using his magic seemed to be making Aspen's reserve of power grow because he was less exhausted than usual after our latest excursion. When Rourke escorted us to our room, he asked us to be ready in forty-five minutes for dinner, and Aspen nodded, looking as weary as always. When I closed the door behind us, he pounced on me, lifting me up the wall in a fierce embrace while devouring my mouth with his.

"We don't have time," I breathed, feeling his hardness beneath me as warmth flooded my core, wishing we did have time.

"I'd better be efficient then," he growled against my neck, biting lightly and causing a shiver to run down my limbs.

"After dinner?" I asked, pushing his face gently from mine. He groaned, putting me down gently, and strode away into the bathing chamber grumbling about dinner parties. I heard the water running and assumed he would be taking a very cold shower. I smiled at the thought as I tried to cool my burning desire to a low simmer until after dinner.

I dressed hurriedly in my red gown which Ember always said looked like fire. It was appropriate now, I thought, that this was one of my favorite gowns, although I smirked a little, realizing Ember's name was more suited to a fae who could wield fire than my own.

I decided to wear my hair loose and pinned a golden comb adorned with roses on one side. I finished by glamouring the gown to flicker like flames as I moved.

When I was ready, I sat on the bed and tested pouring out some of my magic into my hand. The trick would be to pour out just enough to temper the flames simmering inside me without actually setting the room ablaze.

I contained the flame to my palm and practiced lighting and extinguishing it, moving the flame like a ball around my fingers and wrist until I felt confident that I could control its direction for short periods. I wasn't brave enough to test more without the safety of cold water, and my dream of Aspen's charred remains flashed back to me every so often, making me afraid to push further.

I wondered if I would always be frightened of this magic, or if I would grow to let it become part of me, like Ember's healing and Aspen's earth.

"You look like a fire goddess," Aspen said from behind me. I turned to see him leaning against the doorframe to the bathing chamber, arms crossed and a towel slung low around his hips. Days of using his magic and laboring in the fields had made his muscles even more defined, and my mouth went a little dry at the sight of him, damp hair curling at his nape and a boyish grin lighting his features.

He strode over and kissed me gently, tilting my chin up to meet him. I hummed in appreciation and he chuckled. "This had better be the shortest dinner of our lives," he growled, voice filled with promises about what 'after dinner' might entail.

Chapter 21: Aurelia

ASPEN WORE GREEN IN an homage to his magic, and we looked quite the pair as we followed Rourke in his dwarven leathers down for dinner. Knox was waiting for us when we arrived, scowling at Thorn who was still very much alive and present.

"I see our problem remains," he said, glancing at the lord and looking back at me as I went to talk to him. Aspen had gone to chat with Bisera, still hoping to find out anything useful. I doubted we would learn anything from the unseelie under house arrest, but it was worth a shot.

"I think he is working with someone here," I said quietly, dropping a wall of air around us to block our conversation from eavesdroppers. "Do you know who he might be close to?"

Knox frowned and shook his head. "It could be anyone," he replied. "Most of the council moves freely between the mountains as they wish." He looked at me, cocking his head. "Something is different about you," he said, taking my arm and leading me to dinner. "Are you well?"

"Yes, very," I blushed, trying not to look at Aspen as we took our seats. "I suppose I am sleeping better." Knox nodded, still frowning slightly.

"My friends," said King Holvard from the head of the stone table. "My apologies for your continued confinement here. Rourke has assured me that his messengers confirm no blight has spread this last day. This is good news, for it means we have a chance of recovering our food stores."

"And that someone here is responsible?" Bisera asked sourly.

The king hesitated. "The dwarven council feels it is safest if you remain in the palace until we have found the culprit or evidence of his identity," the king said. Bisera and several other unseelie glared but didn't object.

Whoever was responsible was clever, I'd give them that. They had waited until the unseelie were deeply suspected, then stopped killing off fields once they were confined to solidify the suspicion against them. We still had no idea which unseelie might have the kind of power Aspen suspected of causing the blight. I had only seen Hadrian control death so completely.

"What kinds of powers do the unseelie have?" I blurted out, curious if anyone would hesitate to demonstrate. The king raised his eyebrows at me but said nothing.

Knox cleared his throat. "We have the opposite of your powers," he said, creating another flower of ice in his palm and placing it gently on my plate. "Where you are powered by warmth and light and growth, we derive our power from death, darkness, and decay."

Bisera nodded next and held up a mushroom, pulling the moisture from it until it sat shriveled in her hand, a small pool of water on the table beneath it. One by one the other unseelie demonstrated their gifts. One placed his hand over a crystal and snuffed out its light, another pulled the color from a green nettle leaf until it was gray, and a third turned a mushroom to dust, but none seemed to have the same power over death that we had seen displayed in the fields.

"Your Majesty," I said, addressing the king, "is this display not enough to convince you of your council's innocence? You have loyal subjects here who openly show you that they do not harbor the kind of magic that we have seen in the blight."

The king frowned as the unseelie nodded in agreement, looking at me approvingly.

"The scholars have found something that may help us," said Rourke gruffly, producing a paper from his jacket and passing it to Aspen. Aspen unfolded a page with illustrations of tiny vials and swooping, illegible script that had to be Dwarvish.

"It's dwarven blood magic," Rourke rumbled. The other dwarves at the table murmured uneasily. "It's been outlawed for centuries, but supposedly, the blood of different creatures can be used to affect the earth and the water and the air."

"May I?" asked the king, reaching for the paper. Rourke tensed, but Aspen handed it over. The king looked at the paper gravely. "Very concerning," he said, looking up at the assembled guests, and folding the paper into his jacket. "I wish to wait another day. Should the blight return despite this unfortunate situation, then I will lift the order," he said.

Knox clenched his fists tightly under the table, and Bisera looked murderous, but none protested as we endured the rest of yet another awkward dinner.

The only bright spot was that Lord Thorn seemed unable to make headway in gaining any favor with the king, now that he had shown a dislike for dwarven cuisine. He poked sourly at the meager meal before him, casting threatening glances at me.

"How do you feel about traveling further tomorrow?" I heard Rourke ask Aspen across the table.

He looked at me before answering. "How far are you thinking?"

"There are lichen fields a half day from here down through the cave system, impossible to fly to," Rourke said in his gravelly voice. "There is some hunting there too. Cave rats and bats." I tried to hide my grimace at the thought of eating cave rats or bats at the next dinner party, praying to the Goddess that none of the tiny cubes of meat I had eaten had been anything that lived in a cave.

"We will have to camp out there, but we can be back in time for your friends to arrive if they are not caught in a storm."

Aspen nodded, glancing again in my direction. "Lord Thorn should accompany us," he said. I raised my brows at this, and Rourke narrowed his eyes.

"You do not trust this male," he said in his heavy accent. "Why do you wish to bring him with us?"

"Because I don't trust him here either," Aspen said. "At least there I can keep an eye on him."

Rourke nodded as if contemplating the wisdom of this. "Lady Aurelia, will this be well with you?"

I nodded, glancing at Aspen, and said, "Keep your friends close and your enemies closer."

"A wise saying," Rourke laughed, a grin spreading over his face. "I will make the arrangements to leave at first light."

"In that case, we should retire," Aspen said, giving a polite nod to Bisera, who pouted at his departure. He offered me an arm which I took, giving Knox a smile and a nod as well. He eyed Aspen warily, but he didn't protest as Aspen led me away.

I waited until we were back in our room to ask if he had learned anything from Bisera.

"Nothing useful," he grumbled. "Just some drivel about her lineage and her family's fertile, child-bearing hips."

I choked on a laugh. "Her what?" I wheezed. Aspen scowled at me and prowled over to where I sat to remove the comb from my hair. Stepping behind me, he unbuttoned the dress and gently pushed the straps down my arms until my back was bare to him.

He leaned down and kissed my neck and shoulders. "She thought the information would tempt me," he rumbled, making heat pulse up my thighs and through my core. "But it just made me think about you."

I turned to wrap my arms around his neck and met his kiss. "Do you wish to talk about my child-bearing hips?" I teased.

He scooped me up, still half dressed, and dropped me on the bed, leaning over me to kiss down my bare front. "Not as much as I wish to explore them," he growled, pulling the dress off me and removing his coat and shirt.

I lay there, bare before him except for the daggers strapped to my thighs. I leaned down to unbuckle the straps, but he stopped me with a hand.

"Don't," he said, grinning wickedly as he bared his chest to me. "You might need them."

Heat blazed within me again at the suggestion as he lowered his mouth to mine and then trailed it down my body. He sucked each gently-peaked nipple into his mouth, making me moan and gasp, and then kissed a line of fire down my stomach to my navel.

He paused at the scar from the iron dagger, kissing it tenderly. "I may kill Thorn on this trip," he said, voice promising violence that made me shiver with...delight? There was something seriously wrong with me. He continued his path downward until he was kissing the inside of each thigh above the straps of my daggers.

"Aspen," I breathed, "what are you doing?"

He looked up at me, eyes dark. "If I hurt you, stab me," was all he said before he parted the hair between my legs and placed his mouth against my throbbing core. I arched shamelessly into him as he licked and kissed and ran his tongue over the center of me, wringing another gasping moan from me.

"If we are camped tomorrow, and have Seline and Vanth here the next night," Aspen said, lifting his head and speaking between gentle licks and nips, "then this is the last time I'll be able to do this for several days."

"You won't tell them about us?" I asked, gasping as he swept his tongue gently inside me and out again.

"Oh, I intend to," he said, still teasing me mercilessly with his tongue. "I just doubt we will have enough privacy for me to make you properly scream my name." He lowered his head again and feasted on me, seeming to draw satisfaction from every moan and cry he wrung from me until I was panting and thrusting my hips against his mouth. As the sensations grew to be too much, I tried to push his face away a little. He smirked up at me and flicked his head, drawing vines of ivy seemingly from nowhere to wrap my wrists and hold them above my head.

"Oh Goddess, please," I begged as he continued licking and sucking. He gripped my waist with one hand and moved a finger to my entrance, gently pushing and making me gasp with pleasure as he began to fill me. A second finger soon joined, and he began pumping them in time with his licks and kisses until I was coming apart at the seams. I screamed his name and fire erupted along the vines, burning them away and releasing my hands, blessedly dying out before it could scorch the bed.

I sank my hands into his soft hair and held on through the pleasure that rocked me, panting as he continued to lick and kiss. He grasped one of my freed hands in his as he pushed the fingers of his other hand back inside me.

"What—" I started, ending with a moan as he worked me up to a second release. He didn't answer but continued worshiping me until I was coming apart a second time, rocking my hips to his thrusting fingers as I cried out for him.

With a satisfied male noise, Aspen removed his fingers from me and kissed his way back up my body, licking and teasing each sensitive nipple on his way to my mouth. I shuddered beneath him, limp and sensitive.

"Tell me you're mine," he growled, sinking his teeth gently into my neck and sucking lightly as he moved back to my ear. I felt his hard length resting against me as he kissed me, and I wriggled to try to shift it to where I wanted it to go. He chuckled, pinning my hands with his and looking into my eyes. "Tell me you're mine, and I'll give you what you want," he commanded, blue eyes flashing with something primal in his desire.

"I'm yours," I breathed, feeling a hum snapping between us as he finally thrust into me and moved, still kissing my neck, my shoulder, my jaw.

"Again," he commanded, moving faster and stroking deeper with each thrust.

"I'm yours," I gasped again, feeling that coiling tension building for a third time as he moved. I wrapped my legs around him, trying to get even closer than we already were. He groaned against me as he moved a hand to cup my rear and pound out his pleasure. Release shuddered through him, and I cried out with the pleasure of being so close, so loved, so wanted by him.

"And I'm yours," he murmured into my neck when we had both quieted, bodies slick with sweat from our lovemaking. "Always."

Chapter 22: Aurelia

THE EXPEDITION THAT HEADED out the next day was large, consisting of me and Aspen, Rourke, an extremely unwilling Lord Thorn, and at least twenty other dwarven soldiers and laborers who lugged supplies and saddled up the small army of cave dragons we would be taking. By our request, Knox had been permitted to attend as well, and he looked thrilled to be out of the palace.

I had spent twenty minutes trying to purge some of my fire in the shower that morning, and I felt like I had a bit more control than I had the previous day. Nothing had burst into flame accidentally, and I'd managed to contain my burning to the stream of cold water that instantly doused me.

Aspen complained that I smelled like a campfire when he kissed my head, but I argued we would be camping that night anyway, and I'd smell like a campfire regardless. We managed to squeeze in one gloriously long, sensual kiss before Rourke knocked for us. I sighed, strapping on my various daggers and hiding two down my boots as we set off.

I had decided to call today's cave dragon Poppy because she had a little brownish-red spot on her nose that looked a bit like a flower. I patted her scaly head and she hissed happily as we headed out of the city.

"Ember won't let you keep a herd of cave dragons," Aspen reminded me from my left as I crooned to Poppy about all the nice things cave dragons might eat in the Seelie Realm. "And I don't think they'd like the sunshine much."

"But they're so adorable," I whined.

"Only you could find a cave dragon adorable," Aspen drawled.

"They universally seem to like you," Knox said, riding up on my right and smiling. Aspen frowned at him, unwilling to warm up to my friend. The way Knox kept glancing at me hopefully might have explained that, but I pretended not to notice.

"Maybe they sense that I'm a kindred spirit," I said, scratching Poppy's scaly eye ridge.

Knox chuckled. "Can you breathe fire too?" he joked, and I laughed unconvincingly. Aspen raised his brows in warning.

"I mean my fiery temper, of course," I said, smiling innocently. Aspen scoffed.

Thorn was riding some distance ahead with Rourke keeping a close watch on him. Every so often he glanced back at us, and Aspen looked ready to gut him at the first provocation.

"This male who is not your husband," Knox asked me in a low voice, also looking at Thorn, "do you think he may be responsible for the iron thefts? And the blight?"

"I can't be sure," I confessed, "but I don't think it's a coincidence he is here at the same time Aspen and I have come."

"Hmm," Knox said, shooting a glance at Aspen before turning back ahead. "Stay close to one of us while we are out here, Aurelia. I don't like the idea of the lord getting too close to you."

I laughed. "Believe me, neither do I," I said, smiling. Knox looked so serious that I dropped my smile and added placatingly, "I promise, that while I am perfectly capable of taking care of myself, I will stay near you or Aspen or Rourke."

Knox frowned again.

"Do you not trust Rourke?" I whispered, frowning at the back of the sturdy dwarf riding ahead of us.

"I want to. Rourke and I were childhood friends," Knox said with a sigh. "But it occurs to me that Rourke had access to all iron weapon shipments, to all the fields and crops of the realm, and to unhindered and untracked travel at all times." His voice pitched lower so it was hard to hear over the crunching of the cave dragons on the stone floor. "He is one of the few dwarves who could pass such orders without his father's notice or approval."

I frowned, nodding and filing away this suspicion to tell Aspen later. Aspen didn't trust Knox, and Knox didn't trust Rourke. I sighed at the tangled web of distrust we were weaving around us.

The path became significantly bumpier at that point as the dragons traveled over rugged terrain and loose scree. It was a miracle they didn't lose their footing, but I supposed that was a perk of having claws. Talking became difficult, and we traveled in near silence except for the sounds of the dragons moving and grunting at each other in the dark. Once or twice I felt Aspen lay a comforting hand on my shoulder or my back as he got near enough to touch me, but for the most part, it was like traveling alone through the darkness. I didn't remember much about shadow walking when Hadrian had rescued me from Thorn's estate, but the darkness reminded me of the emptiness of the void through which he moved when he used that power.

After a while, a faint glow appeared in the distance, and I gasped in awe when I realized what it was. The crops were endless fields of luminescent mushrooms, glowing faintly white and blue and purple and pink all over the walls and floor and across the ceiling of a gigantic cavern. There was no window of light carved in the wall, and we must have been too deep for light to reach us—my ears had popped several times as we descended,—but the glowing fields made it bright enough to see as if it were day in the Crystal City. I dismounted from Poppy and gaped at the fields.

"It's lovely, isn't it?" said Knox reverently as he stopped beside me. "We call it the Glowing Sea."

"It's beautiful," I said. "But how is all of this here and healthy? Is this not enough to sustain you?"

"Most of these cannot be eaten," growled Rourke as he made his way back to us through the crowd of dwarves. "Only the white ones are edible. The rest are poisonous."

I looked again and saw an area of pure white mushrooms that glowed a little more faintly than the others. This must be the section that was regularly farmed, and it appeared healthy enough. There were a few dark patches throughout, but it was hard to tell if they were patches of blight or just rocks sticking out of the ground.

Aspen came up next to me and gave me a subtle caress on my behind as Rourke gathered us to discuss the plan. Half the dwarves would serve as a survey and collection team, collecting the edible fungi and marking the blighted patches on a map for Aspen to study. Aspen would focus on growing, and Thorn would irrigate the crop to speed the process and provide maximum growth.

Rourke would lead the rest of the dwarves deeper into the caves to hunt the rats and bats that lived there. Apparently, they might even catch a cave mole, which was supposed to be a delicacy. All of these meat sources churned my stomach a bit, and I was secretly grateful for our provisions of dry bread and cooked nettle stew.

The parties would reconvene at sundown, which the dwarves marked by the color of the Glowing Sea. It dimmed as night fell, although no one really understood why. We would then make camp and repeat the process in the morning before packing up whatever food we were able to gather.

Thorn looked none too happy to be a part of any plan in which he answered to Aspen.

"I'm not comfortable being left alone with the male who stole my bride," Thorn said spitefully. Rourke nodded.

"Then you must come with us to hunt the cave rats," he said placatingly. "You can be the bait." The assembled dwarves laughed and Thorn grumbled something about insults and uncivilized brutes.

We split up as planned and I spent the majority of my time as I had on previous excursions, running back and forth from the large storage baskets the dwarves had brought with them, depositing mushrooms that had been magically enhanced in size after releasing their spores to be regrown by Aspen's magic. It was tiring and boring work, and I was sweaty and sore by the time the sea dimmed, signaling nightfall.

The hunting party had returned with a number of kills, and they set up cookfires to roast the cave rats. I declined a leg, but Aspen took one. I grimaced at him as he tore into it.

"What?" he asked, mouth full of cave rat. "Meat is meat." Knox nodded in agreement, one more thing on which they could both agree.

The mushroom sea had dimmed enough to make glowworm orbs necessary, and we lay our bedrolls around the several smoldering fires somewhat haphazardly. Rourke set a rotation of dwarven guards to keep watch through the night, and I settled my bedroll between Knox and Aspen. I tried not to think about the things Aspen and I had done and would certainly not be doing while on this expedition.

"You seem to be getting along better," Knox said, gesturing toward Aspen with his chin. Aspen was deep in conversation with Rourke, pouring over the survey of the blighted sections of the field and showing him where he expected regrowth in the morning.

"We are, I think," I said, trying not to make my lie obvious. It was technically the truth, and Knox didn't need to know exactly how well we were getting along. "It helps that he feels useful here and that I can help in some small way."

"Do you not feel useful in the seelie court?" Knox asked, resting on one arm so he could look at me.

I lay on my back, eyes trained on the ceiling. "It's different," I said hesitantly, wondering why there was a grain of truth to what Knox said. I did feel more useful here. Maybe now that my magic had emerged I would be more use to Ember and the war effort when we returned.

"You could stay, you know," Knox said quietly. I turned to face him, and he looked at me sadly. "You could be happy here, I think."

I shook my head. "Knox, I..."

He nodded, turning to lie on his own back. "I understand," he said, glancing at Aspen as he bade Rourke goodnight and headed toward us. "It's hard to leave someone you love."

I didn't argue with him. I did love Aspen, even if the only time I had said it aloud was a whispered secret as he fell asleep. It wasn't fair to lie to Knox and hurt when eventually I left, or to give him false hope that I could someday love him the same way.

"I'm sorry," I said quietly.

He shook his head next to me. "If I can't have your love, I'll settle for your friendship," he said, facing me again with a sad smile.

"You have it," I said quietly, and I meant it. He smiled and turned over, facing away from me, and consequently from Aspen who sat down next to me.

Aspen raised a brow at me and jerked his head toward Knox. I dropped an air shield around us surreptitiously so we wouldn't be overheard. "I feel terrible lying to him," I whispered. It wasn't necessary with the air shield, but it felt wrong to speak louder.

"Have you told him that you love him? That you want him?" Aspen asked, raising a brow at me. "If not, then you haven't lied. It's not your fault that he sees what I see and fell in love with you."

I looked at him steadily, his eyes burning brightly in the light of the glow worms, his unspoken confession hanging between us.

"Vanth and Seline should be here tomorrow night," he said quietly, settling himself on the bedroll next to me. "And Thorn will hopefully get what's coming to him."

"I don't know," I said quietly, frowning as I thought about our situation. "Why did Thorn come here anyway? It can't have just been to taunt or spy on us. What is he getting by being here that we are not seeing?"

Aspen shook his head wearily. "I don't know, and I'm too tired to figure it out tonight," he said, turning to face me and cushioning his head on one bent arm. He yawned. "That is a problem for future-Aspen to figure out."

We were silent for a moment. "Do you feel useful at home?" I asked, letting Knox's words bother me more than I should have.

Aspen frowned. "Yes," he said. "Obviously I'm not as useful as Ember or Hadrian, but I have a purpose. So do you."

"Do I?" I asked skeptically. "When this is over, what will my role be?"

"Builder of the royal hearths?" Aspen joked, smiling a little. He saw my frown and brushed my hand, holding it in the dark. "I will help you find whatever purpose you want." He whispered. "We will go wherever you want, do whatever you want until you know as well as I do how important you are."

I smiled, reaching up to stroke his face in the darkness. "Good night, Aspen," I whispered, lifting the air shield from around us.

He kissed my fingers. "Good night."

I lay awake for a while, watching Aspen drift off in the dim light of the Glowing Sea. Tomorrow, we would take the next steps we needed to figure out Thorn's plan and motives. Tonight, the best thing I could do was get a proper night's sleep.

But when the morning arrived, we were not able to put our plans into action. Two of the cave dragons had gone missing in the night, along with several sacks of food and a bedroll, and the sentry had been knocked out cold.

Lord Thorn was nowhere to be found.

Chapter 23: Aurelia

"I SHOULD HAVE KILLED him when I had the chance," Aspen raged, pulling off his soiled clothes and daggers as we returned to our room that evening.

The king was not hosting a dinner that night since so many of us had returned late from the overnight excursion. I was relieved to not have to perform for anyone, but Aspen wanted someone to shout at. Yay for me.

"Rourke said he won't get far without a guide," I said placatingly, removing my daggers and moving to stand before him. I gave his arm a little squeeze and looked up at him. "No one else was missing."

"There were two cave dragons taken," Aspen growled, looking at me with his furious blue gaze. "That means he had help."

"Probably," I conceded, still stroking his arm consolingly. "But he can't do much damage if he's on the run."

"Unless he is the one blighting the fields," Aspen growled. I sighed. He was determined to be furious and nothing I could say would change that. Although maybe something I could do, would. I lifted onto my toes and kissed him gently, then stripped off my soiled shirt.

Aspen's eyes went wide at the sight of my bare breasts and his hands unconsciously floated up to cup them. I smiled. "Let's get cleaned up, and then you can shout at me some more," I whispered, standing on my toes to kiss him again.

"Who's shouting?" Aspen rumbled. "I would never shout at you."

"My lord? My lady?" I cursed and threw my shirt back on as someone knocked on our door.

Aspen glowered. "Vanth, is that you?" he shouted, going to unlock the door. Vanth and Seline stood there, grinning at us in their spiked black unseelie armor with an escort of dwarves.

"Are we interrupting?" Vanth said hesitantly, seeing Aspen's furious face.

"No," I assured him, smiling at the same time as Aspen growled, "Yes."

The dwarven guards bowed, leaving us as Seline swept into the room. She grinned, her silver braid swinging behind her, and hugged me. Vanth clasped Aspen's arm in greeting and bowed to m e.

"My lady, I am glad to see you well," he said in his rough voice.

I smiled and hugged him. "It's 'Aurelia,' Vanth, you know that," I corrected, "and I am glad to see you too, my friend." Vanth had been sent to protect me by Hadrian when I had been undercover at Thorn's estate, and I knew his quick thinking and dedication were the reason I had survived my injury. Vanth would also be annoyed that Thorn had slipped our clutches.

"I think we have much to discuss," said Seline in her velvety voice, looking expectantly between me and Aspen.

"Later," Aspen said pointedly, giving her a glare I didn't understand. "Tell us how your flight was."

"Uneventful," Seline said, perching on the arm of the couch. "Vanth was sick the whole way."

"I hate flying," he grumbled sourly, making me laugh.

"We brought enough flour and grain to feed a small army for a week, but it won't keep the whole realm going for long," Seline continued. "Ember wanted me to tell you that they tested Hadrian's blood, whatever that means."

"And?" Aspen asked.

"The patch of soil kills everything she tries to grow there now. Even Mother Vervain couldn't lift the blight from the land," she said, eyes narrowed at Aspen. "You think this is the cause of the blight?"

"I do," he said, nodding and leaning against a wall. The room was rather cramped with four of us.

"I think we may need a bigger room," I said, scowling as Vanth dropped dirt all over the cream sofa. "We should ask Rourke if there's any other room that could be spared."

"It will have to be a suite," said Aspen. "I don't want any of us unguarded."

"First, tell me," said Seline, looking at us piercingly again. "When did this happen?"

"When did what happen?" I asked.

Seline exchanged a glance with Aspen and pointed between us. "This," she said again, gesturing between us. "Your bond."

"Bond?" I asked, looking at Aspen in confusion.

He pursed his lips. "I wasn't sure, which was why I wrote to you," he said to Seline, completely ignoring my confusion. "It's not official yet."

"It feels official," Seline said, moving around us and examining something that none of the rest of us could see.

"Please tell me what you are talking about," I said, getting more annoyed at being left in the dark. Seline glanced at Aspen and raised a brow.

"We will go secure a bigger suite for all of us," she said, pulling Vanth, who looked equally confused, out of the room. "Tell her, Aspen."

I stared at her retreating form, then whirled on Aspen. "Tell me what?" I demanded.

He sighed, running a hand over his face and gently pushing me to sit on the bed by my shoulders. "Remember when you said you were mine?" he asked softly, cupping my cheek with a gentle hand.

"Yes, I said it several times," I agreed, blushing slightly at the memory of those moments. Heat flooded me, but I pushed the feeling aside. For now.

"Did you mean it, when you said it?" Aspen asked. "Or was it just the heat of the moment?" He looked so serious I started to worry.

"I meant it," I said adamantly. "Every time. Aspen, just tell me whatever it is. It can't be that bad."

He sighed. "I swear I didn't mean to do it," he began, and I tensed. He was looking at me so tenderly, so lovingly that I didn't think he was about to hurt me, but whatever he was about to tell me was big. "When you said you were mine, three times to be precise, and I reciprocated," he continued, "I think it locked in a mating bond."

"It what?" I said, rising to my feet and retreating a step, eyes wide in confusion. "Mating bonds have ceremonies. They are chosen in front of witnesses."

"I know," Aspen said. "That's what I thought too. But the other night, I felt something between us. Do you remember? I asked if you felt it too."

I did remember and I blanched, mentally tugging on the thing between us. It hummed, and he smiled. "Yes, that," he said, standing and closing the distance between us. I felt another tug and he gestured to himself. "That one was me. I asked Seline when I wrote to Ember if there were other ways to form the bond. Less well-known ways. I think I know her answer."

"I said I was yours," I whispered, still feeling the thrumming between us. "And you said you were mine."

"I am yours," Aspen said, cupping my cheek again and gently kissing me. "Please say you are not upset." A tear trickled down my cheek and he cursed, swiping it away with his thumb.

"No," I said quickly, smiling up at him. "No, it's alright. I'm not upset." I let another tear fall, rising to my toes to kiss him as deeply as I could. He wrapped his arms around me tightly and kissed me back, tangling his fingers in my hair. "I love you," I said, stepping back and placing my hands on his cheeks. I brought his forehead down to mine. "I choose you. I always have. I chose you at Midsummer, and I knew I would never choose another after."

"I love you," he breathed, "so damn much it terrifies me." His breath skated across my lips as he kept his face bent to mine. "You have no idea, Aurelia, how long I have loved you. I was cruel and cold because I felt like my heart had been ripped from me when you married him." Aspen didn't say Thorn's name, but I knew who he meant. "I am so bleeding sorry for doubting you, and for tormenting you. Say you will be my mate. My love. That you aren't angry at me for this."

"How could I be angry when it's what I have always wanted?" I replied, pressing another gentle kiss to his lips.

"Can we come in now?" called a gruff voice from behind the door. Vanth poked his head around the corner. "Seline said it wouldn't take this long."

I laughed, opening my arms to hug Vanth and Seline as they shared in our happiness.

ONCE WE WERE SETTLED in a bigger suite, one that was reserved for royal dignitaries, which Aspen argued with Rourke that we very much were, we told Vanth and Seline the whole story. Sitting around a coffee table with a meager meal, I may have glossed over some of the more explicit details, but Seline grinned like she knew exactly what would have had to happen for a bond to be formed this way.

"It's called a claiming bond," she explained. Vanth blushed furiously and she rolled her eyes at him. "In giving yourself three times, Aurelia," Vanth went nearly purple at this, "you created a ceremonial offer of binding. Aspen must have accepted at least once for it to take. It's very rarely done like this nowadays. Most fae prefer the ceremony and pomp of formally recognized bonds."

"Will ours not be formally recognized?" I asked, realizing I was concerned that there could be any doubt of it.

Seline shook her head. "Oh no, it will," she assured me. "I can see it clear as day." Seline's spell-breaking power from her mother gave her the ability to see and sense spells that most of the fae could not. If Seline saw that the bond was present, then it was. I relaxed a little, and Aspen stroked a thumb over the back of my hand absently.

"So when is the wedding?" Vanth asked through a mouthful of bread, earning an elbow to the ribs from Seline, who was perched next to him, and a glare from Aspen.

"Let me ask her first, you great oaf," Aspen said irritably.

I laughed and patted his hand. "Wait for a more romantic time," I said coyly, fluttering my lashes at him. He raised a brow but said nothing.

"Now that that's all settled," Seline said in a velvety calm voice, "tell us about Thorn. And the blight. And the dwarves. And anything else important."

Aspen launched into a detailed explanation of everything we had discovered, which was very little, and everything we were trying to find out, which was a much longer list.

Vanth growled when Aspen told them about our first meeting with Thorn at breakfast, and Seline patted his hand. I wondered for not the first time when they would finally admit their feelings for each other as well.

"So what is our next move?" Vanth asked, looking between us.

Aspen shook his head. "I don't even know," he said, looking suddenly exhausted. "We don't know who is smuggling the weapons, we don't know who is behind the blight, and we have no leads on Thorn. All we know for sure is that an unseelie fae with

Hadrian's power is spilling blood to cause the withering. What's been going on at home since we left?"

"The king seems to be keeping his armies put," said Seline, looking between Vanth and Aspen. "But our scouts have been reporting greater activity along the border. The Unseelie King has put a hefty bounty on any Seelie fae found in his territory."

"Why?" I asked, confused as to why the king would suddenly be actively hunting for our kind. "Has something happened?"

Seline glanced toward Vanth again. "We aren't sure. Several scouts have gone missing," she said somberly. "Hadrian hasn't been able to find out anything from his spies, but we fear the worst."

Aspen and I exchanged a heavy look. I had a feeling that if they had been captured by the king, they wouldn't make it out of his castle alive. Vanth let out a sudden yawn, and I stood.

"Let's figure out the rest tomorrow," I suggested, patting Vanth's shoulder. "You need some sleep, and there's no point in rehashing anything else tonight." He nodded, rising along with Seline and Aspen.

"We should keep watch through the night," Seline said seriously. "I'll do the first shift."

"Thank you for coming," I said, smiling at her. I felt much safer with our friends at our backs.

The suite we had been moved to contained a common area, where we sat with Vanth and Seline, as well as two adjoining bedrooms. It was similar to our first suite, except that there was no balcony or stairs to the city. We were now on the same floor Thorn had been, and the thought had crossed my mind to try to sneak in again, but I wasn't sure how to get there.

I had suggested to Rourke that he search Thorn's rooms when he was moving us to the new suite, but he said the process was already completed, so I doubted there would be much to find anyway.

"I forgot to tell Vanth and Seline about my magic," I gasped, moving to turn back to the common room.

"It can wait until tomorrow," Aspen rumbled, taking my hands and placing a kiss below my ear. I shivered at the promise in that small kiss and agreed that this last piece of news was completely unimportant after all.

He walked me to the edge of the bed and sat down, still holding my hands in his while he looked up at me. "How should I worship you tonight, my love?" he asked huskily. "Slow and sweet, or fast and hard?"

"Hmm," I said, pretending to think. I dropped slowly to my knees and began untying the laces of his breeches. "Maybe instead tonight I should worship you."

Aspen's brows shot up as he realized what I was doing, and something I could only describe as a purely male smile curved his lips. The smile died when I freed his length and pressed my lips to him for the first time. He stilled and sucked in a breath as I flicked my tongue over his head.

"Aurelia," he groaned as I moved over him, working my tongue up and down his length and over his head again, flicking the bead of moisture that had pooled at the tip into my mouth.

"Hmm?" I asked, closing my lips around him and gazing at him with wicked intent. He groaned, falling back on the mattress as I moved along his length, sucking gently and teasing with my tongue until I felt his hands fisting in my hair and his breathing grow ragged. Heat pooled in my core at the power I had over him in this moment, as he lay completely at my mercy for once.

"Aurelia," he groaned out again, half plea and half prayer to continue and finish what I had begun.

"Tell me you're mine," I said teasingly, caressing him with my hand and squeezing slightly. He swore, gasping in another breath. "And I'll give you what you want." I waited, poised over him.

"I'm yours," he breathed, lifting up on his elbows to watch me. Slowly, I licked up to his head again. He growled, unable to be so out of control any longer, and pulled me to him, twisting me face down on the bed and moving over me.

I helped wriggle off my leggings and then he was sliding home, gloriously buried to the hilt in me. I cried out as his fingers searched for the place between my legs where my pleasure built, and he moved against me, stroking me with one hand while bracing us against the mattress with the other, all while licking and nipping at my neck. He roared his climax at my back, and pressed against me, still moving and stroking gently as he helped me find my release. The band between us seemed to glow warmer and brighter as I felt him spill into me.

In the afterglow, I laid across his bare chest as he stroked my back and my hair, perfectly content as I felt his heart, my mate's heart, beating in time with my own.

Chapter 24: Aurelia

I WAS WOKEN FOR once not by a dream, but by a crash in the common room. I heard males shouting and the thud of a weapon, and I scrambled to throw on some clothes.

Aspen was up too, and I heard him pulling on his pants and sliding a dagger from its sheath. We crashed out the door to see both Seline and Vanth held at knifepoint. A dwarven guard lay motionless on the floor, and several others flanked the doors.

Rourke stepped forward. "Drop your weapons," he said in his gravelly accent. "I do not wish to hurt your friends."

I looked in panic to Seline and Vanth, both of whom held their hands up in surrender as dwarves held iron daggers to their throats. Seline had a cut under one eye that was already beginning to close, and Vanth's burned neck had torn open, although it seemed like it was mostly superficial. The dwarf on the ground looked like he had been drained of life. I blanched, looking at Vanth. He had told me once his power was terrible, and he refused to use it unless necessary. Now I knew why.

Aspen dropped his dagger and raised his hands. I poured fire into my own, and Vanth and Seline's eyes went wide.

"What is this, Rourke?" Aspen said, voice serious as he glanced at our friends. "I thought we were all allies here."

"We are," he said, sheathing his weapons and motioning toward Vanth and Seline. "Put out the fire please, my lady. I do not wish for any of us to get hurt by magic or by iron."

I realized the guards carried iron manacles, and I looked to Aspen, who nodded, tight-lipped. I doused the flame and felt myself panic as my magic fled me when the iron clapped around my wrists.

"That seems unlikely since you are holding blades to our friends' throats," Aspen said, sagging as he was similarly cuffed. Rourke motioned for the guards to lower their blades, and I breathed a momentary sigh of relief.

"The halls are secure," came a voice from the hallway. My heart sank as Knox strode into the room and bowed to Rourke.

"No," I gasped. "Knox, what is this?"

"I'm sorry, Aurelia," he said, looking genuinely apologetic. "Rourke says he will explain everything."

"Where is King Holvard?" I shouted as a guard pushed me ahead of him.

"Dead," Rourke said emotionlessly. "His time of poisoning my realm has passed. I now protect the Dwarven Realm."

"What's the plan then, Rourke?" Aspen spat. "Do you intend to ransom us back to our Queen for supplies? She certainly won't view you as an ally after this."

Rourke frowned. "I will not be ransoming you, Lord of Earth," he said. "But I need you to not get in my way while I settle things in my court."

We were marched down the hall to the king's council room, where the unseelie members of the council, including Bisera, and several dwarves were also being held prisoner. It seemed that Rourke had the support of only a fraction of the court, but he certainly controlled the upper hand.

"Traitor," Bisera shouted at Knox as he pushed us into the room. "You would side with this murderer against your own people?"

"The dwarves are my people, as they are yours," said Knox in a hard voice, pushing Seline and Vanth down to kneel next to me and Aspen.

"Were you selling weapons to the Unseelie King, too?" I asked, looking at Knox and realizing that I hadn't known him any better than I had known Rourke.

"And tainting the fields?" Aspen asked.

"No," he said quietly. "You have to believe me, I knew nothing of either plot." Aspen laughed derisively.

"Enough," Rourke boomed. "All will be made clear soon."

"You were working with Thorn," I said, realizing that I shouldn't be surprised by Rourke's treachery after being arrested and shackled, but still feeling its sting.

Rourke didn't bother answering me, and I set to work trying to wriggle out of my cuffs. I tried accessing my power to melt them, but it was like my magic had been snuffed out completely by the iron.

Rourke called for several guards, including Knox to follow him, leaving six solid-looking dwarves on rotation guarding the room.

Knox nodded, meeting my eyes. He was still crouched next to me, and he put his hand on my cheek in a too-familiar gesture. I flinched back and he grabbed my wrist. "Know who your allies are, Aurelia," he said quietly, dropping something ice-cold into my hand. He rose and followed Rourke out as I stared after him.

"What is our play here?" Vanth rumbled, moving closer to me and Seline.

"If we can stick together, we have a chance of overpowering the guards, even without magic," Aspen said, twisting his wrists as he also tried to escape the cuffs.

"If you escape, I'm going with you," came a voice from behind me. I turned and saw that Bisera had moved closer as well.

Seline raised her eyebrow at me as if to ask "Who is this?" and I shrugged.

"There's no way we will all be able to get out together without our magic," Aspen whispered. I listened with only half an ear while wriggling and straining at my cuffs. "Our best chance is to overpower the guards by sheer numbers and make for the rookery. We can fly the rocs back to the Seelie Realm. How many here will follow you over Rourke?"

"They'll all follow," said Bisera confidently. "All of us here were loyal to King Holvard, despite our differences. We wanted Rourke to take over eventually, but not like this."

"How many followers does Rourke have?" I asked, finally hearing a click as I moved Knox's gift to my other wrist.

"I don't know," Bisera whispered as a dwarven guard walked past us. "He has the guard though. Some of our people did feel we should side with the Unseelie King in this conflict. That he had more to offer us. They may be allied with Rourke. Only those of us who have seen the cruelty of the Unseelie King firsthand knew better."

"What about Knox?" I asked, still feeling the loss of my friend.

Bisera shrugged. "He came here as a babe," she reminded me. "He has never known the truth of the Unseelie King as the rest of us have."

"And the blight?" Aspen asked. "Do you know who is responsible?"

Bisera looked affronted. "You know I don't, I already told you as much," she snapped.

I glared at Aspen and he shrugged at me apologetically.

"It doesn't matter," said Seline. "Whoever is causing the blight must have been working with Rourke to undermine King Holvard. What we need to figure out is how to get out of this before Rourke decides to sell us to the Unseelie King. Once we are in his clutches, we will not leave alive."

"That's going to be tricky without our magic," Aspen grumbled, shaking his bound wrists in emphasis.

"Luckily, we still have a friend who can help with that," I whispered, smirking as I held the thin skewer of ice in my now free hands. Aspen opened his eyes wide but nodded as I moved to pick his cuffs next. I was wary of the ice melting or breaking, and I knew if we moved too quickly or excitedly we would attract the attention of the guards, so we had to work slowly and carefully. By the time Rourke returned with his men, all of us were free except Vanth and the council members.

"Leave them," Vanth hissed, nodding at the cuffs as the new Dwarven King entered. "I'm better with fists anyway."

I felt a gentle tug on the bond between me and Aspen. I hadn't realized it had been dulled by the iron, but now it returned bright and full and insistent. I looked at him and he nodded subtly to the floor and walls. I wasn't sure what he was planning, but I got his message well enough.

Brace yourself.

"My lord and lady," Rourke said, sending Knox over to collect me and Aspen. "Come with me, if you please."

We stood, the iron cuffs falling away with a clang before Rourke could register the magic Aspen had already tapped into. With a mighty crash, the mountain came down around us.

"Run," I heard Aspen shout as he brought down the palace walls in a deafening crash, the mountain rumbling ominously beneath us. He had carved a new exit from the room and was creating a wall of thorns to hold back Rourke and his men.

"Knox, grab her and run," I heard him shout again. I felt a tug on my arm as Knox followed his orders and pulled me to the new exit.

"No," I shouted, trying to surge for Aspen's side.

"He's coming," Knox reassured me. "He's behind us, but we have to run now."

The dwarves moved slower than the fae due to their height, but I knew the advantage wouldn't last long if they mounted cave dragons or rocs. We ran as one out of the path Aspen had carved for us through the castle, the dwarves leading the way into the city. Several veered off, I assumed to find families or loved ones and get them out too, but we kept moving.

I looked back and Aspen was there, running furiously to catch up with us. The sounds of pursuit had started to follow us in the distance and we sped up, barreling through the long tunnel before crashing out of the side of the mountain into the freezing dark. I shot a burst of flame straight up to light our way as we all ran for the rookery, more and more dwarves fleeing with us as word reached them that their king had been murdered.

"Each roc can carry five," I gasped as we ran up the slick stairs to the rookery above us. "Will there be enough?"

"No," Knox replied breathlessly, "but some will get out other ways." I nodded, pausing and causing Seline and Vanth to nearly crash into me.

"What are you doing?" Knox shouted back at me as I paused.

I shook my head. "Get as many out on the rocs as you can," I shouted back. "Head to the Seelie palace. Tell the queen that Aurelia says to guard her left. She'll know I sent you."

Knox hesitated as Aspen finally caught up to me, looking between the four of us and at Vanth's hands still bound in iron.

"What are you going to do?" he asked, looking around wildly as violent shouts reached us from the bottom of the stairs.

I glanced at my friends—my family. Vanth nodded, grinning wickedly. "We are going to cause a distraction to give you as much time as we can," I said. "Leave Notus for us, and make sure all the other rocs are set loose so no one can follow. We will see you in the Seelie Realm as soon as we can."

"Go," Aspen shouted, waving him away. "We have this."

Knox nodded and ran, dragging the stragglers onto Caelus's back as he took off.

"I hope you know what you're doing," Seline said darkly as she eyed the giant bird still waiting in the rookery.

"Me too," I said, as I built a wall of flame, blocking off the top of the stairs, and then pushing it down the mountain. "Vanth and Seline, saddle Notus. Aspen, take down the stairs."

We got to work, weaving our magic to create an avalanche of rocks and fire that destroyed the staircase. Screams reached us as dwarves careened down the mountainside, and I savagely hoped that Rourke was among them.

"Time to go!" Seline shouted over the wind. Vanth had freed his hands from the cuffs and was strapping the saddle on the great bird as we ran toward the rookery.

Notus squawked in protest as I patted his beak with cold fingers to wake him. He ruffled his head and snapped at me, but I was prepared with some of the raw meat that had been left frozen next to his pen.

"Here you go, boy," I said, throwing him the frozen flesh. He caught it, snapping it up in his beak as we climbed onto his back.

Once all four of us were settled atop him, Vanth looking rather green as he found himself back on a bird, I took the reins and gave him a little kick. With a huff, the bird lunged forward, flapping his great wings and launching us into the starry sky. The earth shrank below us until it was too dark to see anything but a faint pinprick of flames on the mountainside.

I patted Notus's neck and crooned soothingly at him as he flew. "Take us home, boy."

Chapter 25: Aurelia

THE FLIGHT FROM THE mountain was the coldest and most miserable I had ever been. Even pressed to Aspen's front, I was shivering without my fire to heat me, and I couldn't risk lighting one midair in case it caught the bird or my friends.

By the time the sun began to rise, I could barely feel my fingers and toes, and my stomach ached with hunger and thirst. I directed Notus down to land, or more likely Notus decided it was time to land, and he alighted in a patch of snow surrounded by pine trees. Getting off his back was a test of patience. All of us were stiff and cold, and Vanth was heartily sick against a tree when he finally got down.

I patted Notus's side and he took off to hunt. I hoped he wouldn't be too conspicuous flapping around the forest while we rested, but there was really no alternative.

"We will be too conspicuous flying him during the day," I said through chattering teeth. "We should wait until nightfall."

"We need to get warm," Seline gasped, shivering in the freezing snow. Vanth nodded and pointed to the tree line, and we trudged through the thick snow until we were under the cover of trees.

Since neither Vanth nor Seline had magic that would provide shelter or warmth, Aspen and I set up camp. Aspen bent several tree branches toward us using his magic, growing more where they grew sparsely until we had a rudimentary shelter. I set a ring of fire around the inside of the shelter, melting the snow as best as I could. The ground was still muddy and wet in places, but it would be better than sitting in the cold.

I lit a fire, helping the wet branches catch fire with the last of my magic, and the four of us huddled under the shelter together. Aspen bent a few more branches around us before his power was also spent, but we finally had a chance to thaw a bit.

"You two sleep," Vanth grumbled next to me. "Seline and I will take the first watch." Aspen began to protest, but Vanth replied, "I haven't spent all my magic, and neither has Seline. You two recharge."

I already felt my eyelids drooping shut as I rested my head on Aspen's shoulder. He wrapped one of his arms around me and shifted against a tree trunk. He smelled like pine and snow and spring and honeysuckle all wrapped up together, and I let the warmth and safety of his arms lull me to sleep.

When I woke, I was on my side, and the sun was setting. I sat up, rubbing my eyes as a clanging sound came from outside the shelter. Seline was also asleep on her side, and I poked my head out to see Aspen and Vanth skinning a brace of rabbits. Notus was asleep, his head curled under a wing beneath the cover of the trees.

I stuck my head back in the shelter and realized how hungry and thirsty I was. If I could find a way to hold it, I could melt some snow to drink. I set about looking for a large leaf or a piece of rounded bark as a makeshift pot.

Aspen and Vanth came back with the bloody rabbits.

"What are you doing?" Aspen asked bemusedly, watching me hunt around the tiny shelter.

"Finding something I can melt water in," I said irritably. "And shhh, you'll wake Seline. Can you shape some tree bark for me? If it's alive, you can manipulate it, right?"

He shrugged. "I can try," he said, concentrating on the nearest tree and growing a panel of bark into a funnel shape. I beamed at his triumph and asked him to do it again until I had four funnels of snow melting by the fire for us to drink.

"Does anyone know how far we are from the Seelie Realm?" I whispered as Vanth began roasting the rabbits.

"We only traveled a few hours on the bird," Vanth replied wearily. "I assume we are still a fair distance from the border. If we keep traveling southwest, we should eventually reach Seelie territory."

"If we undershoot it we could end up in unseelie lands," Aspen said darkly.

"At least then we can head south and pray to the Goddess we make it before the king finds us," Vanth said. "I vote for that."

Aspen nodded and I shrugged, assuming the decision had been made. After eating and drinking something I felt almost properly alive again. Aspen yawned as he stretched out his long legs in front of him.

"You should sleep," I told him, squeezing his cold hand. "I'll stay up for a bit and keep the fire going." He nodded, squeezing me back and laying down next to the fire. Soon he was asleep, and I scooted next to Vanth, who was still picking at the bones of the rabbits.

"I'm sorry we got you into our mess," I said. "If we hadn't sent for you, you'd both be safe." Vanth chuckled quietly.

"Safe is relative in our line of work, Aurelia," he said. It startled me a bit to hear him speak my name, but it was nice like we were finally real friends. "And it's our job to protect the royal family. You are part of it now."

I smiled at him, feeling a warm glow in my chest that had nothing to do with my fire magic or my bond with Aspen. The little family we had formed when Hadrian and Ember had been mated was one of the best things to come out of their union. I loved my parents dearly, and I was lucky to still have them, but they didn't understand me the way my friends did. I cherished it.

"When are you going to tell her that you love her?" I said quietly, flicking my eyes to Seline, who was still fast asleep. Vanth chuckled again, this time without mirth.

"She's a fool if she doesn't already know," he said, flicking a bone away and looking up through the boughs of our tiny shelter. "But she's not ready to accept it yet. Her loss is still too fresh."

I frowned. "It's been decades though," I said, remembering that she had lost her mate while Hadrian was still young. "Maybe she'd be open to that now." Vanth shook his head sadly.

"Losing a mate is not the same as losing just any lover," he said, glancing over at her as well, something sad and tender in his expression. "She lost part of herself with him. She has to find that again before she'll be ready."

I contemplated what it would be like to lose Aspen now, after all we had shared. To lose that warm tug in my heart that connected me to him. To never again feel his lips or his hands on me, to smell him or see him smiling. My heart cracked a bit for Seline, realizing the depth of her loss. Maybe it wasn't so strange that she wasn't yet ready.

"She'll come around," I said, patting Vanth's broad arm.

He patted my hand in return and sighed deeply. "I'll still be waiting when she does."

ONCE THE SUN HAD fully set, we climbed back on Notus and took off. It was impossible to see in the darkness where we were going, but I told him we needed to go to our realm, and I hoped he understood my instructions well enough to let his sense of direction guide us.

The flight was still freezing and miserable, and we landed again as the sun began to rise, even more stiff and cold than we had been the previous morning.

With a pat, Notus flew off to hunt, and we camped a second day in much the same way we had the first, finding a sheltered patch of pine trees to bend into a makeshift hut and warming it with my fire. Aspen and I took the first watch this time, and I rested my head on his shoulder as he told me stories about his time away at university, what he remembered about me as a child, the first time he learned to ride, and his father.

We hadn't spoken about his father since he had fled seelie lands to swear loyalty to the Unseelie King.

"Do you think he's there, at the unseelie palace?" I asked, wondering how Aspen's father might have made such a trek with only a few servants to help him.

"I don't know," Aspen said. "And I don't much care. Truthfully, he wasn't much of a father anyway."

I frowned and wrapped my arms around him tighter. Aspen and Ember had drawn the short end of the stick when it came to their family, except for each other, and I thanked the Goddess again that I had known the love of not one but two caring parents.

How Aspen had turned out warm and kind and good despite his snake of a father was beyond me. I supposed Hadrian had managed it too. Maybe the truly good males were good no matter their upbringing.

A twig snapped beyond our hut and we stilled, listening for anything or anyone that might pose a threat. Several minutes passed. I hoped it had been a squirrel or an owl or some other creature hunting for its lunch. I shifted, shivering slightly in the cold.

"Shh," Aspen hissed, cocking his head to hear whatever noise was making him tense. "Wait here."

On near-silent feet, Aspen crept out of the hut.

"I'm not waiting here," I whispered fiercely, following him as he listened for any more noises. "Where you go, I go." He rolled his eyes but took my hand as we crept through the tree line. I heard another crack and I turned toward it, but there was nothing there.

"Aspen," I hissed, turning back to him.

Something struck my head with a thunderous crack, and darkness consumed me.

Chapter 26: Ember

WITH VANTH AND SELINE gone to help Aspen and Aurelia, the castle felt strangely empty and lonesome. Hadrian had taken over their duties training the recruits, and I spent most of my mornings, including this one, watching him spar with them. I took the opportunity to train my apprentices on battlefield healing when he inevitably beat them.

I loved watching Hadrian spar, and only part of it was seeing his chiseled chest in all its glory. Hadrian fought like it was a dance, every move precise and smooth. It warmed me to see him using his shadows like an extension of himself, not hiding them from anyone until he had bested them.

I never joined him in the ring. He and Aurelia and Seline had all attempted to teach me to fight, and all had eventually given up at my hopelessness and unwillingness to learn. I didn't like the idea of wielding a dagger or a sword, preferring to use my magic for healing. Still, it didn't mean I didn't get a bit of a thrill from watching my mate demonstrate his physical prowess.

"My Queen," came the timid voice of one of my apprentices.

I smiled at Nella as she approached me in a hurry. Nella had been my apprentice when I was just a rebel working for the resistance against the Unseelie King, and she had been the first to follow me to the palace when I had been revealed as the Seelie Queen. "Yes, what is it?"

"We can't seem to stop the bleeding on one of the soldiers," she said breathlessly, pointing back to where a cluster of my apprentices were gathered around a very pale-looking Seelie male.

I sighed, grabbing my medical bag and gesturing for her to lead the way. None of the injuries this morning were that serious, hopefully including this one, but it wasn't a total waste of our time. I was hoping to be able to imbue items like bandages and tinctures with my healing powers, and minor injuries were a good way to test it. I'd had some success already with bandages that sped healing.

The poor recruit looked worried as I approached. I shooed the apprentices out of the way and demonstrated the correct way to tie a tourniquet, stopping the bleeding from a gash in the recruit's thigh. He sighed with relief, and I turned him back over to my apprentices as Hadrian left the sparring ring to take a break.

Hadrian's pale skin glowed almost white in the winter sun, and sweat dripped down his chest as he gulped down water and splashed some on his face. He flicked his wet fingers at me as I neared him, laughing as I wrinkled my nose, and placed a sweaty kiss on my cheek. "My love," he said, smiling and wrapping an arm around me as he drank again. "Always a pleasure to entertain you and your apprentices."

I glanced up at where my apprentices had all stopped to watch me and Hadrian. As one, they giggled and blushed, bustling off to continue their work.

I rolled my eyes. "This wouldn't happen if you wore a shirt while training," I scolded, taking in his bare chest and not feeling that convicted about my rebuke.

"Hmm," said Hadrian, kissing me deeply, heedless of the watching recruits and healers around us. He smiled his wicked half-smile at me. "But you like it when I don't wear a shirt."

"True," I said, sighing dramatically and tracing a finger over one well-defined pectoral muscle. "It is the highlight of my day."

He laughed loudly and kissed me again, squeezing me around the waist. "I don't suppose you might want to take a break with me right now," he murmured seductively.

I laughed. "It's the middle of the day," I protested, folding my arms and raising my brows at him.

"So?" he asked, mimicking my posture and gazing down at me heatedly.

"We have work to do," I pointed out, gesturing to the recruits waiting to resume training.

"They can wait," he purred, stepping closer to me and skating a barely-there kiss over my lips.

"My Queen," came Nella's voice from where the apprentices worked. Hadrian groaned, pressing his forehead against mine.

I sighed. "Later?" I whispered as his fingers brushed my ribs.

"Later," he agreed, growling a little as he made his intent obvious by pressing his hardness against me through our clothes.

I groaned a little as I spun to go and tend to the latest emergency, hearing Hadrian chuckle darkly behind me.

The emergency was, of course, not really an emergency, and after two more hours of patching up bruised ribs and minor gashes, I dismissed the apprentices and packed up our makeshift infirmary.

I found myself at a bit of a loose end the rest of the day. My wrists were tired from rolling bandages, and I needed a break from the various smells and fumes from the herbs in the infirmary and kitchen. Nisha had already been brushed and cared for by now, and I could have taken her out riding, but I hated using precious palace resources for my own fun. I considered reading or taking a bath, but I felt like I ought to be doing something useful and queenly rather than taking an admittedly well-earned break.

If I was honest with myself, I felt a little useless outside of the infirmary. Hadrian and the Commander were much more versed in military strategy than I was, and I trusted them to plan our campaign. We had no news of the Unseelie King moving south yet, and it made sense to wait and fight a defensive war, rather than going on the attack. I couldn't train the soldiers, and Aurelia and Aspen had taken on our only major mission. I sighed heavily, weighing my options.

I decided to practice flying in the training yard, where I could keep an eye on any injuries and work on my wing strength. My grandmother had told me I must work on flying every day if I had any hope of being able to fly long distances. Since my wings had been hidden since birth, I hadn't had the time most other queens had to master their wings in childhood. At this point, I could fly short distances fairly easily. My problem was stamina. I had been remiss in practicing lately, so it was almost certainly going to hurt. At least if I could fly some distance, I might be able to pull injured soldiers from the field and fly them to safety.

I returned to the training yard to see Hadrian taking on recruits five at a time, pausing to occasionally instruct them in strategy and form as he repeatedly bested them handily. The Commander was running training drills with the others, so no one paid me much attention as I fluttered up and down the barracks, alighting on the roof before returning to the ground over and over.

After thirty minutes of this, I felt like my wings might fall off. I lay on the roof, panting in exhaustion as my wings burned, a little worried that I might not be able to fly down.

I gazed into the sky, noticing a small speck flying from the east. I frowned. It was late in the winter for birds to be migrating, and this appeared to be a small flock. As the speck grew closer, I realized it wasn't a small flock of birds. It was one, lone, very big bird, and it carried something in its beak.

I shouted down to Hadrian as I fell more than flew to the ground.

He caught me nimbly, shadowwalking under me as he saw my frantic descent. "What?" he asked, frowning at me and checking me for injury.

I waved him off and pointed to the roc that was descending swiftly toward the palace.

Chapter 27: Aurelia

FIRE BURNED AROUND ME, but I didn't fear it as I once had. I watched the fire burn to embers as a palace rose from the ashes around me, vines twisting up the walls, holding them together as they rose. Ash floated on a breeze, coating the tiled ground in gray snow as I walked through the palace, watching in awe as it rose and mended around me. I stopped at a staircase, pushing the ash aside with my foot to see the edge of a great moth's wing, ringed with the phases of the moon and stars. A snake coiled around the banister, looking like it was waiting for me to climb the stairs.

I followed the snake up, watching as the smoke and ash dissipated, leaving gleaming marble in its wake. The snake led me further, stopping at a door I didn't recognize.

"Wake up, Aurelia," said a voice through the door. I pushed it open, and blinding pain filled my head. It throbbed and I was cold and hungry, and wherever I was, it was dark. Something cold and metallic was clamped around my neck, but my head hurt too much to try to move to feel it.

"Aurelia," I heard the voice say. It was a voice I knew, and loved. "Aurelia, wake up, my love."

I opened my eyes to darkness no different from when they were closed, but a figure bent over me whose face was so dear and well known to me there was no mistaking it, even when I could only make out its edges in the blackness.

"Aspen," I rasped, my throat raw and sore. I tried swallowing, but it was painful, and the metal cuff around my neck made it even harder.

He held a cup to my lips and I drank greedily, coughing and spluttering as I took too much too fast. "Easy," he said, lowering my head, which he must have been holding up, gently to the ground.

I reached up to touch his face, his soft hair. He gripped my hand with his, and I knew whatever this was, it was no dream. "Where are we?" I croaked. It was cold, although not as cold as the woods had been, but when I tried to access my fire I was met by that empty hollow pit of nothing. The band around my neck must have been made of iron.

"The dungeon of the unseelie palace," Aspen said quietly. He had a band around his neck too, I noticed, and his face felt swollen to my fingers, although I couldn't see anything to be sure. "You've been out for two days. I'm fairly sure that blow would have killed a human. There was a lot of blood."

He gripped my hand hard, as if afraid I might not have woken. I touched my head gingerly with the other hand and winced. It should have healed if it was a two-day-old wound, but I supposed the iron was slowing down my rapid fae healing as well as killing my magic.

"Did they get you too?" I asked, feeling Aspen's swollen cheek under my hand.

"Not as bad as you," he said. "I was more ready to fight after they took you down. They didn't make it easy though, and there wasn't much I could do once they had you at knife point. I was afraid they would slit your throat and I wouldn't be able to stop them. As soon as we got here, they put the damn collars on."

I felt gingerly around the collar at his neck for a lock or mechanism or anything that could release the collar. It was simple in design—just a hinged band of iron held together at the back by a padlock. I cursed, wishing for one of Knox's ice picks right now.

"Seline and Vanth?" I asked, remembering we had left our friends in the shelter while investigating a sound.

"Not here," Aspen rasped back. "I'm hoping they made it to the Seelie court and told Ember what happened. If they assume we were taken by the Unseelie King, they can hopefully come up with a way to get us out of this."

"I wouldn't be so sure," said an oily voice from the dark hall outside the cell we were in. A lock clicked open and a fae male accompanied by an unseelie guard in spiked black armor stood in the silhouette of the door frame. Aspen growled.

"Always a pleasure, Lord Aspen," Thorn said dismissively, keeping his distance from us despite the iron collars. "What luck that the king's forces were able to retrieve you after your little friends aided in your escape. Now you can return what you have stolen from me."

"I was never yours," I spat at him, a gesture that lacked a certain bite when I was too dizzy and weak to sit up properly.

Thorn tsked and dared an additional step into the room. "Under unseelie law, you are mine by marriage," Thorn said condescendingly. I ground my teeth and Aspen squeezed my hand until I was near the point of pain. "And since we are in unseelie territory, the king has already agreed to return you to my custody, once this charade is done."

"What charade?" I gritted out, unsure whether or not I should be entertaining this by speaking to him.

"Oh, I shan't ruin the surprise," Thorn said, far too gleefully for my comfort. "Enjoy your last hours together with my wife, Lord Aspen." Aspen lunged for him, but the collar around his neck was bolted to the wall.

Thorn laughed as Aspen attempted to reach him, tutting again. "Desperation doesn't suit you, Aspen," Thorn said, looking at me and licking his lips. I shuddered in revulsion and Aspen tried to lunge again to no avail. Thorn left laughing mercilessly, and the door slammed shut with a deafening thunk.

"I swear to all the gods and goddesses, Aurelia," Aspen growled as he returned to my side and took my hand again. "I will wring his miserable head from his neck." I squeezed Aspen's hand as he stroked my hair gently.

"Not if I do it first," I croaked.

TIME PASSED SO SLOWLY in the dark that I wasn't sure it was passing at all. Aspen stayed with me, stroking my hair and my face as I felt the wound in my head knit back together too slowly under the influence of the iron cuff. I think I dozed off some of the time, but I always woke up with Aspen's hands on my face or in my hair or holding my hand.

"He's going to kill us, isn't he?" I said during one stretch of interminable nothingness. I wished I could feel the bond between us tugging, but I felt nothing from Aspen as he replied.

"He's going to kill me," he said, sighing. "You'll be turned over to Thorn. And then you have to kill him for me, Aurelia."

My throat tightened at the idea of Aspen being killed in front of me, and I resolutely refused to accept it. "I should have killed him when I left his house on fire," I said bitterly, regretting that I'd let him get the upper hand on me. "If I had, none of this would have happened."

"It's not your fault," Aspen said, leaning his head back on the wall behind him. "You should never apologize for not killing."

"That was my job," I said darkly, still feeling the bitter pang of regret. Aspen squeezed my hand, unable to think of something to say to that. He knew it had been my job, and I strongly suspected he wished I had killed Thorn when I'd had the chance.

"Someone will come for us," I whispered, belying the tear that trickled down my cheek. "Vanth and Seline got out. They can get to Hadrian."

"I hope so," Aspen said gently. "But if this is all the time we have, then I will spend every waking second of it holding you." I turned my face into his hand as he lay next to me on the ground, wrapping his arms around me as I cried quietly. I didn't like to cry in front of him. I liked to go out and assassinate my problems head-on. But with the iron collar keeping me weak and Aspen powerless, I felt like that version of me may not ever make it out of this castle.

What would the Commander say, seeing me lying here and giving up?

"Tears are for the weak and hopeless, Aurelia," she had said to me once after I had failed a mission and nearly been killed in the process. "Hone your terror into a blade to strike your enemies down."

I took a shuddering breath, then another, and felt myself calm. I would become a blade for Aspen like I was for Ember. I would turn this terror into a weapon to protect the male I loved. And anyone who dared to take him from me would feel its razor-sharp edge.

"Help me think," I said, pushing back the panic and trying to clear my head. "Why would Rourke be working with the Unseelie King? What could be his motive for poisoning the land?"

"Power," suggested Aspen, shrugging next to me. "Maybe he wished to become king so badly he had to undermine his father with a crisis. Have the council replace him."

"That makes sense," I said, frowning. "But Rourke never struck me as power hungry."

"We didn't know him at all," Aspen said, wrapping an arm around me.

I nodded, still trying to puzzle the whole thing out.

Chapter 28: Aurelia

AFTER WHAT COULD HAVE been hours or days—it was impossible to tell in the unending darkness of the dungeon—we were hauled before the Unseelie King.

I had never been in this part of the unseelie palace, but Ember had described the throne room to me enough from her time here that I wasn't surprised by what I saw. The room was cold, barely warmed by the fireplaces that lined the walls, the symbol of the two-headed raven carved above them. Unseelie lords and ladies, and some Seelie nobles, I realized, lined the hall and watched our progression toward the great spiked throne on the dais at its end.

Aspen and I were marched forward, necks still banded in iron and wrists bound with rope. Thorn was standing smugly near the dais, looking at me with evil intent. I had a feeling that I wouldn't last long as his wife if I were sent with him. If my choices were to die at his hands or the Unseelie King's, I thought I would choose the king.

"What a pleasant surprise, to find the Lord of Spring and the Lady of Summer in my humble court," mocked the king as we approached. Aspen's face was still bruised and swollen, and I'm sure I looked no better as the iron slowed our healing to human speeds. Despite this, I plastered my most haughty mask to my face and looked disdainfully at the king.

"Your hospitality is lacking, Your Majesty," I said, mustering all the bite I could. The king laughed, a cold horrible sound. He was ancient and gruesome, and I could barely make out his eyes in his wrinkled face. Oily shadows writhed around him, sending bolts of disgust through me.

"I hear you have a fiery tongue to go with that gift of yours," the king said, waving someone forward from behind him. Thorn stepped toward the king, bowing magnanimously.

"Lord Thorn," said the king. "You still wish to claim this female as your bride?"

"I do, Your Majesty," Thorn said, stepping forward with a look of pompous importance.

The king made a show of considering this, a wicked grin spreading across his ancient face. I noticed a two-headed raven land on the throne behind him. It squawked loudly, seeming to communicate something with the king.

He laughed. "It seems she is claimed by another," the king said, gesturing toward Aspen. Had that demon bird told him of our mating bond? Could the raven see it?

"She was mine first, by law," spat Thorn.

"Hmm," said the king, still play-acting for his court. "What to do. One male claims to be her legal husband, another her mate." He clapped his hands gleefully. "I have a solution. What I should do is send your heads to my upstart daughter-in-law, but it's been terribly dull here of late, so I'll offer you a bargain. You can provide tonight's entertainment by fighting for the lady."

Thorn visibly paled. "My King, it is not a fair fight," Thorn said, indicating the collar around Aspen's neck. "It would not be sportsmanlike for me to kill him while he is imprisoned."

"I will gladly accept the challenge," Aspen rumbled, staring at Thorn with a murderous intent that made me a little frightened. "Just give me a weapon." I felt my stomach clench as I saw the wicked gleam in the king's eye. Aspen was strong and fast, but not when he had been held prisoner for several days.

"No," I said, stepping forward to face the king. Aspen squeezed my hand, trying to pull me back. I shook him off. "I request the right to fight for my freedom," I said, shooting Thorn a death glare as the old iron wound in my side gave a phantom pang. "I owe him a death."

"Brilliant ideas all around," said the king, waving to a guard, who nodded and went to retrieve something. "The lady will fight for her own honor. Both of you will be armed, and both of you will be chained as you fight to the death."

"No," Aspen shouted as the guard returned and produced a second iron cuff and two iron daggers. My stomach hollowed out, both in fear for my life and fear for what Aspen might do if I died.

"I can do this," I told him, placing a kiss on his lips as a guard dragged me forward.

Thorn spluttered and protested as two of the king's guards held his arms and snapped the collar around his neck, locking it in place. "My King, this hardly seems right," Thorn cried, trying again to change the terms of the bargain. "If I kill my bride, what prize do I earn?"

The king looked thoughtfully at me for a moment as I took the iron dagger I had been handed and the chain was removed from my collar.

"We do need terms," the king agreed. "If the lady wins, she and her mate may live one more day." I nodded. "If she dies," the king continued, nodding to Thorn, "then you may kill Lord Aspen."

Thorn attempted a sneer, still pale as he faced me across the aisle in front of the king. He knew as well as I did that there was no getting out of this. One of us would have to die.

"Begin," the king commanded.

Thorn lunged, overconfident because of his previous victory against me. I dodged lithely and spun, trying to catch Thorn around the back. Despite his lack of muscle, Thorn was fast, and he lunged with the desperation of a male who knew the alternative was death.

The unseelie fae in the crowd cheered and jeered, exchanging money and insults as they placed bets on the outcome of the fight. The Seelie seemed more reserved. I started as I realized that I recognized one of them: Aspen's father was in the crowd, watching stone-faced.

Thorn lunged again and I dodged, catching him on the back of the skull with the blunt end of my dagger and causing him to stagger forward. I tried to stab my blade into his heart, but he jumped out of the way.

"You failed to kill me once, wife," Thorn spat, glaring at me with hatred. "What makes you think you can kill me now?" He swiped at my ribs and I darted back.

"I am not your wife," I growled, lunging after him and missing as he dodged. "And it's you who failed to kill me."

"What shall I do with your precious lord when you are dead?" he spat, circling me with more calm than I expected. "Maybe I'll carve out his heart and feed it to my dogs."

"You will not touch him," I snarled, dodging his attack and using the momentum to spin around him and grab a fistful of his hair. He cried out, and I twisted, holding his neck firmly as I pressed the blade to his throat above the iron collar. A drop of blood welled at the top of my blade. "And you will never touch me again." With one clean swipe, I dragged the knife across his throat, letting hot blood spill over my hands.

I let Thorn fall, blood gurgling from the wound as he took his final breath. The court was silent as they were forced to watch the male die. Lines of black corruption spread above his collar and up his face, moving more quickly than they had for me or Hadrian when we were wounded, probably due to the iron band around his neck.

The king clapped slowly, standing, and the crowd erupted into cheers and boos and jibes as winnings and losses were calculated and collected. I glanced over and saw Aspen's father still looking on. He nodded to me with faint approval.

"Well done, Lady of Summer," said the king, signaling his guards to take the body and secure my hands again. "You are a fiery pet indeed. You and your mate may live for one more day."

He waved us away and we were shackled and marched back through the crowd of jeering onlookers. Blood dripped from my fingers, and I saw Aspen clench his hands tightly as if he had been the one to make the fatal blow.

Killing was never easy, even when borne of hatred, and I knew it would have haunted Aspen, no matter that it wouldn't really have been his choice. Better for me to bear that burden, having already placed several souls on my conscience.

"Are you hurt?" Aspen asked softly when we were back in our cell, taking my cheek in his hand and examining my face. I shook my head. "That was damned foolish," he continued, a little harder this time. "Don't ever put yourself in danger like that again, Aurelia."

I looked up into his eyes, which glittered in the darkness. "You can't command me, my love," I said, taking his hand in mine and lowering it from my face. "And I had a debt to repay."

"Did Thorn touch you?" he growled. When I didn't reply, he added, "I heard what you said to him. At the end."

"He tried," I said, words clipped at the memory of my arrival at Thorn's manor when he had tried to force his tongue down my throat and I had pushed him away, trying to hide my revulsion with false timidity. He lost interest in me after that, essentially rendering me useless as a spy.

Aspen growled and I placed my hands on his face to soothe him. "He didn't do anything," I said, "but I owed him for the stabbing anyway."

"Is it wrong that watching you kill him turned me on a little?" Aspen asked pressing his lips to mine in a bruising kiss. I laughed when he let me go.

"Almost certainly," I said, running my hands across his iron collar and turning my attention to our escape. "We need to use our time to figure out how to get out of these," I said, brushing my iron collar with my fingertips. The metal bit into my skin, and I knew my throat would be red and raw when I finally got it off. "Will your father help us?"

Aspen scoffed. "Not likely," he said, pressing his forehead to mine. "Did you see him?" I nodded, and Aspen sighed deeply. "His loyalty lies with whoever can provide him with the most power. Right now that's not me."

"Ember will come for us," I said resolutely. I had to believe it was true, even if the chances were small. "She and Hadrian are stronger together than the Unseelie King. They won't leave us to our deaths."

"If they don't come..." Aspen said seriously, lifting his forehead from mine and cupping my face in his hand. "If that monster gives you a choice, you save yourself. You let me go and you find a way to get out." I shook my head, the idea of leaving him to die so unthinkable I couldn't even process the request.

"Promise me," Aspen said firmly. "Promise that if he makes you choose, you save yourself and let me go."

"Why are you asking this?" I said, a tear running down my cheek as he forced me to hold his gaze and agree to this awful request. "You know I can't."

"Because watching you die will kill me," Aspen said, brushing my cheeks with his thumbs. "But knowing you have a chance will make my death worthwhile."

I shook my head, refusing to make such a promise to him. I knew deep in my heart that if Aspen died tomorrow, I would too. Maybe not physically, but my soul would never recover from the loss.

We sat like that for several hours, holding each other until I lost track of time and fell asleep.

Chapter 29: Aurelia

In the darkness, I thought I heard someone whispering. I sat up and looked at Aspen, who was asleep. A pale face appeared at the door to the cell, then disappeared as a key clicked in the lock. I nudged Aspen, who woke with a start as the cell door swung open.

"I swear to the Goddess, boy, you make one bad decision after another," came the voice of an older male from the shadows of the door. A cloaked figure walked forward, stopping before us as we scrambled to stand. "Are you greatly injured?"

"Who are you?" I whispered, still struggling to identify the voice of the male, which was somehow familiar. Aspen grabbed my hand and squeezed.

"Father," he said coldly. A jolt of shock ran through me as I finally recognized Aspen's father. "Are you here to gloat?"

"Gloat that my only son and heir is now a prisoner and likely to be killed tomorrow?" his father asked, laughing humorlessly. "Not likely."

"Then why are you here?" Aspen said coldly, pushing me back behind him slightly.

"I'm here to help you," his father replied with a sigh.

"You've never helped anyone a day in your life," Aspen replied caustically. "You didn't even help my mother when the king came for her."

"You know nothing about your mother," his father hissed. I frowned, sensing anguish in him I hadn't heard before. "I've had to make difficult choices in my life, boy, and I made them for you."

Aspen scoffed, and his father smacked him across the face. I growled, trying and failing to fill my hands with flame, the iron collar still dampening my magic.

"It was your mother or you," Aspen's father growled, looking murderously at his son. "She made the choice. She wanted you spared." While I hated this male, I suddenly understood some of his displeasure for his son. If he blamed Aspen for losing his wife, it's no wonder their relationship was complicated.

"How can you help us?" I asked warily. I had known Aspen's father a long time, and based on what Aspen and Ember had told me, he never did anything unless he could gain from it. Still, he sounded genuinely concerned.

"I can get you out of those collars, but not until tomorrow night," he said. "After that, you'll have to get out of the castle on your own."

"What do you want in exchange?" Aspen said suspiciously. "Why help us?"

"Because I made a promise to your mother that I'd keep you alive," his father bit out. "And I intend to keep that promise." Aspen blinked at this new information, and his father continued. "If I help you, I want a full pardon from your cousin," he said. "She's the queen now, and I want the respect my rank deserves."

"Not finding life in the Unseelie Realm to your taste anymore?" Aspen asked, voice shaking with suppressed fury and shock. I squeezed his hand in comfort.

His father laughed coldly again. "The king's power is waning," he said, sounding disgusted. "There are rumors that he is dying. He will be unlikely to defeat your Queen and his son in battle if it comes to it. I intend to be on the winning side when this war occurs."

"And you would get us out, in exchange for Ember's pardon?" Aspen said quietly, squeezing my hand as he thought through his father's plan. My eyes narrowed on the male who sired my beloved, trying to work out his character. He seemed to be both incredibly loyal to his late wife, and unbelievably self-serving at the same time.

"I said I would try," his father corrected. "I can promise nothing. I also want my manor back."

"Fine," Aspen said. "I don't want it anyway."

His father sneered. "I'm doing this so that our family position remains," he said. "Have you no honor or pride in your family name?"

"I do," Aspen said, grasping my hand and bringing it to his lips for a kiss. "Just not yours."

His father chuckled darkly. "Be ready tomorrow," he said, sweeping from the room.

THE DAY PASSED INTERMINABLY once again. At one point I heard faint screams coming from somewhere else in the dungeon, and I huddled close to Aspen, hoping it was no one we knew being tortured.

We were brought before the king for a second time, the room and guests seeming identical as they had on our first visit. I noticed a slight thickening of the shadows in one corner, and felt hopeful that Hadrian was watching.

"My guests," said the king, holding out his arms in a mockery of welcome. "You are just in time for tonight's entertainment."

We were pushed forward by the guards until both of us were on our knees before the king.

"A rather interesting development has occurred," said the king, staring at us beadily from his tiny black eyes. The king waved someone forward, and Aspen's father was dragged by two guards in front of the dais. He was bloodied and beaten, and my heart sank. I knew whose screams had plagued us all day. I glanced at Aspen, and his face was ashen.

"My loyal servant here was found skulking around the dungeons," the king said, gesturing to Aspen's father, who sneered faintly, spitting blood into the carpet.

"This is a mistake, Sire," cried Aspen's father, desperation lacing his words. "I swear."

"Silence," said the king, sending his oily shadows to bind Aspen's father. "You will be tried by combat for your guilt," the king continued. "And I have found the perfect person to execute your judgment."

"Lord of Spring," the king said, turning to Aspen with a malicious gleam. "I offer you a new choice tonight since your lady fought on your behalf last night. You may execute your father for his crimes against me, or you may sacrifice yourself in his stead."

The king held out an iron dagger as Aspen was pushed forward by the guards.

Aspen took the dagger and turned toward his father, who was pale and shaking. Nausea roiled in my gut. Aspen was going to have to take a life, and it would torment him.

"Well, boy," spat his father, "is this how it ends?"

"It is," said Aspen, seemingly emotionless as he stared at his father. Aspen didn't move, and the king began to grow impatient.

"Choose now, young lord, or I will make the choice for you," he said, snapping his fingers and having the guards lift me and put a blade to my throat. I let out a muffled shout as Aspen turned to me, eyes wide.

"Yes, save your whore, boy," spat Aspen's father. "You always did think with the wrong head."

Aspen turned back to him, eyes wide with shock.

"You don't have it in you to kill me," his father continued, goading him, I realized. With a glance at me, his father continued. "I always knew you were weak. Useless," he spat. "You'll die a coward, just like your mother."

With a roar, Aspen plunged the dagger into his father's heart. Blood covered his hands and dribbled from the lord's mouth as he said something, so quiet only Aspen could hear it.

The room was silent as he died. Aspen breathed heavily, blood dripping from the blade where he had pushed the dagger home.

The king rose, clapping slowly as he had done the previous night, and the crowd broke out into a smattering of applause and murmuring. "Well done, young lord," he said, snapping his fingers in my direction. The guards released me. "You have earned one more day for you and your mate. Tomorrow you will not be so lucky."

With a wave, the king dismissed us. I was pushed back down the hall as several guards dragged the body of Aspen's father away from the throne room. Aspen was silent, his gaze steely as he stared straight ahead.

We didn't speak until we were back in our cell, hands unbound but collars still in place. Aspen sat heavily against the wall, head between his knees.

"Aspen," I rasped, feeling like I didn't have the words to properly express what had just happened. "Aspen, I'm so sorry."

He didn't say anything, just shook his head numbly as if in shock. I knelt before him and wrapped my arms around him. He was trembling slightly.

"I'm so sorry," I whispered again, pressing my forehead to his neck. Aspen broke, sobs wracking his body as he grieved what he had just done. His hands were still bloody as he wrapped his arms around me, but I didn't care.

"I've never killed another," Aspen whispered hoarsely as he held me.

"I know," I said sadly, understanding exactly how he felt; relief and remorse and terrible grief all wrapped up together.

"I didn't have a choice," he said, feeling the need to justify himself. I put my hand on his cheek.

"I know, Aspen," I said, drawing his eyes up to meet mine. "The king would have killed you if you hadn't agreed." Aspen nodded, but I knew my reassurance would not be enough to mend the emptiness left by delivering a fatal blow. Only time could do that.

"I'm sorry," he croaked, gripping my hand tightly. "For judging you before. When you did this for the resistance." A part of me I hadn't known was still broken began to mend at his words.

"You bought us a day," I replied, brushing my lips gently against his.

"Am I a monster now?" he asked me hoarsely when some of the anguish had subsided. I cupped his face in my hands and shook my head.

"No, my love," I said. "You were protecting me. Protecting us."

"He was my father," Aspen rasped. "And I killed him."

"I know," I said, resting my forehead against his. "But in the end, he wanted you to live, I think. That's why he said such horrible things. To make you do it."

We sat there in the dark and the silence for a long time until I finally had the courage to ask him the question I had been waiting to voice.

"What did he say to you?" I whispered.

Aspen looked at me, face pale and almost impossible to make out in the darkness of the dungeon. "Protect your family."

Chapter 30: Aurelia

FOR THE THIRD TIME, we were hauled before the king and the unseelie court. Tonight there were no jeers or laughing. There was a tension in the room as if the unseelie nobility realized that any of them could be part of tonight's entertainment.

Aspen and I already knew that there would be no more reprieves. The king's patience undoubtedly grew thin, and he would want to send a message to Ember and Hadrian for defying him.

We knew that tonight was likely the last chance our friends would have to come for us.

When we arrived in the throne room, my stomach dropped. Rourke bowed before the Unseelie King, a contingent of dwarven guards flanking him.

"Ah, my guests," said the king, gesturing to us as we were pushed forward. "We have a mutual friend here now, as you see. King Rourke claims that you escaped from him recently, and would like to have you back."

I looked at Rourke, whose face was as impassive as ever.

"But since you are such great friends with my daughter-in-law," the king drawled lazily as we were brought before the dais, "and my errant son, I would be remiss to neglect to ask for your help with their wedding gift." He smiled wickedly as the raven alighted on his shoulder. The guards behind us pushed us down roughly until we were kneeling before him.

"I think your heads in boxes might do," said the king, waving forward an unseelie male in forbidding black spikes carrying a heavy iron ax. The male's features were hidden by the spiked black helm, but menace poured off him as he strode toward us and stopped next to the king. I saw Rourke stiffen out of the corner of my eye.

"That is not what was agreed upon," Rourke said stiffly. My heart sank. Of course, he had been working with the Unseelie King.

"So that's how you did it?" I asked Rourke, throwing caution to the wind. If I was to die, I wanted answers to my questions, rather than letting them plague me in the hereafter. I also hoped that if I could keep him talking, Hadrian would have more time to intervene.

"Did what?" asked the king lazily, swirling a goblet of wine in his hand.

"Poisoned the Dwarven Realm," I said. "We know it was unseelie magic. You gave it to him?"

The king smiled maliciously. "What a mind you have, pretty pet, to be asking such things as you are about to die," he said. "When the Dwarven King asked for my blood in exchange for iron weapons, I gladly accepted. Now his son comes requesting a new bargain. I find I'm tired of all dwarves."

I frowned, confused by his meaning. Did he mean Holvard had asked for his blood—or Rourke?

"It was King Holvard," I said, seeing Rourke nod subtly next to the king. "He planned the blight, not Rourke," I said, finally letting the pieces slide into place. "He used the Unseelie King's blood to blight the land."

"I told you," Rourke growled, "that his time of poisoning my realm was done." In a move far faster than I thought possible, Rourke had his warhammer in his hands, swinging at the unseelie guards protecting the king. At the same time, our would-be executioner swung his ax, taking down the guards next to us, and pulled up his visor.

"Time to run," shouted Vanth, swinging the ax around again as the guard behind us unlocked our collars. I turned and saw pale blue skin and dark blue hair.

"Knox," I breathed, smiling for the first time in days as all hell broke loose in the throne room. Unseelie fae turned on each other, and dwarven guards surged forward in a mass of warhammers and iron shields. Darkness spilled from a corner of the room as Hadrian appeared, roaring in rage at his father. Light exploded next to him as Ember appeared, holding out her hands to push the king's darkness back.

"Get them out," she shouted, and I felt another hand grab mine and pull me along the room.

"Seline!" I gasped. "How are you all here?"

"Less talking, more running," she shouted, whisking me into shadow and re-emerging at the end of the throne room, then re-turning the same way with Aspen. We ran, shooting vines and fire and darkness and light in all directions as we fought our way out of the throne room and into the freezing night. I shot a column of fire behind me, smirking in triumph as I took down several of the king's guards. I might like this even more than my daggers.

A flock of rocs descended upon us as we emerged from the castle. Notus squawked happily as he recognized us, landing heavily amid the chaos.

"We have to go," said Seline, jumping onto Notus's back and pulling us up after her.

"What about the others?" I panted as Notus launched us into the sky. He turned south and began flying at breakneck speed away from the unseelie palace.

"They'll meet us," Seline shouted back, holding on for dear life as Notus swooped out of the way of a volley of fiery arrows that trailed after him. A mighty explosion rocked the night, and I looked back to see darkness and light pouring from the windows of the castle as Hadrian and Ember battled his father.

"We need to help," I shouted, tapping Seline on the shoulder. She just shook her head as we kept flying.

Soon we were out of reach of the castle and over the border between the realms. I felt weak and nauseated as I dismounted, and I wondered if there might be some truth to Mother Vervain's superstitions about tea.

We landed on the border of a forest and Notus flapped off with a squawk, presumably to hunt.

Hadrian appeared suddenly, Ember in his arms. "Be right back," he said as he disappeared again. I threw my arms around Ember as she ran toward me.

"You came for us," I choked out through tears of relief and terror.

"Always," she replied, patting my back and opening an arm for Aspen.

Hadrian reappeared a moment later with Vanth, who ran toward Seline before remembering himself and slowing his pace to a less frantic stroll.

"You alright?" he asked her gruffly. She nodded, saying nothing as he looked at her. My heart leaped a little for them.

"Where are Knox and Rourke?" Aspen asked. "And all the others?" There had been at least twenty dwarves and unseelie fighting on our side, and while Hadrian was powerful, I knew he couldn't shadowwalk that many back to the Seelie palace.

"They got out on the rocs," he said, panting with the strain of moving us all so far. "Looks like we have our aerial cavalry now."

"The king?" I asked. "Did you kill him?"

Hadrian looked darkly at Ember, then back at me, and shook his head. "No," he said. "He sensed me coming in time to shield himself. I think he knows I will kill him if he faces me openly."

"Let's discuss it at home," Ember said, placing a hand on his arm.

"I'll need to borrow a lot of power," Hadrian said, looking at Ember. "I'm almost drained."

She nodded and grabbed my hand. I reached out for Aspen and held on tight as Hadrian swept us all into shadow.

HADRIAN COULDN'T GET US all to the palace in a single jump, and it took almost three hours with Ember lending him most of her power. When we finally arrived in the kitchen of the Seelie Palace, both were drained and breathing hard, Ember looking whiter than usual in the pale light of dawn.

Mother Vervain was there, pouring tea into flowery cups as if expecting us for a party rather than as refugees from a terrifying ordeal.

"Ah, there you all are," she said placidly, her weathered voice making her sound frailer than I knew she was. She shucked the shawls up around her shoulders and smiled. "Tea is ready. You should never travel the realms without it."

She pushed us all into seats and stools around the hearth, plying us with various teas based on whether we were Seelie or unseelie. I felt like this was a superstitious practice, but Ember swore by the power of Mother Vervain's teas, so I drank mine without complaint.

We sat in stunned silence, drinking our tea and feeling rather nauseated after shadowwalking so far.

"Well," she said briskly, looking around the room at us. "You all look terrible." I choked on my tea and looked around, realizing she was right.

Ember and Hadrian looked pale and drained, having used all of their magic to get us back. Vanth was covered in a sheen of blood from his fight with the guards, and Seline had a gash in her side from a knife she must have taken in the ribs while getting us out. It wasn't an iron injury, but it looked painful. Aspen was pale and thin, but finally healing with the iron band removed.

Ember set to work ordering us all around. She sent Seline to get stitched up by one of the apprentices, despite Seline's protests that she was fine. She sent Vanth away to get cleaned up, promising he could come and keep Seline company after he was no longer drenched in blood.

She turned to me and Aspen next, pinning us with a critical glare. "Food and rest," she said. "We will explain everything later."

I opened my mouth to protest, but Hadrian cut in, his shadows leaking out in his exhaustion.

"I promise, it will all make sense soon," he said, "but Ember is right. Tomorrow you will debrief us about your time in the Dwarven Realm, but today you need time to recover."

Ember cast Hadrian a grateful look and he smiled at her tiredly.

The little flutter of jealousy I always felt looking at them reared its head, then settled back down as Aspen placed a hand on my shoulder and murmured in my ear. "Come to bed, Aurelia."

I sighed, letting him lead me away to my room in the palace.

"Mine, not yours?" I asked as he opened the door. Everything was as I had left it, and I sighed, feeling suddenly that my life was too big and too different to fit into this room again.

Aspen rested his chin on the top of my head. "My room here is just a soldier's barracks," he said teasingly, "but if you prefer a rock-hard cot, I'm happy to take you there."

"Hmm," I said, pretending to think about the offer. "Will there be other rock-hard things there?"

Aspen barked a laugh and turned me to face him, kissing me soundly. "Tonight, no," he said tiredly. "But tomorrow," he promised, kissing me again. "Tomorrow, you may have whatever you want."

Chapter 31: Aurelia

I WOKE UP IN my bed for the first time in what felt like years, even though it was only a few weeks. Aspen was next to me, chest bare and golden in the wintry morning light, his curls adorably tousled as he slept.

I curled into him, resting my head on his shoulder and stroking a hand over his chest.

"Why are you awake," he groaned, throwing an arm over his eyes to block out the light.

I chuckled. "Because it's morning," I said quietly, sitting up a little and kissing his chest, moving across him in a lazy arc.

He lowered his arm and looked at me skeptically. "Ugh," he said, making a noise that I couldn't replicate if I tried. "Why is your room so pink?"

"Ember decorated it," I said, still kissing across his chest. I lifted my hands to stroke where I had kissed and he tangled his fingers in my loose hair. "Why have you been staying in the barracks here instead of a proper room?"

"Because I didn't want to be tempted to come to you in the middle of the night," he said seriously, scratching my scalp gently with his fingers. "But today we are asking for a bigger room. A less pink one."

"We?" I asked coyly, quirking a brow at him.

"Yes, we," he said forcefully, wrapping his arms around me and flipping me so I was beneath him. I squeaked in protest but stopped when he began to kiss my neck, the place behind my ear, my collarbones.

"It's a good plan," I said, knocking a pink ruffled throw pillow off the bed as I shifted to give him better access to me.

He chuckled, moving further down to my breasts and gently licking until my nipples peaked beneath him. "I did say you could have whatever you wanted today," he said, still kissing his way around each breast without touching the most sensitive part. I wove my fingers through his curls in pleasure at his touch. "So tell me," he continued, gently flicking each nipple with his tongue. I gasped. "What is it you want, my love?"

"Hmm," I sighed, reveling in the pleasure of his touch. "Something rock hard, I think."

He barked a laugh. "That can be arranged," he growled, sucking one nipple into his mouth gently, then the other. He kissed down my stomach, across the iron scar, and down my abdomen until he was positioned between my thighs. I held my breath a bit as he looked at me, something molten and heated in his gaze.

"How about we start with something softer?" he teased, leaning down and stroking his tongue over my center. I gasped, throwing my head back at the touch, and trying not to wriggle away from its intensity. He chuckled thickly and stroked again, beginning a steady circular rhythm with his tongue against my center.

I raked my nails over his scalp at the feel of him working me and moaned, not caring if anyone outside my room heard us at this point. I guessed that Seline had already told the others we were mated. Frankly, it was a miracle Ember hadn't come in here cheering yet.

"You taste like life," Aspen growled, still licking and sucking in that steady rhythm. "I could survive on this taste alone." I bucked a little, so aroused by his tongue and his words that I wanted more of him.

"Aspen," I breathed as he flicked his tongue inside me, stroking and thrusting with delicate sweeps. I gasped as he reached deeper than I thought he could, the sensations stoking something blazing hot in me. I struggled to tamp down my flames as he moved, his wicked tongue circling relentlessly, then flicking on that spot between my thighs that made me shudder.

"What does my mate wish?" he asked again huskily, looking up briefly, his eyes dark and wild.

"More," I breathed, and he growled as he inserted a finger into me and pumped gently, flicking that spot again with his tongue. I thrust my hips forward and he inserted a second finger, pumping me as I rode his hand, brazenly seeking my release.

"That's it," he said, pressing his free hand down on my abdomen to keep me in place as he worked. I moaned, the sensation both too much and not enough, and release shattered through me as he pumped, wringing every drop of pleasure from me that he could.

"I think I could do that every day," he said, pressing a kiss to my inner thigh, then my hip, and finally my stomach before resting his chin on my abdomen. "And never need anything else."

"Nothing?" I breathed, panting a little as I caught my breath from the peak he had just pushed me to. He kissed my stomach again, licking my navel and making me squawk in protest.

He laughed. "You sound like one of the rocs," he teased, kissing lower again until he was back and licking me again with that wicked, deadly tongue. I gasped at the sensation, still riding the wave of my previous release as he worked me up to a second.

I cried his name as I shattered a second time, and my breaking seemed to shatter his restraint as he growled and lifted himself above me, pushing my knees up and thrusting to the hilt. I kicked my head back in pleasure and a bit of pain as intense pressure filled me, and he stilled for a moment, letting me adjust. He was trembling with the restraint of holding himself still.

"Don't hold back," I breathed, hooking my legs around him and pulling him close. He growled, withdrawing slowly and pushing in again hard and fast, increasing his speed with every thrust of his hips. A third release shimmered through me as he crashed into me again and again. This was what I wanted, for now, and forever—just to be held and loved and claimed by this male for the rest of time.

He spilled into me with a roar that he muffled against my neck, clutching at my back as he pumped into me. I shuddered against him, at the feeling of being one with him, until he finally relaxed, lowering himself onto me and kissing my neck.

"I love you," he breathed, kissing and nipping at the sensitive flesh there as I stroked his back, legs still wrapped around his hips as he slowly pulled out of me.

I cupped his face and smiled at him. "I love you, too," I breathed.

He leaned down to kiss me, and I reveled in the taste of myself on him. "You are radiant," he said, lifting himself a little to look at me again. "A goddess. What did I ever do to deserve you?"

I kissed his lips gently, pouring my love and devotion into the embrace. "You were you," I replied.

As MUCH AS I wanted to just stay in bed with Aspen the rest of the day, I knew that eventually, we would need to find Ember and Hadrian and the others and begin unraveling the story of everything that had happened to us.

We showered together, and I moaned in pleasure as Aspen took me again against the wall, his desire from the morning still unsated as he claimed me fast and hard.

"I'm sorry," he said, breathing heavily against me as the hot water washed away the evidence of our lovemaking. "I meant to be gentle."

I laughed, still amused that Aspen thought I wanted him to be gentle with me. "I told you I wanted something rock hard, didn't I?" I teased. He kissed me, and I turned the water to cold lest he get any more ideas and delay us further.

It was nearing lunch by the time we finally made it downstairs, clean and somewhat presentable for the Queen and King of All Fae.

When we entered the sitting room, Ember and Hadrian broke apart guiltily, faces flushed and lips swollen. I smiled.

"See?" Aspen said teasingly, throwing an arm around my shoulders casually. "They wouldn't have minded if we had waited a bit longer." Ember blushed even more pink and Hadrian growled slightly, his shadows curling protectively around Ember's waist. Aspen put up his hands placatingly.

"Peace, cousin," he said, addressing Hadrian with a smirk as he led me to a sofa. "I just meant that I would have liked to spend time similarly with my mate." My heart did a little flip as Aspen referred to me as his mate in front of others for the first time. It had already been acknowledged, so I don't know why it affected me so, but something flowed happily within me at the way he called me his mate, and I beamed at Ember as she rushed to hug me.

"I knew you would be mates," she cried smugly as she attempted to strangle me with her love. I laughed, pushing her back a little and blushing at Aspen. He smiled indulgently and stretched his arms along the back of the sofa, crossing an ankle over a knee in such an Aspen-ish gesture that I laughed.

"Tell me everything," Ember said excitedly, sitting before me on an ottoman while Hadrian leaned against the mantelpiece.

"Wait for Vanth and Seline, my love," he said, looking at the door. "They should be here any second."

As if summoned by his will, Vanth and Seline strode through the doors glowering darkly as if they had been fighting. I frowned at Seline, but she smiled upon seeing me and embraced me almost as warmly as Ember.

"We were so worried when you went missing in the woods," she said, voice shakier than I was used to hearing it.

"I told you they'd be fine," Vanth said behind her, shooting me a grin.

"Being locked away and forced to kill by the Unseelie King is fine?" she asked, fury radiating from her small form as she whirled on Vanth.

"Whoa," Hadrian said, appearing between them as he shadowwalked across the room. "What's the matter, Seline?" He looked down at his sister, who was several decades older than him, in concern. She flashed a look to Vanth and deflated slightly.

"Nothing," she said, sitting next to Ember on the ottoman and turning her attention to me. Vanth and Hadrian exchanged a look, and I had a feeling I'd be hearing third-hand about whatever it was they were arguing over.

Ember looked at Seline with concern but turned back to me with a smile and sighed. "Well, I think you'd better start from when you left the palace," she said.

Aspen and I wove the tale as well as we could, discussing the flight to the Dwarven Realm, our first investigations of their fields, Thorn's arrival and the confinement of the unseelie, and the moment we thought Rourke had betrayed his father.

The others interjected with questions every so often, and we tried to fill in as many gaps as we could.

"So, Rourke is trustworthy?" I asked, still feeling a little confused by the events of the last few days. "It was Holvard blighting his own fields with the Unseelie King's blood?"

Ember nodded. "Rourke will explain his part better than I can, and your friend Knox, I think, was caught up in the intrigue much like you were," she said thoughtfully.

"What happened after we were captured?" I asked, looking at Vanth and Seline. They didn't meet each other's eyes, and Vanth eventually took up the tale when it became clear Seline wouldn't.

"We hunted for a full day before Rourke found us by roc," he said, sitting on a chair and leaning forward with his elbows on his knees. "Notus led him right to us, the traitorous vulture. At first,

I tried to gut the dwarf, but he finally convinced us he was there to help by offering to let the bird bring us back here with him in his beak."

"Did he?" I asked.

Vanth smiled darkly. "He did. It was very satisfying."

"Anyway," cut in Seline, frowning at Vanth, "Rourke convinced us, and we realized you must have been captured by unseelie forces. We had unknowingly crossed into unseelie territory, so Hadrian did reconnaissance and found out you were at the palace the night you killed Thorn."

"And good riddance," Vanth interjected.

"At that point, we knew we had to get you out," Ember said, "but it took time to get everyone in place, even with the rocs. Hadrian was ready to pull you out that day, but it would have been impossible with those iron bands, so we needed a way to get them off you first."

"We would have gotten you out no matter what," Hadrian said, looking seriously at me. "I'm sorry it took so long."

I shook my head. "It was brilliantly done," I said. Then I remembered the cost of our second night. "Except..."

"I heard," Ember said gently, putting a hand over Aspen's. "I am so sorry, Aspen. You know I had no love for your father, but I know in the end he wanted to protect you." Aspen nodded tightly.

We sat in silence for a minute, letting the events of the last few days wash over us. Ember insisted we all eat lunch, and then sent us to take a nap while she found a "more appropriate suite for a mated couple."

When we were back in my room I reached up on my toes to kiss Aspen gently. "It's alright for you to feel sad," I whispered, seeing the conflict on his face. "He was your father."

"I know," Aspen said tightly, sighing and dropping his forehead to mine. "I know. It's odd. I hated him most of my life, and in the end, he did the best thing he could have ever done for me."

"Save your life," I said, brushing the hair from his temple tenderly.

Aspen shook his head. "No," he said, cupping my cheek, his blue eyes blazing down at me. "He saved yours."

Chapter 32: Aurelia

I LEFT ASPEN TO take a nap in the afternoon and went to the infirmary to look for Mother Vervain. Something was still bothering me about the dream, and I wanted her opinion on it. I hoped Ember would go with me, but she was bustling around making arrangements for new sleeping quarters and the construction of a rookery, so I went alone.

Mother Vervain was sitting by the fire, knitting something pink and fluffy, the same thing she had been working on before we had left for the Dwarven Realm.

"It's about time, child. I was wondering when you'd get here," she said in her characteristic, all-knowing way. I sighed, sitting across from her as she continued to work.

"I suppose you already know why I'm here then?" I asked resignedly, taking a sip of the tea she had already made and left out for me. It had a bitter aftertaste, and I was about to ask her what she put in it when she tied off whatever she was knitting and put it aside.

"There are several things we should discuss, my dear," she said portentously, "but let's start with your dreams."

I smiled. "Well I suppose the dreams were about my magic," I said, sipping the bitter tea again. "The fire is sort of obvious. The snakes may have been related too. You said they were a symbol of rebirth. Maybe the rebirth of my powers?"

"And transformation," Mother Vervain added, sipping her own tea and looking at me over the rim. "I hear there are a lot of those going around."

I laughed, blushing a bit. "You mean me and Aspen?" I asked.

She shrugged noncommittally. "What else was in your dreams?" she asked, pulling a poker from the hearth next to her and beginning to sketch a little design in the ashes.

"Well," I said, frowning as I thought over the dreams. "Fire, obviously, and ash falling, but I assumed that was related to the fire. Sometimes one snake, but sometimes two, and there was also an element of earth each time, like a rockslide or vines of ivy. And in one..." I paused, swallowing as I remembered the vision of Aspen dead next to me. "In one, Aspen had been burned."

"Hmm," said Mother Vervain seriously, still sketching in the ashes. "Snakes for transformation and your celestial bond." She drew two squiggles in the ash that I assumed represented snakes. "Vines of ivy," she looked at me and smiled faintly, "for fidelity, devotion, and loyalty." She added some more squiggles, which I assumed were supposed to be ivy. "Earth is fertility and life," she added looking up briefly and away again as I frowned, "and ash is repentance. Redemption and forgiveness." She circled her drawing with the poker and admired it for a moment before scrubbing it away with her foot.

She looked at me then. "How is the tea?" she asked, catching me so off guard I blinked a few times in surprise before answering.

"It's fine," I said hesitantly. "A little bitter."

"Hmm," she said again. "Well does the dream seem to fit what you have experienced? A series of dreams of this complexity is almost certainly a sign from the Goddess you should heed."

I put down my teacup and considered it for a moment. "Well, my magic emerged, so that could be rebirth," I said, "and Aspen and I are obviously the ivy and the ashes. Redemption and for-giveness and fidelity all around I think."

"Very good," she said encouragingly as if waiting for me to come to some revelation.

I shook my head. "Other than Aspen's power, I'm not sure I understand the earth," I said. "I also had a dream about the seelie palace, rising from ashes, when we were trapped in the unseelie dungeons. Do you think that might mean we will be successful in our war? Or maybe our successful escape. And why did my magic take so long to emerge anyway?"

Mother Vervain sighed as if no one in the world was brilliant enough to understand her. "Dreams are often symbolic," she said, rocking in her chair. "But sometimes, they are just manifestations of our conscious anxieties." I nodded, not sure I actually understood what she was saying. "I think your magic waited until you were whole to use it," she continued. "And the tea is bitter because it's made with red raspberry leaf," she added, making me feel like I had conversational whiplash.

"Okay," I said. "It's not very nice."

Mother Vervain barked a laugh and smiled at me warmly. "It's not, you are correct," she said, wiping away a tear of mirth from the corner of her eye. "But it is very good for expectant mothers."

I paused with the teacup almost at my lips when what she had said registered with me. "What?" I whispered, putting the teacup down.

"Three cups a day will make sure the babe is born healthy," she said gently, reaching over and patting my hand. "And that you weather the labor with ease."

"I'm not," I started, furiously counting months in my head. "I can't be..."

I blanched.

"Never trust a male to mix his contraceptive tea correctly," Mother Vervain said, waggling a finger at me. "I'm sure your mate meant to do it correctly, but he certainly did not succeed."

Fae cycles happened only once or twice a year. My last had been twelve months ago. Nearly thirteen.

"My dear girl," said Mother Vervain kindly, reaching forward to pat my hand, "do not worry yourself. All will be well, and Ember and I will be here to assist with the birth. Aspen will be thrilled when you tell him."

From her small table, Mother Vervain picked up the pink fluffy thing and put it on my lap. I opened it with trembling fingers. It was a tiny hat.

"It's a girl," she said, beaming at me.

I REMAINED IN A state of partial shock for the rest of the day. Aspen kept shooting me concerned looks at dinner while Ember chatted away about the progress on the rookery, and Seline and Vanth discussed how to utilize an aerial cavalry with Hadrian. I begged fatigue and went to our new room, which Ember had picked out and furnished more quickly than I had ever known anyone to furnish a room.

There was a big, four-poster bed with creamy white blankets and a small sitting area with an elegant sofa and cozy hearth. A bathing chamber was attached, tiled in white marble and complete with all the amenities we could possibly need.

There was a large, floor-length mirror in one corner of the room, and I stood before it, flattening my hand over my belly. There was no evidence yet that I was with child, other than Mother Vervain's omniscient intuition and the lack of my cycle. Aspen entered behind me and I turned around guiltily, dropping my hand.

"Tell me what's wrong, Aurelia, and don't tell me it's nothing," he said, striding toward me purposefully and putting his hands on my shoulders. "Whatever it is, we will figure it out. Did I do something? Say something?"

The concern in his eyes cracked something in me, and tears welled up unbidden.

"My love, please," he said, getting to his knees before me, "tell me what I have done and I'll move the earth to fix it."

This proclamation had the opposite effect of the one I'm sure he wanted, and I cried even harder, dropping to my knees with him and burying my face in his shoulder. He held me, whispering soothing words and endearments and stroking my back until my sobs had quieted. I clung to him, afraid of the truth I was going to have to reveal, not because I didn't want it to be true, but because I was afraid he might not share my happiness.

"You made the tea wrong," I whispered, not certain how else to explain and latching on to the part of this that was definitely not my doing.

"I...what?" he said, holding me back a bit to look at my face. "What tea?"

"The contraceptive tea," I said, reaching into the pocket of my dress and pulling out the fluffy pink hat. I pressed it into his hands. "Mother Vervain thinks it's a girl."

Aspen stared down at the tiny pink ball as if he had been struck momentarily dumb. He looked up at me, and down at the hat, and up at me again. "I made the tea wrong," he said, comprehension alighting in his face.

I laughed at the ridiculousness of this announcement, and the laughing turned into more tears.

"Aurelia," he said, scooping me up into his arms and sitting with me on his lap on the bed. "Are you sure?"

"No," I sniffed, wiping my eyes. "But she is. And I'm late."

I risked looking up. Aspen was looking at me with wonder and adoration, not the shock and terror I feared he might have felt. I gave him a watery smile. He laughed—a joyful ecstatic sound—and kissed me, holding me tighter as he poured his joy into me through that kiss.

"My darling," he said, kissing my tear-streaked cheeks and my eyes and my nose. "My love." He pressed his forehead to mine. "You're not unhappy, are you?" he asked, lifting his face to study mine.

"No," I whispered. "I just wasn't sure what you would feel."

Aspen's face broke into a wide smile. "I am more happy than I could ever express to you in words," he rumbled, kissing me again, deep and plundering as he shared his relief and joy with me through our bond. He rested a hand on my still flat stomach and looked up at me, his eyes damp with emotion. "A girl?" he asked.

I nodded, laughing a little, and he kissed me again.

"Marry me," he breathed, breaking the kiss and looking at me seriously. "I know it's not a romantic proposal, and everyone has been asking and this isn't the right time, but please." He dropped his forehead to mine. "Be my wife, my partner, my mate. Mother of my beautiful girl. Keeper of my whole heart."

"Where will we live?" I asked, unable to focus on his much more important question. "And what will we do? I don't want to be an assassin anymore, and I don't want you to be a spy."

"We can live here or at the manor or wherever you want," Aspen said, brushing away the tears that fell down my cheek and punctuating each option with a kiss. "And we will do whatever you want. You can train rocs, or be a lady, or serve as a soldier for the resistance, or work in the infirmary, or be a mother. We don't need to have all the answers right now. We have the rest of our lives to figure all of that out." He smiled down at me, so much hope and joy in his face that I couldn't help but smile back.

"I love you and I want you and I choose you, Aurelia, for now and for the rest of my days," Aspen said seriously. "Please, my darling, tell me you're mine."

I smiled at the familiar request and kissed him again, imagining the future we might have now. I remembered the discussion I had with Knox back in the Dwarven Realm, about not feeling useful. But a tiny spark in me ignited at the idea that a whole new world of possibility was opening up to me, and part of it would include being a mother and Aspen's mate.

I looked up at Aspen and kissed him. "I'm yours."

Chapter 33: Aurelia

I WANTED TO TELL Ember before the dwarves arrived, but they came earlier than expected, and I had to keep the news to myself. Aspen was fairly bouncing on the balls of his feet in excitement, and Ember asked him three times if he was alright before I elbowed him in the side and told him he had to calm down.

Rourke had arrived, clasping arms with Vanth in a way that was far more friendly than I expected. Knox followed and jogged over to me, grinning and throwing his arms around me. Aspen did his best to restrain his growl, but he clasped my hand and kissed it very obviously when Knox released me. I rolled my eyes at the male marking his territory.

"I see he finally earned you," Knox said, nodding to Aspen somewhat coolly. "You don't deserve her," he added to Aspen. I was about to protest, but Aspen cut me off.

"I know," he said. "I don't. But I will work every day for the rest of my life to be worthy of her." Knox nodded and offered his forearm to Aspen, who clasped it. I rolled my eyes again. Fae males and their ridiculous posturing.

It took a while to get everyone settled and ready to hear the full story. Dwarves and unseelie fae flew in one after another until I counted ten rocs and forty bodies, including Bisera, who greeted me with a cool nod.

"Bisera," Aspen said, pulling me over to her despite my groan of protest. "I'm sorry for leading you on in the Dwarven Realm. I shouldn't have done it, and I apologize."

She raised a silver brow at him, glancing at me before looking back at him. "What?" she asked, seeming to genuinely not understand him.

He sighed in frustration. "You know, in the Dwarven Realm, you were very forward. I should not have reciprocated," he said, somewhat awkwardly.

"Oh, that," she said, waving a hand at him as if she had forgotten all about it. "Please, you're fine. I was only trying to make your lady jealous."

"What?" I hissed, fury rising in me. Aspen's sleeve caught fire and he yelped, patting it out and glaring at me. "Sorry," I added.

Bisera laughed and shrugged. "I thought if you saw your friend enjoying me, you might want to join in," she shrugged. Aspen stared in open-mouthed shock at her. She sighed and rolled her eyes. "I prefer females," she said, clearly and slowly as if to a child.

I laughed, relief and a little embarrassment cooling my anger. "I am happily taken, I'm afraid," I said.

Bisera shrugged. "Let me know if that ever changes," she said with a wink and a little wave. Aspen stared after her retreating form, and I suppressed a grin.

"I have so many ideas right now," he said. I poked him in the arm. "Ow," he said, frowning at me. "What?"

"You're about to be a father," I hissed at him, following the crowd of fae and dwarves who were gathering to debrief our rescue.

"I still have eyes," he murmured, earning another scowl from me. "Only for you, my love," he amended, giving me a playful peck on the cheek.

We gathered in Ember's private sitting room once all of Rourke's people had been settled. Ember and Hadrian took places near Rourke, and Aspen and I sat opposite, hands intertwined. Knox perched on the window sill while Vanth and Seline stood guard at the door. I still hadn't had a chance to talk to Seline about her argument with Vanth, and I made a note to make sure I cornered her later that day. The Commander joined us too, taking a position near Seline.

"King Rourke," said Ember formally. "Please explain for the benefit of our friends and allies how you came to overthrow your father and come to the aid of Lord Aspen and Lady Aurelia."

nodded stiffly and turned toward us. "I am sorry, my friends," he began, his gravelly voice lighter than the last time I had heard it. "If it is any consolation, you repaid me for my unwillingness to confide in you earlier with that avalanche you orchestrated." I felt a smug tug on our bond and poked Aspen in the ribs.

"Before I begin, Lord Aspen," Rourke said, turning to Aspen and holding out a tiny, empty glass vial. It was stained red with something that had been stored inside it. "Can you please confirm that this is the same magic you found in our blighted fields?"

Aspen took the tiny vial, unstopping it and sniffing. I saw him close his eyes so he could reach out with his magic, and he suddenly recoiled. "Yes," he said, handing the vial back to Rourke. "What is it?"

Rourke nodded in grim satisfaction. "Let me start at the beginning," he said, taking a sip of ale. "When the blight began, I traveled to many of our fields to hunt for the cause of the sickness. I know this is one of the many reasons you suspected me. I know now that Knox told you he suspected me as well." I nodded, glancing at Knox who blushed faintly, and Rourke took this as permission to continue.

"The locals all reported similar things. One day, the fields were fine, and the next day the blight began, with no obvious cause." He paused, taking another swig. "When you told me that the blight was the result of unseelie magic, I began to suspect the truth.

314

I knew that none of our unseelie friends had such magic, but I also knew that my father was a scholar. He knew of blood magic. He must have learned the effect of unseelie blood on our crops, or at least suspected it."

Rourke picked up the tiny vial again and shook it. "You have just confirmed for me now that I was correct," he said, placing the empty vial on the table. "We found many such vials in my father's study the night I was forced to kill him. I think it is likely he paid others to deliver and spread the poison, then had them arrested or killed."

"How exactly did you prove this to Ember?" I asked. "You didn't know for sure what the blood was."

Rourke nodded, pulling a stack of papers from his jacket and laying them out on the table. "I investigated the missing weapons when you told us about the iron shipments. I agreed with you that the two events must be connected," Rourke said, pulling a paper from the stack and passing it to me. "Only my father or I could have made so many weapons completely disappear without a trail of signatures, and I knew it wasn't me. So I did some digging."

"Your father just kept these damning papers lying around?" I asked, passing the paper to Aspen to examine. It was a trade agreement, signed in blood with the Unseelie King, detailing the exchange.

"No, of course not," Rourke said, taking the paper back from Aspen. "These took weeks to find. I didn't want to confide in you until I had enough evidence to be certain."

"Why do this?" Aspen asked. "Why poison the land and then call on our queen for help?"

"My father was a politician," Rourke explained. "The council had been discussing his abdication for almost a year before the blight started. I believe this was a ploy to stay in power, and seem like a hero, by calling you in to fix it. He must not have anticipated you would find out about the iron shipments."

"Why did you kill him? Why not make him stand trial?" I asked.

Rourke sighed sadly. "He forced my hand," he confessed. "He discovered me searching his rooms and tried to kill me. I had to kill him first. That was the night I detained you."

"You arrested us," I corrected accusingly. "You cuffed us in iron."

"I did," Rourke said, unapologetically. "I assumed if I did not, you would attack me with magic before asking questions or letting me explain. Would this not have been so?"

Thinking back on it, Rourke had never actually said anything to make us doubt him. We assumed he was guilty, but he never actually threatened us, except for Seline and Vanth, and remembering the husk of the dwarf Vanth had killed, I couldn't exactly blame him for that.

I nodded. "Fair enough," I said.

"I did not wish to kill him," Rourke said quietly. "He was still my father." I reached for Aspen's hand and gave it a small squeeze.

"What about Knox?" I asked. "He helped me pick the locks on the cuffs. He escaped with us."

"I did," Knox said, placing a hand on the back of his neck and frowning. "I also believed Rourke was guilty until he showed the remaining councilors his evidence. I helped you escape because..." He trailed off, looking at me meaningfully.

"Because we are friends," I finished for him. Aspen tensed, but Knox just nodded.

"Aye," Rourke said, frowning at Knox. "I couldn't tell anyone until I was sure the councilors were not complicit. My apologies, friend." Rourke held his arm out to Knox, who grasped it gratefully.

"Forgiven, My King," he said loyally.

"Anyway, to make an extremely long story short," finished Rourke, "I sent my evidence to your queen, relaying what had happened and asking her to shelter my people until I could fully explain the situation. I went looking for you in the mountains and found your friends alone. They told me they suspected that you had been taken."

"How did the Unseelie King know where we were?" I asked.

"Thorn," Aspen said, turning to Rourke. "I assume your father helped him escape?"

Rourke shrugged. "I assume, but I do not know," he replied. "Without the male to question, we are still missing some information. Do you know where he is?"

"Dead," I replied unemotionally.

nodded. "That is for the best then," he said.

"How did you even know we were taken?" I asked, turning to Vanth. My head was starting to pound with all of this new information I had to process.

"When we couldn't find you, we knew something had happened," Vanth said, shifting against the wall. "There were signs of a struggle and blood in the snow."

"Your king suspected where you might be and scouted the palace," Rourke said, nodding to Hadrian. "We thought that asking the Unseelie King to hand you over to me was unlikely to succeed, but we needed a way to get my forces into his palace either way to get you out."

I closed my eyes, rubbing my head and leaning back into Aspen.

He looked down at me with concern, patting my shoulder gently, then stood. "Aurelia needs to rest," he said, turning to Ember and Hadrian.

"Of course," said Ember, rising and coming to me with concern. She put a hand on my brow, feeling for fever. "Are you well?"

"I'm fine," I assured her. "Just exhausted. I promise I'll be better after a good night of rest." She nodded, seemingly unconvinced. Seline glanced between me and Aspen, eyes widening almost imperceptibly.

Somehow, she knew.

"Let's all retire then," said Ember, nodding sympathetically. "Can we begin preparations tomorrow?" she asked, turning to Rourke. He nodded, standing stiffly.

"Preparations for what?" I asked, looking at Ember for an answer.

She smiled sadly. "For war."

Chapter 34: Aurelia

I WOKE ON THE heels of a dream that was, for once, not new.

It was the same dream I'd had in the unseelie palace. I was standing in the great hall, watching as a fire burned to embers and the Seelie palace rose from the ashes around me, vines twisting up the walls, holding them together as they rose. Ash floated past me, and a snake coiled around the banister, looking like it was waiting for me to climb the stairs.

I followed the snake up, watching as the smoke and ash dissipated, leaving gleaming marble in its wake. The snake led me further, stopping at a door I didn't recognize. This time, I opened the door. Aspen was there, standing in the middle of the room with a tiny bundle in his arms. He turned, golden curls like a halo around him as he smiled at me.

I woke up feeling more peaceful than I had in a long time. Glancing at my mate—now my fiancé—I ran my hand over my still-flat belly, certain now that Mother Vervain was right about the pregnancy. I needed to tell Ember about it today.

She was busy the whole day planning and strategizing and discussing ways to attack the Unseelie King with minimal loss of life. I sat in meetings with her feeling like I was lying to her by not telling her my secret.

"We can add two hundred fighters," Rourke said gruffly, "plus fifty mounted rocs, but it may still not be enough."

"The King's power is waning," Hadrian said. "I felt it in his palace. He should have sensed me slipping in and out through the shadows, but he either didn't notice, or he didn't think my power was a threat. I'm betting it was the former since I know him to be extremely paranoid. Once he is gone, the others like him will easily fall."

I was only half listening as I worked on my plan for how to tell Ember I would need to retire as her assassin. I had faithfully visited Mother Vervain that morning, and she happily presented me with a cup of red raspberry leaf tea and questions about my mood and my symptoms and several other private topics. There was no way to know for sure I was with child until I told Ember, she said. Ember would be able to sense the life inside me. I was already sure, though, and a new tiny part of me glowed with happiness at the knowledge.

I was also trying to figure out what I would do next. I wanted time to be a mother and to be with Aspen, but I also knew I wanted to do something for myself. My whole life had been spent serving the rebellion, and now that my priorities would have to shift for a baby and a husband, I wanted to do something more fulfilling with my life and my power. I just wasn't sure what.

"What about the wild fae?" Aspen said, bringing me back to the conversation. "Most of them were driven out by the war. Surely they would side with us."

"Are you already itching for another job as my emissary?" Ember said, smiling at her cousin.

Aspen blanched, glancing at me. "I think my days as an emissary are over," he replied, looking at me and smiling affectionately. Ember frowned and glanced at me, and I pretended to be very interested in the map before us.

"The wild fae are used to fighting for survival," Vanth said thoughtfully. "They could be valuable allies if they could be convinced to support us. And that's if we have time to recruit them before the Unseelie King strikes us first."

"Are you volunteering to make the journey?" Hadrian asked seriously. Vanth nodded. If Hadrian asked him to walk to the end of the realms, Vanth would do it.

"They won't be easy to convince. Cut off from the magic of the realms for so long, they'll be unpredictable," Vanth said thoughtfully. "The journey will be dangerous. I'll have to contend with the wild shifter packs and the creatures of the Deep Wood."

"We," Seline said. "I'll go with you." She looked at Vanth, then quickly looked away. Vanth nodded his agreement, unsmiling. Something was going on between the two of them, and I couldn't tell if it was good or bad.

"Are you sure?" Hadrian asked, looking at his sister with concern. "I won't be able to come for you out there. It might be a fruitless mission if you can't convince them."

"I know," Seline said. She looked again at Vanth, who was still studying the map.

"We'll offer them a home," Ember said confidently, smiling at her mate. "And protection and new lives. Surely that will be enough to convince them."

"I don't know," Hadrian said, frowning. The talk returned to troop numbers and unseelie spies in the palace, and how to get rid of the king without full-fledged warfare.

"I still think we should have poisoned him when we had the chance," Ember said acerbically, glaring at Hadrian and the Commander, who had made the call to not attempt it.

I chuckled quietly as Hadrian sighed in a beleaguered way. "Not all problems can be solved by poison, my love."

It was late when I finally had a chance to talk to Ember by myself. She had been shooting me glances all day, trying to figure out what was wrong, and she insisted we have dessert for dinner like we had before I left for the Dwarven Realm.

"So," she said conspiratorially when we were finally alone. "Tell me how exactly you and Aspen made up." I laughed, giving her the non-explicit version of the story. She pressed for the juicy details and I obligingly gave her some, but not all, explaining about the claiming bond and Seline's discovery of our relationship.

"So it's good then?" Ember asked, waggling her eyebrows suggestively. I laughed, remembering I had asked her the same thing about Hadrian.

"Do you really want me to tell you about that?" I said. "He's your cousin."

"Oh, I suppose not," she said, making a face. "Fine, then tell me what's wrong. You've been out of sorts all day, and Aspen has been bouncing off the walls."

I sighed, trying to decide what to tell her first. "What do you want my role to be here?" I asked. She frowned, so I pressed on. "I mean, am I always to be your assassin? Fire warrior? Lady of Summer? Something else?"

"Aurelia, you can be whatever you want," she said warmly, taking my hands. "If you don't want to be an assassin anymore, no one would blame you."

I looked into her dear face and smiled. "I want to help with the rocs," I said, remembering the joy I had found in flying. "And maybe try to breed an army of cave dragons."

Ember laughed. "Of course you do," she said, squeezing my hand. "We will make it happen."

I sighed, looking at her again. "He asked me to marry him," I said.

Ember's gasp became a little squeal as she said, "I knew it!" about five thousand times. I smiled indulgently. "Wait," she said, frowning. "Do you not want to marry him?"

"Oh no, I do," I said. "There's just a bit of a complication."

"A complication?" she asked.

I nodded, moving to sit next to her. "Can you do something for me?" I asked. I took her hand and pressed it to my stomach. "Can you stretch out your magic and tell me what you feel?"

"Is the iron wound bothering you?" she asked, concentrating on her magic. "Because I can...oh!"

She stopped, looking up at me, eyes wide. She placed her hand back on me and felt again. Her magic was light and tingling, and I felt it like a warm flush traveling through me. "Oh, Aurelia," she said, looking up with tears in her eyes. "Does he know?"

I nodded, smiling and she threw her arms around me, full-blown sobs wracking her body. I was surprised by her reaction and I wrapped my arms around her. "Oh, Em," I said, frowning and starting to panic. "What's wrong? Is something wrong with her?"

"No," Ember said, pulling back and drying her tears. "Her?"

"Mother Vervain says it's a girl," I said, shrugging.

"Of course she does," Ember said, sniffing and wiping her eyes. "And of course, she was the first to know. No, there's nothing wrong." She tried to beam, looking rather guilty and waterlogged rather than genuinely happy.

"What?" I said, taking her hand and squeezing it.

"I am so happy for you," she said, smiling sadly. "It just surprised me. Hadrian and I...well, we've been trying. We need an heir, and I want a baby so desperately. So does he."

I smiled. "That's wonderful," I said, imagining our children playing together, mine blond and hers dark-haired. I frowned, seeing her sadness. "It's not happening?" I pressed quietly.

She shook her head. "I feel wretched for even saying anything," she said, looking at me apologetically. "It's only been a few months and I know it can take decades. This is your happy news. I don't want to spoil it."

"You're not," I said, squeezing her hand. "Of course I understand."

She shook her head, lip trembling a little. "It's just...Mother Vervain says it might be difficult," she said quietly. "Our magic is so different, she thinks I may not be able to..." She trailed off and I wrapped my arms around her.

"I'm so sorry," I said, feeling deeply for my friend. Ember was like a sister to me and her pain was so clearly written upon her face.

It would be cruel if she weren't able to have a child with the male she so desperately loved.

"But I have faith in the Goddess," I said resolutely. "You and Hadrian were not brought together to suffer heartache. He loves you more than anything. If anyone should be blessed with a child, it is you two."

She smiled at me, squeezing my hands. "Oh!" she cried, jumping out of her seat. "You will need a bigger room! And we need to build a nursery! And plan the wedding!" I smiled as she rattled off plans, clearly distracting herself.

I played along, arguing about floral arrangements and nursery layouts, and the effects of using fire magic during pregnancy until it was nearly midnight. Hadrian came looking for her and dragged her to bed, giving me a peck on the cheek and a soft "congratulations," as he took her off.

Aspen was waiting for me in our room when I returned. "How did it go?" he asked, rising to greet me with a kiss. I told him about Ember's confirmation of the pregnancy and her enthusiasm, but I kept her fears private for now. Some worries were meant only for best friends and not for cousins.

Aspen gave me a little spin when I told him that Ember said the baby was well, and he kissed me soundly when I chastised him for lifting me in my condition.

"True. You are a delicate flower now that you are carrying my child," Aspen teased, scooping me up in his arms and carrying me to the bed. "I have to take extra special care to be gentle with you."

I laughed and kissed him soundly. "What if I don't want you to be gentle?" I asked suggestively.

Aspen smiled wickedly, kissing me slowly and sensually as he began unbuttoning the back of my dress. "Tell me you're mine, and I'll give you whatever you want," he promised, kissing me below my ear, in the hollow of my shoulder, and down my throat.

I lifted his face and kissed his lips, marveling that this male was finally mine. "I'm yours," I whispered. "Always."

Chapter 35: Ember

THE DAYS AFTER ASPEN and Aurelia's return were busy and chaotic. Between meetings with Rourke to discuss numbers and weapons and mobilization of the roc cavalry, and treating injuries of the dwarves and fae who had been hurt in the rescue from the unseelie palace, I was busy most days until late in the evening.

This night had been no different, as we had entertained the dwarves with a formal dinner to thank them for their alliance and help. Rourke had poked suspiciously at all the meat and vegetables, and Aurelia had happily chattered away at him, explaining what everything was and comparing it to familiar dwarven delicacies she had tried in his realm.

Aurelia had described some of the ways the dwarves had grown food beneath the mountain, and I was fascinated to learn more, but my heart and mind were just not in a place to be good company.

Aurelia had shot me furtive glances and smiles, clearly worried that I was upset about her and Aspen's happy news. I had plastered on my brightest smile, eager to reassure her that I was thrilled to be an aunt and that I was overjoyed for them. And I was.

And also I wasn't.

"You're doing it again," Hadrian said murmuring into my hair as he lay behind me in bed long after the dinner had ended. "I can practically hear you thinking."

I sighed. "Sorry," I whispered, squeezing his arm. "Go back to sleep." His shadows were curled around me, and they flickered slightly as if seeking my attention too.

"You act as if I was ever asleep in the first place," he replied, brushing a light kiss against the back of my neck as he stroked a hand down my thigh. "What's wrong?"

I sighed, feeling like the worst friend in the world for what I was about to admit to him. "I was thinking about Aurelia," I said. "And the baby."

"Ah," he said, rolling me over so I was facing him in the warm circle of his arms, shadows adjusting like a blanket around us. He kissed my nose lightly. "We've talked about this."

"I know," I said, frustrated with myself that I couldn't let it go. I leaned into him, pressing my face against his pale chest. "I know, I'm the worst friend of all time."

"You're not," he said, stroking my hair with the hand that was not resting on my hip. "But as I've said before, I'm rather glad I don't have to worry about you being pregnant right now. As much as I want a hundred children with you," he continued, placing another kiss on my nose, "and believe me, my love, nothing would bring me more joy. But if you were with child right now, I don't think I could let you do what you will have to do in this war."

"I know," I said again, trying to burrow deeper into his chest. I knew Hadrian was right, and that now was not the right time for us to have a baby, but it didn't stop the twist of longing I felt every time I looked at my best friend. I knew it could take years to have children, especially as a fae, but it had happened so quickly for them, and now that I was the Seelie Queen, I felt this overwhelming pressure to produce an heir to make sure the realm's magic was secure. My grandmother's dire predictions about our potentially incompatible magic didn't help either.

Hadrian told me I was being ridiculous and that we had all the time in the world. He tilted my face up to his and brushed a kiss against my lips. "You're still thinking loudly," he said, moving his lips to my cheek and then my ear, and planting soft kisses along the way. "Let me help you get your mind off it."

I smiled and rolled my eyes. "Truly, that's all you think of," I teased, feeling the evidence of his thoughts against my thigh.

He huffed a laugh against my ear. "If your mate was this beautiful and perfect, you would think of nothing else as well," he said, sliding his hand down my thigh to cup the back of my knee, and pulling my leg up over his hip. I felt warmth coil in my belly at the move and smiled despite myself as he rolled on top of me, kissing me languidly and teasing my arousal from me.

"You are beautiful and perfect," I assured him, cupping his face in my hands as I wound my other leg around his hip.

He kissed me again, smiling against my lips as his shadows curled around me. "Then we are agreed," he said, moving down to tease my peaked nipple with his tongue. I shuddered, feeling warmth coiling low and shooting sparks of desire up my spine. I arched into his touch as he teased me, moving his mouth to my other breast.

"Plus, we should practice," Hadrian added between searing kisses and licks and nips, moving down my stomach to kiss my navel, then the mound above the apex of my thighs. He looked up at me, eyes flashing silver in the dark room, then lowered his mouth to me again.

"I'm not sure this really counts as practice," I gasped as he stroked his tongue up my center, groaning at the wetness he found there.

"It most definitely does," he replied thickly, continuing to lick and suck until I was writhing against him. He reached his hands up to roll my nipples between his fingers as he worked me, and I felt lightning pulse through me as he gently teased me to a frenzied, pulsing desire.

"Hadrian," I gasped.

His shadows wrapped around my waist, holding me in place as I tried to grind against him, making the sensations more intense the more they held me. "Come for me," he growled against my center.

I shattered against him with a cry, and he quickly rose to capture it with his mouth, thrusting into me at the same time and making me cry out more at the pleasure and pressure of it. He moved, thrusting steadily into me as I moaned against him, biting down on his shoulder to muffle the noise I was making as I held him tightly to me.

He chuckled darkly, pressing his teeth to my throat and nipping lightly as he moved in me, gripping my rear to move me faster until he was coming undone just as I had. He groaned into me as he filled me, kissing my neck and my jaw as he breathed through his pleasure.

I stroked his back, lifting a hand to brush the hair from his damp forehead. He lifted his face to kiss me again, and we stayed like that for a few minutes, enjoying slow and tender kisses as we came down from the passion and intensity of our joining.

"That was nice," I breathed, holding him close as he chuckled against my neck.

"Only nice?" he asked, turning to lie on his back and pulling me with him until I was resting with my head against his shoulder, the shadows draped over me again like a cloak.

I smiled. "More than nice," I corrected as he kissed my temple.

"Hmm, clearly we need more practice if that's all the praise I get," he said tiredly, cupping my rear as he held me to him. I laughed.

"It will happen when it's meant to happen for us, my love," he said, speaking against my hair as he stroked my arm with his other hand. "And even if it doesn't, there is no one I would rather spend my life with than you, My Queen, however long we have."

I let his steady heartbeat and warm shadows lull me to sleep as he continued to stroke my arm. As slumber took me, I felt determined that our lives and those of our family would be long and happy and filled with love, and I vowed to hunt down the Goddess and make her suffer if she didn't agree

Epilogue: Aurelia

THE FIRST BUDS OF spring were blossoming on the trees when Aspen and I said our vows. The ceremony was lovely and small. Our family was there of course, and King Rourke and several of his councilors had been invited, including Knox and Bisera. They brought several barrels of dwarven ale for the celebration, which Mother Vervain strictly forbade me from drinking.

Aside from Aspen marrying me, the best part of the day was Rourke's gift. A beautiful, snowy-white roc was presented to me, smaller than the other I had seen. He squawked happily as I patted his beak.

"He is only a hatchling," Rourke said, "but he will grow soon enough. You'll need to train him for riding if you want him to be at all useful."

"Oh, you are lovely, aren't you, Foxglove?" I said, scratching his beak and ruffling his feathers. Aspen rolled his eyes at the endearing creature's new name but said nothing.

"I wanted to bring Honeysuckle," Knox said, smiling up at my new roc, "but he would have had a miserable time flying." I nodded, laughing at the idea of a cave dragon flying on a roc.

"I'll just have to find a type of dragon that likes to fly," I said excitedly. Aspen choked on his dwarven ale and Knox laughed, slapping him heartily.

As the sun began to set, I found Aspen alone on the terrace overlooking the party. A soft swell had begun to show in my low belly, and Aspen ran his hands lovingly over it as I came to stand with him.

"You look radiant," he said, kissing my neck and stroking down the blue silk of my gown. I had asked for honeysuckles to be embroidered on my wedding dress, and I felt like I embodied the spring with the tiny life growing inside me.

"My wife," he murmured into my neck, making a shiver travel down my spine. "Hmm, I like saying that."

"I like hearing it," I said, reaching up on my toes to kiss him. He rested his forehead on mine as we basked in the warm glow of the sunset.

"Vanth and Seline will be leaving soon," I said sadly, turning to look off the terrace at our friends, who were talking quietly. Both wore their characteristic black armor, and I wondered if Seline even liked soft dresses or pretty things. I bet she did. I made it my goal to find her something beautiful to have before she left for the Wilds.

"They'll be fine," Aspen assured me, moving behind me and wrapping his arms around me to rest his hands on my stomach. "They're brave and strong."

"And stubborn," I sighed. They had fought about something and had seemed on cooler terms than normal. Seline had repeatedly said everything was fine, but Vanth continued to gaze darkly after her, and I knew something must have happened.

I had cornered him in the rookery the other day to make him tell me. He had sighed mightily. "I kissed her," he said, returning to the birds he had brought raw steaks for.

I gasped. "What? How? When?"

"When she was injured after the rescue," he admitted. "She was bleeding and exhausted and I just lost all self-control and kissed her," he said frustratedly.

"And?" I said, pressing for more detail. "It was bad?"

"No, it was fucking magical," Vanth said angrily, "until her head caught up to her and she pushed me away. She told me she doesn't want that with anyone."

"Oh, Vanth," I said, heart cracking for him. He had been pining after Seline for years, but this was the first time I thought he had acted on any of his feelings. "I am so sorry."

He shook his head angrily. "It's my own damned fault," he said, throwing the last of the raw meat at the birds and putting the bucket down. He crossed his arms and turned toward me, glowering. "Now she's avoiding me and it's awkward."

I sighed sadly, patting his arm. "She looks," I said, remembering what Seline had said about Aspen weeks ago when I was ready to give up on him. "Don't stop trying, Vanth."

Aspen kissed my neck again, bringing me back to the present and pulling me from my melancholy thoughts. "Let's go to bed," he whispered in my ear, sending a shiver down my neck.

I laughed. "It's not even dark yet," I protested as he trailed more kisses down my throat.

"Hmm, I need the light for some of the things I plan to do tonight," Aspen replied, making heat curl low in my core.

"Really?" I teased, lighting a little ball of flame in the palm of my hand and letting it roll between my fingers. "I can always provide the light."

"Torturous female," Aspen groaned, scooping me up in his arms. I gave a little yelp and he kissed me soundly, heading toward our new suite of rooms that Ember had provided for us.

My heart still ached a little for her. She was going to be such a wonderful aunt, but I knew she longed to be a mother as well. I hadn't thought about the difficulty her mating an unseelie fae might cause. As far as I knew, it hadn't been done often. Our people had been kept apart for three hundred years by war, so there wasn't a lot of information about cross-realm couplings. But I couldn't believe that they could be brought together by fate or the Goddess or whatever force commanded the universe just to suffer heartache.

"The Goddess will make everything right, won't she?" I asked Aspen as he deposited me on our bed. "For us and our friends? For Seline and Vanth and for Ember and Hadrian?"

"I don't know," he said honestly, kneeling before me and removing my heeled shoes. I ran my fingers through his blond curls, smiling at his tender affection. "But I know if she doesn't, you will make it so for them," he added, kissing me soundly. "And I have faith that it will all turn out well."

"Me too," I whispered. He kissed me then and I let my worry slip away as Aspen reminded me that I was his as only he could.

The story continues in A Dream of Frost and Fury, book 3 of Queen of All Fae, featuring Vanth and Seline in a second-chance, friends-to-lovers romance.

Acknowledgements

Once again, my first thank you has to go to my husband, who put up with long afternoons and evenings of writing and always offered to assist me with "research."

This book would not have been possible without my earliest readers. Thank you Aurora and Shelly, for giving me feedback and encouragement and helping me find Aurelia's voice.

Thanks also to my amazing volunteer ARC team, who crushed it by sending me typos and giving me valuable feedback and early reviews.

To my friends, who read A Dream of Stars and Darkness and encouraged me, thank you for believing in and supporting my journey.

Thank you Jen and Katie for fangirling over my work, and thank you to the countless colleagues and friends who started reading joyfully and enthusiastically. Without your encouragement, this would not have been an easy or enjoyable task.

And once again, thank you for supporting indie authors and taking a chance on an unknown writer to tell you a story. I know opening a book can be a leap of faith, and I hope this leap was worth it for you!

About the Author

MADELEINE ELIOT LOVES TO read and write spicy romantasy with all of the best tropes. Dubbed the "Queen of Cozy" by her readers, Madeleine enjoys writing romantasy that is all vibes and spice, with a dash of adventure and world-building. She is always working on her next book, which is probably another spicy romantasy. Follow her adventures and latest works at instagram.com/madeleineeliotwrites

Also by Madeleine Eliot

Queen of All Fae

A Dream of Stars and Darkness
A Dream of Earth and Ash
A Dream of Frost and Fury
A Dream of Sun and Solstice (Novella)

King and Coven

To Hunt a Demon King
To Break a Demon Curse
To Wear a Demon Crown
To Claim a Daemon Lord (Novella)
To Sway a Demon Heart (Novella)

The Whispering Sea Duet

Ballad of Sea and Sky
Hymn of Breath and Bone

Enchanted Hearts

Gold & Shadow
Blood & Roses

It's Beginning to Look a Lot Like Witches

Hex the Halls

Made in the USA
Columbia, SC
08 February 2025

52976387R00212